…NG…

Hold on … s on a number of levels.

—ERIC WILSON
AUTHOR OF *NEW YORK TIMES* BEST SELLER *FIREPROOF*

Mike Dellosso's brilliant light shines into the dark places of the human heart and illuminates our most terrible fears.

—ERIN HEALY
AUTHOR OF *NEVER LET YOU GO*
AND COAUTHOR WITH TED DEKKER OF *KISS AND BURN*

Taut, tense, and frightening. A high-speed ride that will keep you guessing until the end.

—TOSCA LEE
AUTHOR OF *DEMON: A MEMOIR*

Mike Dellosso could very well be the next Frank Peretti.

—C. J. DARLINGTON
AUTHOR OF *THICKER THAN BLOOD*
AND COFOUNDER OF TITLETRAKK.COM

Mike Dellosso, an astonishing new voice in supernatural thrillers, cements his right to be grouped with the likes of King and Peretti.

—SUSAN SLEEMAN
THESUSPENSEZONE.COM

Mike Dellosso has once again brought us an engaging thriller full of gut-wrenching suspense and strong spiritual truth.

—JAKE CHISM
THECHRISTIANMANIFESTO.COM

DARKNESS FOLLOWS

Mike Dellosso

REALMS

Most Charisma House Book Group products are available at special quantity discounts for bulk purchase for sales promotions, premiums, fund-raising, and educational needs. For details, write Charisma House Book Group, 600 Rinehart Road, Lake Mary, Florida 32746, or telephone (407) 333-0600.

Darkness Follows by Mike Dellosso
Published by Realms
Charisma Media/Charisma House Book Group
600 Rinehart Road
Lake Mary, Florida 32746
www.charismahouse.com

The characters portrayed in this book are fictitious unless they are historical figures explicitly named. Otherwise, any resemblance to actual people, whether living or dead, is coincidental.

Cover design by Justin Evans
Design Director: Bill Johnson

Visit the author's website at www.MikeDellosso.com

Library of Congress Cataloging-in-Publication Data:
Dellosso, Mike.
Darkness follows / Mike Dellosso. -- 1st ed.
p. cm.
ISBN 978-1-61638-274-2
1. Fathers and daughters--Fiction. 2. Assassins--Fiction. 3. Political fiction. 4. Psychological fiction. I. Title.
PS3604.E446D365 2011
813'.6--dc22
2010051708

E-book ISBN: 978-1-61638-434-0

First Edition

11 12 13 14 15 — 9 8 7 6 5 4 3 2 1
Printed in the United States of America

For my four girls—
Laura, the creative one
Abigail, the analytical one
Caroline, the courageous one
Elizabeth, an unexpected blessing

Acknowledgments

As always, with every book there are plenty of thanks to go around, too much for just a few pages, actually. But I'm limited by space, so I must make do with mentioning a few who played major roles in seeing this latest book come to life.

Jen, my wife, my rock, my cheerleader. She doesn't have to do anything but just be there to inspire me. So much of the love in my stories grows from the love we share.

My girls, all four of them. Your daddy loves you more than you know, but your Daddy in heaven loves you perfectly. Cling to His love. Let it inspire you and carry you through every trial and valley.

My parents. Their support never grows old. Thanks for never giving up on me.

Phil Dellosso, my uncle and purveyor of Civil War knowledge. Much of Samuel Whiting's journal entries are his creation. His experience with the entries was the event that gave birth to the story idea.

Officer Joe Henry offered advice, knowledge, and wisdom concerning all things police related. If I got anything wrong or if anything is inaccurate, it's my fault not his. Believe me, this guy knows his stuff.

Scott Sadler answered questions about life "inside the beltway" and inside a senator's office. I needed someone like him, and he was a willing victim.

My agent, Les Stobbe. Thanks for sticking with me, believing in me, and championing my ideas.

Eric Wilson, who took a scalpel to my story and made it better than I thought it could be. Brother, your wisdom and advice are always coveted and never taken for granted.

My editors at Strang, Debbie Marrie and Deb Moss, knowledgeable, sweet, and supportive. I'm glad you're on my side. This is *our* book.

The rest of the fine people at Strang who work diligently to bring these books to the reader. Your work is worth more praise than you receive and has more of an impact than you think.

My readers. Without you all this would be an exercise in self-appreciation…or maybe self-flagellation. Anyway, just know I am *your* fan. I appreciate you.

My God. I can't believe how much You love me in spite of myself and all my failures. Thank You for blessing me. Expand my horizons. Keep me from evil.

Foreword

I'M TOLD NO ONE REALLY READS THESE FOREWORDS, THAT they're wasted space, wasted words. I'm told only self-aggrandizing authors write them, thinking the general public actually cares what we have to say about anything. I can assure you, there's nothing self-aggrandizing about me. If anything, the pendulum of my self-image tends to swing the other way into the territory of self-deprecation. Also, I don't believe in wasted space or words. So since this is my story, I suppose I have the prerogative to write a foreword if I wish to. I'm sure some will read it, if for no other reason than to satisfy their compulsion to read a book cover to cover and nothing less. So here goes...

I can't believe it, but it happened again.

Here's how it went down. During the editing phase of my novel *Scream*, a story about the brevity of life and the certainty of death, I was diagnosed with colon cancer—an appropriate battle to wage after writing a book about such a topic. Then during the editing phase of my next novel, *Darlington Woods*, a tale of monsters and fear and our struggle to conquer both, my youngest daughter was diagnosed with idiopathic juvenile arthritis—again, a difficult but appropriate bedfellow for my story. Juvenile arthritis is a monster with its own brand of attitude. So this time around I wondered what, if anything, it would be and questioned how much more our family could take.

Well, yes, it happened again. This story, *Darkness Follows*, is a love story. No, it's not a bodice buster. There are no long-haired hunks with clean-shaven chests, no damsels in distress with flowing hair. You won't find any longing eyes or lingering touches here. So, men, relax. It's a story of the love between a father and his little girl. I have three of them, so I know a bit about the bond between daddy and daughter, the unconditional love that tethers them. So during the editing phase of this book something unexpected, surprising, glorious, and fearsome happened. We found out my wife was pregnant with our fourth—and yes, it's another girl.

Now, knowing what I know of my next book, I must admit I'm a bit leery of what's going to happen during that all-important editing phase. Maybe nothing, maybe something. What could be worse than cancer or juvenile arthritis? I can think of a few things. What could be better than a surprise baby? Not much. Time will tell, but it does beg me to ask the question: Do you think my publisher will go for skipping the editing phase altogether? No, I didn't think so either.

—Mike Dellosso
www.mikedellosso.com

Prologue

Gettysburg, 1863

CAPTAIN SAMUEL WHITING REMOVED HIS GLOVES AND SAT ON the cot in his tent. It had been a long, grueling day of battle, and his clothes were soaked through with sweat. He'd lost more men, good men, family men. Men who would never return home to their wives. Boys who would never again cross the thresholds of their parents' homes.

He leaned forward, removed his boots, and stretched his legs. The air in the tent was still and muggy. At least outside there was a light breeze to carry away the stench of the wounded. In here, the smells hung in the air like a haze. Beyond the canvas walls the sounds of soldiers—heroes—in the throes of agony wandered through the camp like the souls of dead men looking for rest. But there was no rest in a place like this.

A single oil lamp sat on the floor, casting an orange glow about the tent's interior. Samuel turned the knob on the lamp, giving more wick to the flame. The light brightened and the shadows darkened. From a writing box he removed a leather-bound journal, the one his mother had given him before he left to join Mr. Lincoln's army. At the time he thought he was doing the right thing, thought he was fighting for a noble cause.

Now he thought differently. There was nothing noble about this war, nothing honorable about the way it was being fought nor the reasons for which it was being waged.

After dipping the tip of his quill into an inkwell, he put the tip to the paper and began to write. The words flowed from his hand, though they were not born of him but of something else, something dark and sinister, something to which he had finally given himself.

In the corner of the tent a shadow moved. He saw it from the corner of his eye. It was a shadow cast not by the oil lamp's flame but by some other source, a source Samuel did not fully understand but felt.

The shadow glided along the canvas, following the angles of the tent, and came to a stop beside the cot. There it seemed to lurk, to hover, as if curious to see what was being written on the pages of the journal. A chill blew over Samuel, penetrated his clothes and flesh, and settled into his bones.

The shadow began to throb in rhythm with Samuel's beating heart. His quill moved across the paper more rapidly now, the point carving words—vitriol—at an alarming pace. His heart rate quickened and, with it, the pulsations of the shadow.

At once a strong wind ruffled the canvas and brought with it a low howl that sounded more like a moan. It did not originate from outside the tent, from wounded and homesick boys, but rather from within, from the shadow. The wind circled the tent's interior, stirred the pages of the journal, Samuel's hair, his clothes, and finally, as if in one final great sigh, extinguished the light of the lamp.

Captain Samuel Whiting was engulfed by darkness.

One

Present day

Sam Travis awoke in the middle of the night, cold and terrified.

The dream had come again. His brother. The shot.

You did what you had to do, son.

He sat up in bed and wiped the sweat from his brow.

Next to him Molly stirred, grunted, and found his arm with her hand. "You OK, babe?"

"Yeah. I'm gonna go get some water."

"You sure?"

He found her forehead in the darkness and kissed it. "Yeah."

The house was as still and noiseless as a crypt. Sam made his way down the hall to Eva's room, floorboards popping under his feet. He cracked the door and peeked in. The Tinker Bell night-light cast a soft purple hue over the room, giving it a moonlit glow. Odd-shaped shadows blotted the ceiling, like dark clouds against a darker sky. Eva was curled into a tight ball, head off the pillow, blankets at her feet.

Sam opened the door all the way, tiptoed to the bed, and pulled the covers to his daughter's shoulders. She didn't stir even the slightest. For a few hushed moments he stood and listened to her low rhythmic breathing.

The past six months had been hard on them all, but Eva had handled them surprisingly well. She was just a kid, barely seven, yet displayed the maturity of someone much older. Sam had never known that her faith, much like her mother's, was so strong. His, on the other hand…

He left the door open a few inches. Farther down the hall he entered the bathroom, where another night-light, this one a blue flower, reflected off the porcelain tub, toilet, and sink. He splashed water from the faucet on his face. Remnants of the dream lingered and stuttered like bad cell phone reception. Just images now, faces, twisted and warped.

After toweling off, he studied himself in the mirror. In the muted light the scar running above his ear didn't look so bad. His hair was growing back and covered most of it. Oddly, the new crop was coming in gray.

From downstairs a voice called Sam's name. A chill tightened the arc of his scar.

He heard it again.

"Sammy."

It was neither haunting nor unnatural, but familiar, conversational. It was the voice of his brother. Tommy. He'd heard it a thousand times in his youth, a hundred ghostly times since the accident that had turned his own brain to mush. The doctor called them auditory hallucinations.

Sam exited the bathroom and stood at the top of the staircase. Dim light from the second floor spilled down the stairs into the foyer below, and the empty space looked like a strange planet, distant and odd. Who knew what bizarre creatures inhabited that land and what malicious intentions they harbored?

He heard that same voice—Tommy's—calling to him. "Sammy."

Sam shivered at the sound of his name.

A dull ache had taken to the length of the scar.

Descending the stairs, Sam felt something dark, ominous, present in the house with him. He stopped and listened. He could almost hear it breathing, and with each breath, each exhalation, he heard his own name, now just a whisper.

He started down the stairs again, taking one at a time, holding the railing and trying to find the quiet places on the steps.

From the bottom of the stairway he looked at the front door, half expecting it to fly open and reveal Tommy standing there, with half his head...

You did what you had to do, son.

He looked left into the dining room, then right into the living room. The voice was coming from the kitchen. Turning a one-eighty, he headed that way down the hall.

At the doorway Sam stopped and listened again. Now he heard nothing. No breathing, no whispers, no Tommy. The kitchen held the aroma of the evening's meal—fettuccine Alfredo—like a remote memory.

"Tommy?" His own voice sounded too loud and strangely hollow.

He had no idea why he said his brother's name since he expected no reply. Tommy had been dead for—what?—twenty-one years. Thoughts of his death came to Sam's mind, images from the dream. And not just his death but *how* he'd died.

You did what you had to do, son.

From off in the distance Sam heard a cannon blast. Living in Gettysburg, near the battlefields, the sound was common during the month of July when the reenactments were going on. But not in the middle of the night. Not in November. Another blast echoed across the fields, then the percussion of rifle shots followed by a volley of more cannons.

Sam walked back down the hall and opened the front door. He saw only darkness beyond the light of the porch lamp, but the sounds were unmistakable. Guns crackled in rapid succession, cannons boomed, men hollered and screamed, horses whinnied and roared. The sounds of battle were all around him. He expected Eva and Molly to stir from their sleep and come tripping down the stairs at any moment, but that didn't happen. The house was as still and quiet as ever.

Crossing his arms over his chest, Sam stepped out onto the porch. Three rotting jack-o'-lanterns grinned at him like a gaggle of toothless geezers. The air was cold and damp, the grass wet with dew. Nervously he felt the bandage on his index finger. He'd slipped while carving one of the pumpkins and gouged his finger with the knife. Molly had thought he should get stitches, but he refused. It was still tender, throbbing slightly, healing up well enough on its own. Here, outside, the loamy smell of dead wet leaves surrounded him. Beyond the glow of the porch lamp, the outside world was black and lonely. The sky was moonless.

Across the field and beyond the trees the battle continued but grew no louder. Sam gripped his head and held it with both hands. Was he going crazy? Had the accident triggered some weird psychosis? This couldn't be real. It had to be a concoction of his damaged brain. An auditory hallucination.

Suddenly the sounds ceased and silence ruled. Dead silence. No whispers of a gentle breeze. No skittering of dry leaves across the driveway. No creak of old, naked branches. Not even the hum of the power lines paralleling the road.

Sam went back inside and shut the door. The dead bolt made a solid *thunk* as it slid into place. He didn't want to go back upstairs, didn't want to sleep in his own bed. Instead he went into the living room, lay on the sofa, and clicked on the TV. The last thing he remembered before falling asleep was watching an old *Star Trek* rerun.

■■■

Sam's eyes opened slowly and tried to adjust to the soft morning light that seeped through the windows. He rolled to his side and felt something slide from his lap to the floor with a papery flutter. He'd not slept soundly on the sofa.

Pushing himself up, he looked out the window. The sun had not yet cleared the horizon, and the sky was a hundred shades of pink. The house felt damp and chilly. The TV was off. Leaning to his left, he saw that the front door was open. Maybe Molly had gone out already and not shut it behind her.

"Moll?" But there was no answer. "Eva?" The house was quiet.

Sam stood to see if Molly was in the yard and noticed a notebook on the floor, its pages splayed like broken butterfly wings. Bending to pick it up, he recognized it as one of Eva's notebooks in which she wrote her kid stories, tales of a dog named Max and of horses with wings.

Turning it over, he found a full page of writing. *His* writing. Before the accident he'd often helped Eva with her stories but had never written one himself. He'd thought about it many times but had never gotten around to doing it. There was always something more pressing, more important. Since his accident he'd had the time, home from work with nothing to do, but his brain just wasn't working that way. He couldn't focus, couldn't concentrate. His attention span was that of a three-year-old.

Sitting on the sofa, he read the writing on the page, the writing of his own hand.

November 19, 1863
Captain Samuel Whiting
PennsylvanIa Independent Light Artillery, Battery E

I am full of dArkness. It has coMpletely overshadowed me. My heart despairs; my soul swims in murky, colorless waters. I am not my own but a mere puppet in his hanD. My intent is evil, and I loathe what the dAy will bring, what I will accomplish. But I must do it. My feet have been positioned, my couRse has been set, and I am compelled to follow. Darkness, he is my commander now.

I can already smell the blood on my hands, and it turns my stomach. But, strangely, it excites me as well. I know it is the darKness within me, bloodthirsty devil that it is. It desires death, his death (the president), and I am beginning to understand why. He must die. He deserves nothing more than death. So much suffering has come from his words, his policies, his will. He speaks of freedom but has enslaved so many in this cursed war.

See how the pen trEmbles in my hand. I move it, not myself but the darkneSs guides it, as it guides my mind and will. Shadowy figures encircle me. I can see them all about the room, specters moving as lightly as wiSps of smoke. My hand trembles. I am overcome. I am their slave. His slave.

I am not my own.

I am not my own.

I am notnotnotnotnotnotnotno

my own

Sam let the notebook slip from his hands and scrape across the hardwood floor. Gooseflesh puckered his skin. He thought of last night's battle sounds, of Tommy's voice and *feeling* the darkness around him—the *darkness.* He remembered the grinning jack-o'-lanterns, the click of the sliding dead bolt. He had no memory of turning off the TV and opening the door, nor of finding Eva's notebook and writing this nonsense.

What was happening to him?

He stood and went to the front door, barely aware of his feet moving under him. With one elbow on the doorjamb he poked his head outside and scanned the front yard, listening.

"Moll?" His voice was weak and broke mid-word.

There was no answer. If Molly was out here, she must be around back.

Then, as if last night's ethereal battle had landed in his front yard, a rifle shot split the morning air, and the living room window exploded in a spray of glass.

Two

Molly was down the steps in no time, slippered feet scuffing the hardwood like fine-grit sandpaper. Her hair was wildly out of place, pushed to one side and matted like steel wool, and pillow crease lines marked her left cheek. Her eyes were wide and bleary, her jaw slack.

"Wha-what happened?" The panic in her voice sent spidery legs down Sam's back.

She stood at the bottom of the steps in blue flannel pajamas, palms turned up, expecting an answer. But Sam didn't have one. He had no idea what had happened. He knew the window had exploded—the glass on the living room floor, glimmering like diamonds in the light, testified to that—but the gunshot...

Was it real? Was it his mind playing war games with him?

He looked at Molly, "I, uh, I'm..." He glanced at the floor then back at her. His damaged brain wouldn't shift into gear.

She took three steps forward, cautiously, as though creeping through a haunted house and expecting a mischievous teenager in a monster mask to jump from the next corner. She looked into the living room, and her hand went to her mouth. "Sam, what happened? The window."

"Mommy?"

It was Eva, standing at the top of the stairs.

Sam was still frozen, his mind a block of ice, unable to make sense of anything that had transpired in the last fifteen minutes.

Molly spun around. "Eva, stay there, baby. Don't come down."

"What happened? Did something break?" She was barefoot in

her Dora jammies, clutching her worn-out stuffed dog in her arms. Max. There was no fear in her eyes, only questions.

"Yes, baby," Molly said. She was in take-charge mode, and Sam knew when she had that look it was best to let her do her thing. "The window broke, that's all. Nothing to worry about. Just stay there, OK? There's glass all over the floor."

Molly looked at Sam again. "What happened? Why's the front door open? How did the window break?"

Too many questions.

"I..."

"Sam?" Her voice was more concerned than accusatory.

For an instant, the briefest moment on a clock, less than one tick of a second hand, Sam almost told her about Tommy's voice last night, about the sounds of war—Civil War—about the TV and the front door and the notebook with the strange entry he'd written in his sleep, but he didn't. He couldn't. He was already enough of a burden to her. She didn't need to know he had lost his footing in this world and slipped into another, that he was now going insane.

"I don't know. I couldn't sleep last night, came downstairs to watch some TV, fell asleep on the couch. I woke up and needed some fresh air."

She put a hand on his arm. Her touch was soft and comforting, a complement to the tone of her voice, and again he almost told her everything.

"I–I heard a gunshot and..." He looked at the opening in the window, framed by jagged shards like the hungry jaws of an unearthly beast. "The glass broke. It just shattered."

Molly's hands rested on her hips.

"Did you hear it?" Sam asked, hoping she would say she had, hoping his mind wasn't really betraying him.

She shook her head. "I didn't hear any shots, just the glass."

"Not shots," he said. "Just one. One shot." He looked up at Eva. She was sitting on the top step now, still holding Max like he would run away if she let go. It seemed she was so far away that Sam could climb that staircase forever and never reach her. He had the sudden impulse to prove this inclination wrong, to bound up the stairs and take her in his arms and squeeze her, to hold her tight and make sure she was real.

Please, Lord, let her still be real.

Molly said, "Do you think someone was hunting? Maybe a stray bullet?"

"I don't know." But he did know. Or did he? He couldn't be sure of anything anymore.

"Did you call the police?"

Sam met her eyes. The police. Should he have called the police? A voice in his head told him to leave the cops out of this, since they would only complicate matters. Questions would be asked, explanations expected, and he had no answers. But Molly was giving him that look, the one that said she was calling the shots on this and the cops were getting notified regardless of what he said. "No. Not yet. We probably should, though, huh?"

"I'll call them." She spun toward the kitchen.

Sam looked at Eva again. He tried to force a smile, but it wasn't anything near genuine. Every time he looked at her he thought of her notebook, the one with her stories about Max and the flying horses, the one with his writings about the man—Samuel Whiting—full of darkness.

I am full of darkness. I am not my own.

He felt that somehow his writing had violated the innocence of his daughter, that it had trespassed upon and poisoned the sacred ground where childlike expression took root and flourished.

"Are you OK, Daddy?" The sweetness of Eva's voice almost brought tears to his eyes. The sincerity. The tenderness. It was the voice of an angel—*his* angel—anchoring him in reality.

"Yes, darling, I'm fine. Are you OK?"

She shrugged and held Max closer to her chest, as if the stuffed dog gave her the comfort her daddy couldn't. "Just a little scared. Did someone shooted our window out?"

Sam ascended the steps and sat next to Eva. He put his arm around her, looked deep into her eyes, and yes, there he found the fear. He pulled her close to his side, and she rested her head on his chest. The smell of her hair was right, the way it should be, the way it had always been. At least one thing hadn't changed. "I don't know, little buddy. I think so. Maybe some hunters were shooting at groundhogs, and one of them missed."

"Why do they shoot at groundhogs?"

"Farmers hire hunters to shoot groundhogs. They dig holes in the fields."

"The hunters dig holes?"

Sam laughed. "No, silly. The groundhogs dig holes."

Eva paused, and Sam knew she was thinking that over. "Is Mommy calling the policeman?"

"Yup."

"Is he going to take you to jail?"

"No way," Sam said, ruffling her hair. "I didn't do anything wrong." If not, why did he feel so guilty? Again the voice was there telling him not to involve the authorities. "They'll come and look around and ask lots of questions. They'll figure out what happened."

"Daddy?"

"Yeah, buddy?"

"Are you OK?"

Ever since the accident Eva had been overprotective of Sam, asking him this question several times a day. Her faith was strong, but she was still a kid, and Sam knew she worried about her daddy.

Sam pulled her closer. "I'm fine, sweetie. Just fine."

He hated lying to her.

Three

Ned Coleman had wanted to be a Pennsylvania state trooper for two reasons: the uniform and the women. Like rock stars, staties had groupies, women who loved the uniform as much as Ned did and gave any man in it plenty of action as long as he was willing. And Ned was always willing. What he didn't like was the graveyard shift, and what he liked even less was Adams County.

He was a senior at Archbishop Ryan High, in Philly, the first time he met a statie. Unfortunately it was on the wrong end of a ticket, for doing ninety in his parents' Beamer on US 95. But he saw the power and intimidation that uniform commanded and fell in love with it. After graduation he tried college for two years because that was what his parents wanted (what his father wanted), but neither his heart nor his mind were in it, and he eventually flunked most of his classes. He quit college, disappointing his parents (his father), and applied to the state police academy. Two months later he received a we're-very-sorry-but-we're-denying-you-admittance letter. Ned Coleman wasn't used to being told no, and neither was his father, a powerful criminal defense attorney at the legal firm of O'Hara & Coleman. In spite of his disappointment, Garrison Coleman pulled some strings and cashed in some favors for his only son, and within a week Ned had received his acceptance letter.

The second blow came when, upon graduation from the academy, he was stationed in the Gettysburg barracks despite his requests to be placed in or around Philadelphia. Ned didn't want to cruise the back roads of Adams County at forty miles an hour, and he certainly didn't want to patrol an area that was one step above Appalachia when it came to nightlife and women. What Ned wanted, and what even his powerful lawyer of a father couldn't deliver, was the fast life in Philly—fast cars on the open highway and fast women on the Philly night scene.

So here he was, one year into his stint in hillbilly land, working the graveyard and maxing out his Crown Vic (most turnpike staties around Philly were getting Mustangs or Chargers) at fifty on the winding mountain roads of northern Adams County. Even the groupies were slow and sparse around here. Life in the fast lane it was not. Someday he'd get a transfer; he just hoped it wasn't to Potter County. The staties there spent their time cleaning up road-kill and busting rednecks for oversized tires on their pickups.

And on top of all that, his partner had gotten sick this morning and upchucked all over the dash and seat of the cruiser. Back to the barracks they went. Jeff took the rest of the day off, and Ned got a new cruiser to finish the two hours left in his shift.

Now the shift was just about over, and Ned Coleman was ready to wrap things up and head home for a morning beer and some sleep.

He was pushing his cruiser around a tight curve and accelerating into a straightaway when the PCO, Police Communications Officer, spoke over the radio. It was Tiffany, a young brunette with a smoky voice who had caught Ned's eye.

"Gettys Nine, copy a call, shots striking a house."

Ned picked up the receiver and pushed the button to talk. "Gettys Nine, bye."

"Got a report of shots striking the residence at 456 Pumping Station Road."

Great. Some hicks were probably up all night drinking and decided to get the guns out. "Any vehicle description or number of subjects involved?"

"The caller says she doesn't see any vehicles or subjects in the area. Do you want the corporal to respond from the barracks?" Tiff's voice made Ned momentarily forget his current plight.

"Negative. We'll see what we have. En route." He pulled into a gravel driveway to turn around.

"Per the corporal. Do you have an ETA?"

Ned backed up the cruiser, shifted into drive, and stepped on the gas. The wheels spun and loose stones clinked off the underside of the car. "Fifteen minutes. Ten if I'm lucky."

"OK."

As he handled the curves and straights, Ned hoped he wouldn't get sick. Man, he hated barfing.

Four

"THE POLICE WILL BE HERE SHORTLY," MOLLY SAID FROM THE foyer.

Sam kissed Eva on the top of her head and descended the stairs. Memories of last night and of following Tommy's voice down these same steps washed through his head like dark ocean waters. It was that voice from the past that had started this whole thing, the voice that haunted him.

Molly walked carefully into the living room, looking around. "What a mess. What a total mess."

It was then Sam noticed the notebook on the floor by the couch, pages splayed and bent like those same broken butterfly wings.

I am not my own.

He wanted to run and pick it up before Molly found it, but he was still barefoot. Molly circled the room, steering clear of the damage. Morning light bent at an odd angle through the broken window and dusted the room in a pink hue. Molly stopped. Sam followed her gaze to the notebook. She tiptoed between the couch and coffee table and picked it up, letting a handful of glass shards slide off. As she turned it over, her eyes traced the writing on the page.

"What's this, babe?" she said, reading the words—those words borrowed from another—that Sam had written.

He swallowed hard. "It's nothing." Such a lame response was all he could produce. He wasn't about to tell her the words were foreign even to him, though they appeared to be written by his own hand. He had absolutely no recollection of penning them.

Molly looked at him, her expression a cross between bewilderment and betrayal.

"Are you writing again?" she said.

Many years ago, it seemed like a lifetime, maybe more than a lifetime, when they had first started dating, Sam had aspired to be a writer. He wrote a few novels, was unable to get the attention of any agents or publishers, and eventually dumped his dream for carpentry, crafting with wood rather than words. No use pursuing an obvious dead end. Molly, though, loved his stories. She encouraged him to keep writing, keep submitting his novels, and never quit. She believed in him...or at least said she did.

Sam shrugged. "I was sorta thinking about it," he lied. "When I couldn't sleep last night, I jotted some things down. Just some ideas I have for a story." He held out his hand for the notebook.

Molly was about to say something when a knock came at the front door. Eva started down the stairs, but Molly handed the notebook to Sam and headed her off. "Oh, no, young lady. You stay on the steps. There's still glass you could step on."

"But Daddy's not wearing any shoes."

Molly gave Sam that be-a-good-example look. "Daddy should get some shoes on too."

Sam ignored the look and opened the door.

A state trooper stood on the porch, notepad in hand. "Mr. Travis?"

"Yes. Sam. And, uh..." Molly was there by his side. "My wife, Molly."

"I'm Officer Coleman." He looked at Molly, then past her into the house. He was already sizing up the situation. "You made the call, ma'am?"

"Yes," she said, nodding. "Sam said he heard a gunshot and then the window shattered."

Sam didn't miss her choice of words. Sam *said* he heard. Not Sam *heard* a gunshot. She doubted him already. Since the accident she hadn't taken him seriously. She would deny it, of course she would, and Sam knew it wasn't intentional, but he could tell. To him it was as obvious as blue fur on a cow.

"May I come in, folks?"

"Oh, yes. Of course," Molly said.

She and Sam moved out of the way, and Coleman stepped through the doorway. No more than thirty, he was a short man but built like a bulldozer. Thick neck, broad chest, and bulky arms. What every cop should look like. When he removed his hat, his close-cropped hair made his head look like it had a five o'clock shadow.

"Is anybody hurt?"

"No," Sam said. "Molly and Eva"—he motioned to his daughter standing on the bottom step—"were asleep when it happened. Upstairs. I was standing by the door here."

Coleman made some notes in his pad. He stopped and looked around. "Is anybody else in the house?"

The cop's left eyelid drooped ever so slightly, like a shade half-closed, and it reminded Sam of Marty Miller in the fifth grade. He had the same lazy eyelid, same side too. Sam remembered looking into that eye right before Marty's fist met Sam's mouth. What he'd found there was hate and hurt and hellfire. Vengeance came at the hands of Tommy, though. After that, Marty Miller and his droopy eyelid never messed with Sam again.

"No. Just the three of us."

"And you said you were standing here at the door."

"That's right."

"Was it open or closed?"

"Open," Sam said. "I was getting some fresh air."

Coleman examined the entryway, then leaned forward so he could see the window in the living room. He was measuring the distance. "What time did this happen?"

Sam shrugged. "Just after sunrise, so what, about six thirty, I guess?"

"And you called us at six fifty. Did any time elapse between the gunshot and the window breaking? Was there a delay?"

"It was instantaneous." Sam snapped his fingers. "The shot, then the glass broke."

"Has this ever happened before?"

"No."

"Did you hear any other shots last night or this morning?"

He had. Of course he had. He'd heard a whole battle taking place. Gunshots. Cannon blasts. Screams and hollers. "No. Just the one."

Coleman glanced into the living room again. "Mind if I look around?"

"Not at all," Molly said. "If it was a bullet, shouldn't there be a hole in the wall opposite the window?"

Coleman walked to the far wall and studied it. "Most likely, yes." He glanced several times between the window and the wall, drawing a line with his eyes. But the wall was clean. There were no holes. Nothing was disturbed. "You didn't find any rocks or anything?" Coleman asked, circling the couch, his eyes running trails along the floor.

"I looked all around the room," Molly said. "Didn't find anything."

Coleman stopped and looked at Sam. "Did you hear anything else besides the gunshot? Any yelling or talking? A car engine?"

Again Sam thought of the sounds of battle. Did the wails of the wounded and snorts of frightened horses count? "No. Just the gunshot."

"You didn't hear a car drive away?"

Sam shook his head.

"You sure it was a gunshot?"

Sam forced a little laugh. "Pretty recognizable sound, isn't it?"

"A lot of things can be mistaken for a gunshot."

"I'm certain it was a gunshot." A musket shot, to be exact, but Sam didn't think that detail would buy him any credibility points.

Coleman scanned the floor and far wall once more. "You have any enemies, Mr. Travis? Anybody you owe money, anybody you may have ticked off?"

Sam didn't like where the questions were going. He just wanted the cop to do his thing and get out. "Not that I know of."

"What do you do for a living?"

"He was a self-employed carpenter," Molly said.

Again Sam didn't miss her choice of words. *Was* a self-employed carpenter.

Coleman caught it too. "'Was?'"

Sam's hand reflexively went to his head, to the scar. "I fell a few months back and injured myself. Been on disability for a little while."

"You ever have any clients complain, file any lawsuits, stuff like that?"

Sam shook his head. "Never. There've been a few jobs where the client wasn't completely satisfied, but I went back and made it right. I always do that."

Coleman glanced between Sam and Molly. He kept his voice low. "You two OK? I mean, marriage problems or anything?"

Molly took Sam's arm in her hands. "No, of course not. We're fine."

Looking at Sam, Coleman kept his expression flat, emotionless. "You seeing anybody's wife?"

Anger rose in Sam's chest. Flashes of Marty Miller taunted him. The lazy eyelid. The fist. The fat lip for a week. "Of course not!"

"What kind of question is that?" Molly snapped.

Coleman shifted his eyes and tightened his jaw. "Sorry, folks. Routine questions. We have to cover every angle."

"What do you think happened?" Molly asked.

Coleman took one last look at the living room. "If there was an entry point anywhere in the room, I'd say it was probably some poachers or groundhoggers with bad aim. But...I'm not sure. I'll file a criminal mischief report and check if there were any similar reports filed in this area recently. I'll check with the neighbors too, see if they heard anything. In the meantime, if you see or hear anything suspicious, call the barracks immediately." He retrieved a business card from his pocket. "That's my name and the number for the barracks. I'm sorry this happened, folks. Not exactly the kind of thing you want to wake up to. Call your insurance company about the window. I'll check the area and make extra checks in the next few days. If anything comes up, don't hesitate to call, OK?"

They both nodded, and with that, Coleman shook their hands. Sam watched him get into the cruiser, back out of the driveway, and pull away.

From the steps Eva said, "Mommy, there's something I didn't tell you."

Five

Sam leaned against the doorframe of the dining room. Molly sat next to Eva on the step. A strange heaviness permeated the house, as if Eva's simple declaration was the precursor to a coming storm of immense proportion. A storm that would devastate, maybe even annihilate, their family.

"What is it, darling?" Molly said, stroking Eva's hair. She apparently could not sense the tempest.

Eva, on the other hand, could. She had an odd look in her eyes, a mixture of fear and concern. She glanced at Sam, squeezed Max tighter, then said to Molly, "It's about Daddy. Can I just tell you? Alone?"

Molly and Sam locked eyes. Since his accident Eva had asked a ton of questions, and Sam and Molly had done their best to answer honestly without adding worry and stress to their seven-year-old. But this seemed different.

Molly said to Eva, "It's OK, baby. You can tell both of us. Daddy can hear what you have to say."

"It's fine, honey," Sam reassured her. "Go ahead."

Eva swallowed hard and leaned her head against her mother's arm.

Molly wrapped her in a hug and set Eva on her lap. "Now, what's this all about?"

"Is Daddy OK?" Eva spoke to no one in particular. She made no eye contact.

Molly looked at Sam, then ran her fingers over Eva's straight blonde hair. "Yes, darling. Daddy's fine. He's gonna be fine."

Sam squatted and put his hand on Eva's back. He could feel

her heartbeat tapping rapidly against her ribs. "I told you I'm fine, buddy. Nothing to worry about."

"I had a dream last night," Eva said. Her voice was low and serious.

And again that sense of an impending storm. Sam could almost hear the thunder in the distance, smell the ozone in the air.

"There was someone in my dream. He was real shiny all over. His name's Jacob. He said he's here to help us." Eva's eyes darted to Sam, then away. There was uncertainty in them, like she was sharing something she'd be mocked or punished for saying. She nuzzled her face against Molly's shoulder. "He told me to tell Daddy I love him every day and make sure he knows it. And he said Daddy's real scared and needs my prayers." She spoke as if Sam were nowhere near, a million miles away.

A jolt of electricity ran up Sam's back, and the hair on his neck prickled. He looked at Molly.

She said, "That sounds like an important dream, baby. You *should* tell Daddy you love him every day. And give him hugs and kisses too."

Eva turned her face toward Sam. In less than an instant that million miles closed to twelve inches. "Are you scared, Daddy? Was Jacob right?"

Sam knew his hesitation said it all, even to a seven-year-old. "Sometimes. All grown-ups get scared sometimes."

"But what about right now?"

"No, buddy." Another lie. He remembered Tommy's voice last night, the reverberation of the cannon blasts, the echoes of agony from across the field. He hadn't been scared of the sounds; he'd been scared of himself. "I'm fine right now."

"I'll pray for you," Eva said. "Like Jacob said."

Pangs of guilt hit Sam like multiple bullet punches. His daughter's faith put his to shame. Since the accident he'd not prayed much at all. Had no interest in it. He swallowed past the baseball in his throat and said, "Thank you, Eva. I think I need your prayers."

Eva sat up straight in Molly's lap and threw herself at him, wrapping her little arms around his neck. "I love you, Daddy. I love you so much."

Behind his eyes Sam's sinuses felt as if they'd been injected with concrete. He held his daughter close and took in the familiar scent of her skin. "I love you too, little buddy. Daddy's girl."

Six

Ned Coleman arrived back at the barracks as the first-shift staties were heading out to comb the highways and byways of Adams County. On his way into the building he ran into John Becker, a five-year war veteran who thought he was the good Lord's gift to law enforcement. According to Becker, he had spent those years training in the army as a Green Beret, seen some covert action in Central America, drug cartel stuff, then came home to hillbilly land to serve and protect. At least that was the story *he* told.

Becker slapped Ned on the back as they passed. "Hey, man, good ride?"

He called a shift a "ride" for no reason at all, except that this was John Becker, supercop, and he said it like he owned the word. It irritated Ned.

"Wonderful. Just wonderful."

Becker kept walking but spun around and backpedaled. He was wearing mirrored aviator sunglasses, the kind that looked cool in the 1980s on Tom Cruise in *Top Gun* but looked ridiculous on Becker. "I heard Santos puked all over your vehicle," he said with a grin. "Bet that was nice."

Ned kept walking and didn't say a word. He pushed through the glass doors, waved a weak hello to a couple other staties preparing for their "ride," and found his desk. He needed to fill out an Initial Crime Report on the shooting, then he could call it a day. That was another thing Ned didn't like: paperwork.

As he waited for the computer to boot up, Corporal Jim Kerr stopped by his desk. "You wrappin' up, Coleman?" Kerr was OK as far as corporals went, but he was a real pain in the butt when it came to procedure. Everything was by the book, no exceptions.

"Yes, sir. Just doing this initial, then heading home. That shooting on Pumping Station held me over."

"Everything go book there?" Kerr's annoying phrase was "go book," meaning "by the book." Everyone knew he was trying to get it to catch on so he could claim he'd coined it. Ned refused to play along.

"Sure. Smooth as glass."

Except it hadn't been as smooth as glass, had it? And it hadn't gone by the book either. There was no entry point on the far wall or anywhere in the room. He'd checked it out good. No slug on the floor either. A shooting with no bullet. And the neighbors had heard nothing. Not that that disproved anything in itself. Out there on Pumping Station the houses were separated by a few hundred yards of farmland on either side. If it was a low-caliber rifle, a sound sleeper could miss the discharge easily.

Something about that Travis guy just didn't seem right, though. Like he was withholding information. Ned hadn't been a cop long, but he'd quickly developed that police instinct and could tell when someone wasn't spilling his guts. In fact, if Travis's wife hadn't played it so cool, he'd have thought Travis was making the whole thing up. 'Course, maybe he was making it up. Maybe Travis had a short fuse and busted the window in a fit of rage, or maybe he was just a klutz and too embarrassed to admit it. Concocting some story about a shooter would keep the cops and his wife off his back and get the damages covered by his homeowners'.

Hey, it wasn't Ned's job to read minds, just the evidence, and while this was weird, it certainly wasn't the weirdest thing he'd seen in Adams County. But that was the problem: the evidence. It didn't support Travis's testimony.

Kerr tapped the desk with his index finger and looked straight ahead. "Make it quick, trooper. You're already pullin' OT."

"Yes, sir."

Fifteen minutes later his report was finished and he was officially off the clock. Ned Coleman wanted nothing more than to head home, jump in the shower, throw back a couple beers and some food—he had leftover Chinese in the fridge—and hit the sack.

Seven

SAM SAT AT HIS DESK IN A STUPOR. THE STUDY'S FOUR WALLS seemed closer than the last time he was in here. How had he never noticed how small this room was? The feel of his desk chair, the curve of the seat, the lumbar support...it all irritated him.

Minutes ago Molly had ordered him to his room like a child so she could clean the mess in the living room. He wasn't sure if she believed him about the gunshot or not. Wasn't sure if Coleman had believed him either. Fact was, he wasn't sure if he believed himself. He could no longer trust his own mind. It was sending false signals to his ears, counterfeit sounds that existed only in the short-circuited sphere of his broken brain.

Anger and frustration bloomed in him like poison flowers. Six months ago he would have been the one cleaning up downstairs, putting plastic over the window, calling the glass guys. Now Molly had taken over that role, usurped it to "protect him." He knew her intentions were good (she *was* only trying to protect him) and that her uncertainty about his mental capacity was justified (since the accident he'd proven himself to be cognitively challenged in more than a few areas), but she needed to give him a chance, let him learn how to function on his own again.

Sam ran his finger along the edge of the desk, leaving a trail in the light dust. He could hear her down there, sweeping glass across the hardwood, brushing it into the metal dustpan, dumping it in the plastic wastebasket. Eva was down there too, mouth going like a high-rpm engine. He couldn't make out what she was saying, but he imagined her telling Molly every last element of her dream. He'd never known someone to remember dreams in such vivid detail. Eva could recount hers as though she'd just finished watching them in high definition on the big screen.

His desk was a mess. That was something he'd lost since the accident—his organizational ability. Bills were piling up, some no doubt overdue. He didn't even know anymore. Molly had tried to commandeer this from him too, but he'd insisted he could handle it, and to her credit she allowed him to try. Finances and bookkeeping had never been his specialty, but he'd managed them adequately. Now, of course, the disability checks were birdseed compared to what he used to bring home.

Atop the envelopes and bills and receipts and other assorted junk Eva's notebook sat like a lump of smoldering coals. That was another thing, the strange writing.

Samuel Whiting. Who was he? *What* was he?

And why was Sam Travis suddenly in Samuel Whiting's head? He'd have to deal with that another time. Soon.

He leaned back in his chair, the wheeled office job Molly got him for his birthday three years back, the birthday after he decided to venture out and experience the life of a self-employed carpenter. He'd loved his work too, until the fall. He still had no memory of it, which drove him batty. He was a fixer, and if he'd made a mistake—a wrong step, a faulty joint, a careless move—he wanted to know about it so he could make a memo to self to never do that again.

But by all reports he'd done nothing to cause such a fall. He tried to imagine it, his foot slipping on a loose shingle (though none of the shingles were loose), his legs disappearing from under him, hands groping frantically to find purchase on something, anything. His body being airborne (the roof from which he fell was twenty feet high), feeling weightless for a mere moment, then striking the ground. His head taking the brunt of the fall, neck snapping but not breaking, brain rattling like an egg yolk in his skull. Then lying motionless, unconscious, while sirens blared and passersby whispered and murmured. But it was only his battered brain that conjured those images; there was no truth to any of them. It may have happened just like that, or it may have been nothing like that.

The morning sun was slanting through the study window, bathing him in warmth, tugging at his eyelids. He hadn't slept well last night, not in his own bed, not on the sofa. Downstairs, Molly was still sweeping glass; Eva was still jabbering away. But Sam's mind focused on the voice from last night.

Tommy's voice.

Had it actually sounded that real? Real enough to pull him from his bed and lure him downstairs, like a magical flute in the hands of a malevolent piper?

Slowly he blinked, and his vision blurred. Fatigue, both mental and physical, washed over him, pulling him into the land of sleep and his own disturbing dreams...

Mom and Dad were downstairs in the kitchen arguing. Always the arguing. Always about Tommy.

Sammy's brother, who bested him by two years and about forty pounds, was at it again. Mr. Aholt (nicknames abounded) had called from the school. Tommy had apparently jammed a dissected rat's head over the nozzle of the water fountain so that water arced out of the rodent's mouth.

Tommy was in his room in the attic now, Black Sabbath's "Iron Man" blaring from the stereo, thumping through the floorboards. Sammy opened his bedroom door and crept to the top of the stairs to hear what Mom and Dad were saying.

"I think he's nuts, Gloria!" Dad said. "Out of his mind. He needs professional help."

Mom's voice came back sharp and double-edged. "How dare you say that about your own son. Your own blood. He's no crazier than you are."

"Me crazy? I'm not the one protecting a kid who cuts the head off a rat and stuffs it on a water fountain."

"He's looking for attention, probably from his father who never gives it to him."

"Don't you tell me about showing my boys attention. I'm busy working my tail off so I can put food on the table, on their *table."*

Sam had heard enough. The arguing made his stomach knot up and gave him a headache. And Tommy was beginning to scare him. His temper had grown hotter in the past few months. He'd never taken it out on Sam, but their Lab, Gomer, had been on the receiving end more than once.

Back in his room Sam shut the door, sat on the edge of his bed, and reached for his rifle. Dad had gotten him his first gun, a Remington .22, for Christmas, and he'd proven to be quite the marksman. He could hit a Coke can right in the C *from fifty yards away without a scope. Dad said he was a natural. Tommy said, "Big deal." The rifle brought a bit of comfort, a sense of safety, though he was sure he'd never have to use it against his own family.*

He was sure of it.

A knock came at his door, and he jumped. He gripped the rifle tighter and felt his pulse pounding all the way to his fingertips.

"Sammy." It was Tommy.

Sam didn't say anything but forced himself to loosen his fingers from the gun. Tommy was no threat. He was his brother.

"Sammy…"

Sam jolted awake and nearly fell off his chair. The feel of the rifle's wooden stock was still imprinted on the nerves of his hand. Tommy's voice, like a distant echo, trailed off and faded to nothing.

After rubbing his face and combing his hands through his hair, Sam walked to the window. The sun was a blazing disk now, hovering above the South Mountains of Adams County. The fall colors, weeks past prime, were muted and browning. More than half the trees were bare, exposing twisted and contorted limbs. In the distance two buzzards carved wide arcs in the sky.

Movement in the left rear of the property caught Sam's eye. A groundhog was rummaging through the weeds at the edge of the field. It was a good sixty, seventy yards off, just a gray-brown ball of fur. Sam thought of his gun, not the .22 but the Winchester

Model 70 he got when he turned fifteen, the one he had used to drop more deer than his dad and Tommy combined. He was a natural, after all.

He went to the study closet, opened the door, and stood with arms hanging limply, eyes glazed over. Behind a stack of Molly's old shoes, next to a curtain rod in the back left corner, the Winchester leaned against the wall. It beckoned him, whispering his name. His palms itched to feel the grain of the wood. His trigger finger twitched.

When he took hold of the rifle, the metal felt alive in his hand, and the weapon seemed to sigh. He hadn't fired it in twenty-one years. For more than two decades the rifle had sat comatose, neglected, abandoned. Now with it in his grip, he felt the life surging back into it. It awakened in him a desire he hadn't felt since the last time he fired it. He wanted to shoot something. He *needed* to shoot something.

After all, he was a natural.

The groundhog. What a perfect target to give rebirth to his innate ability.

Sam remembered the ammunition's location. Dresser. Top drawer, in the back, under his boxers and briefs. He kept his dresser in the study to save room in their bedroom since these old homes had small rooms and even smaller closets.

He crossed the floor in three large strides, pulled open the top drawer, and dug his hands through his underwear. His fingers found the magazine. The feel was unmistakable. In one deft motion, as though he'd been doing it every day for the past twenty-one years, he positioned the rifle in his left hand and snapped the magazine into place with his right. Working the bolt action, he chambered a round.

From the window Sam spotted the groundhog in the same place, foraging among the same weeds. Quietly, so as not to attract Molly's or Eva's attention, he slid open the sash and lifted the screen. Cool air tickled his face. It felt good. Sam raised the rifle and placed the butt against his shoulder. It was a natural fit, like an extension of his arm, of his own skeleton, his own flesh. He sighted the groundhog down the barrel and put a bead on it.

The last time he'd done this he was aiming at...

You did what you had to do, son.

His hands began to tremble, sending the tip of the barrel into erratic little circles.

Sam closed his eyes and slowed his breathing. He focused on a steady inhale and exhale, found the rhythm of his heart. Opening his right eye, he fixed his sights once again on the groundhog. There was no more trembling. His hand was as steady as concrete. His right index finger found the trigger and coiled tightly enough to collapse the fat pad on his fingertip. All it would take now was two pounds of pressure to squeeze off a round and put a hole the size of a golf ball in the little varmint.

The groundhog moved to the right and Sam followed it, keeping the sight on its midsection. He relaxed his shoulders, arms, hands, found the even rise and fall of his breathing again. During exhalation he took his time, feeling the weight of the gun, the texture of the wooden stock, matching its heartbeat with his own. They were one.

On the other end of the barrel the critter was motionless, as if it knew its time had come and there wasn't a thing it could do, as if it accepted its fate and embraced the violence soon to be hailed upon it.

The groundhog, Sam realized suddenly, was about the size of a human head. A figure flashed across his brain's imaging center, causing his eyes to lose focus and the end of the barrel to lose its target.

He couldn't do it. He couldn't.

Eight

Molly Travis dumped the last of the glass shards into the wastebasket. She glanced back at the window, where that mouth of jagged teeth sucked in cool air that said winter was on the way. Normally Sam would have been the one cleaning up and putting plastic over the opening. Since the accident, though, he'd had trouble with decision making and sequencing; that's what the occupational therapist called it.

She sat on the couch and let her mind go for a moment. She was so very tired, more tired than she could remember ever being. Memories of that day, that moment, floated back into her mind as they did on a regular basis.

It had been three o'clock in the afternoon, the sun hot and high in the sky, the air thick with humidity. She'd opened all the windows in the house, but no air moved through the screens as she waited for Beth Fisher to bring Eva home from school. Both moms had agreed the school bus was no place for their daughters and arranged to carpool. Today was Beth's day. The phone rang, Molly answered, and that's when her world was grabbed and shaken violently like a dying rabbit in a dog's mouth. It was Norman Guise, the elderly man Sam was doing some work for. He said Sam had fallen from the roof and been taken to the hospital. It was bad. That's all he knew.

Molly called Beth on the cell, asked her to take Eva home with her, then rushed to Gettysburg Hospital. But Sam wasn't there. The emergency room receptionist said he'd been flown to the regional trauma center.

Trauma center? Molly remembered how those words had

crowded her mind like a granite boulder the whole hour it took her to get there. How far had he fallen? How had he landed? What injuries had he sustained? So many questions with no answers.

When she arrived, she was told Sam had fallen a good twenty feet and his head had absorbed the impact. There were no broken bones, no spinal injuries, but multiple contusions had been found on his brain. "Coup-countrecoup"—that's what the doctor called it. It was when the brain got shaken like yogurt and developed bruises on all sides.

The initial prognosis wasn't good. Sam was in a coma, and nobody knew what dysfunctions he'd have when he came out of it... *if* he came out.

For Molly, it was like being submerged in murky water. That disoriented, suffocating feeling. She prayed, oh, how she prayed. She took Eva to visit her daddy every day. She and Eva cuddled together, cried together, prayed some more together, and for four weeks slept in the same bed together. That's how long it took Sam to climb out of his coma.

But he wasn't the same man when he returned home. Though glimpses of the old Sam surfaced from time to time, for the first month or so it was like living with a stranger. There were times when Molly watched him sit and stare out a window, wondering if she could live the rest of her life with this man she no longer knew. Slowly, though, almost imperceptibly, the old Sam reemerged. There were still deficits with organizational skills, decision making, and that blasted sequencing, but the therapist said those should return in time. Molly just had to hold on a little longer, carry the weight a little farther.

Yes. So very tired.

She rubbed her eyes, smoothed back her hair, and headed to the closet for the vacuum. That's when she heard the gunshot.

Her first thought was that it had originated from outside the house—like the gunshot Sam had heard earlier—and she instinctively ducked and covered her head. Someone was shooting at her.

But as the concussion reverberated in her ears, she realized it had not come from beyond the four walls of her home but from within. Upstairs.

Heart in her throat, mind racing with all sorts of grisly images, Molly dashed up the stairs two at a time.

On the second floor Eva stood in the hallway. "Mommy?"

The sight of her daughter, unscathed, sent a wave of relief over Molly but dread as well. Sam. The door to his study was closed. Would he…?

"It's OK, baby," she said to Eva, trying in vain to control the shaking of her voice.

She listened and heard nothing from beyond the shut door. The only sounds were Eva's hitched breathing and her own pulse tapping in her ears.

"Eva, go back in your bedroom."

"But is Daddy…?"

Molly swiveled and faced her daughter. In Eva's eyes she saw confusion and fear. Eva was seven but no dummy. She knew what Molly was thinking. "Honey, go in your bedroom, OK? Let me check on Daddy."

Eva stepped back into her room, her eyes never leaving her mother.

Molly turned, placed her hand on the doorknob, and pulled in a deep breath. Her heart thumped like a war drum, beating out a rhythm of doom. The knob was cold and seemed to warn her against turning it. She placed her other palm on the door, hoping to feel Sam's heartbeat through the board, but found nothing but lifeless wood. She turned the handle, heard the latch click, and pushed.

The door creaked open on dry hinges, and there, by the window, his back to her, stood her husband. The window was up and Sam was leaned forward, his hands on the sill. Daylight silhouetted his hunched frame and gave him an almost ghostly appearance.

"Sam? You all right?" Her voice sounded weak and thread-thin to her ears.

He didn't turn. "Yeah."

Next to him, his rifle was propped against the wall. The one he'd kept in the closet and never once fired in their thirteen years of marriage.

Molly approached Sam and rested a hand on his back. She looked back to make sure Eva hadn't wandered out of her room. "What's going on?"

Sam shrugged. "Groundhog."

Well, that made sense. He'd seen a groundhog and taken a shot at it. Molly looked out the window and scanned the backyard, but saw no dead fur ball. "Did you get it?"

"Nope."

She could hear the disappointment in his voice, the discouragement, the self-reproach. According to the stories she'd heard, he had once been quite the shot. Had a knack for marksmanship. But it was something Molly rarely spoke of...and Sam never mentioned.

"It wasn't more than seventy yards away," he said. "Shoulda poked it."

He looked at his hand, and Molly noticed the trembling.

"It's OK," she said, but she knew her words fell on deaf ears. They meant nothing to Sam. She didn't even want to broach the subject of why he'd taken the shot. What had urged him to dig his rifle from the closet, load it, and do something he hadn't done in at least thirteen years?

Sam hit the sill with both palms, hard enough to rattle the wall. "It's not OK."

Molly thought he looked older than his thirty-six years. The lines of his face were deeper, his stubble grayer. The distant look in his eyes was one she hadn't noticed before. "You scared Eva and me, you know."

Sam looked at her with those blank eyes. He forced a little smile. "Sorry. Didn't mean to do that. Just thought..."

She waited for him to finish, but his words trailed off like a column of smoke into a starless sky. "Well, no harm done. Not even to the groundhog." Her attempt at humor was ill received. "Where's the plastic for the window? There's cold air pouring in."

Sam paused. She could see he was processing the question, mentally searching the house, the cellar, his supplies.

"On the shelves next to my workbench in the basement." He started to get up. "I can do it, Moll."

Molly put a hand on his shoulder. "Why don't you put that gun away so Eva doesn't get it? I'll get the plastic, and you can show me how to do it. I'd like to learn some home-improvement stuff."

"Fair enough."

She lifted her hand from his shoulder and noticed the notebook from downstairs, open on his desk. "I see you've been writing again."

Nine

Sam slumped into his desk chair and stared at the notebook. There was more writing on its lined pages. Tentacles of fear wormed into his chest and strangled his heart. He hoped his reaction wasn't evident to Molly. "Uh, yeah, I guess I have been."

"Good for you," she said, smiling. "I think it's what you need."

"Yeah."

"I'll get the plastic and meet you in the living room."

"Yeah." It was all he could say.

His mind wasn't on plastic or the living room or the broken window or the cold air pouring into the house. Goodness, no. Those were the last things on his mind. He was thinking about the unusual words, scrawled in his own handwriting, dated July 1, 1863. The first day of the Battle of Gettysburg. He was thinking about how they had gotten there. Thinking about how he hoped—man, he hoped—he wasn't going insane. After all he'd been through and put Molly and Eva through, that was the last thing he needed.

Behind him Molly closed the door on her way out. The click of the latch sounded like a gunshot, causing him to jump, and in his mind he saw the snap of a head and spray of blood.

On the desk the notebook waited. It beckoned him to take hold of it and read, as if it held some cryptic message for his eyes only, as if Samuel Whiting—whoever he was—had solved the mysteries of quantum physics and now reached a gnarled hand through the gulf of time and space, touching him, tapping him on the shoulder, grabbing him by the scruff of the neck.

He picked it up and leaned back in his chair. The words spoke to him from the past.

July 1, 1863
Captain Samuel Whiting
As we came into a field full of wheat and straw, some parts of it were already on fire. We drew into battery, our three-inch ordnances belChing forth a deadly fire at 600 yards. To my left, I saw the 11th Corps streaming toward the town. The rebEls were in close pursuit. I ordered wheels right-right to cover their retreat. At the same time I saw puffs of white smoke coMing at a half mile. Within seconds we were under terrific fire of shot and shell. I ordered the battery to split two left and two right and return fire. Soon another battEry wheeled and silenced the enemy. We took aim at the mass of gray hot on our boys' heels, but they already had forward momenTum and could not be stopped.

By this time the sun was well on its way down. Received orders to withdraw to a hill to the left rear of town. We were forced to leave behind four dead and one fiEld piece (spiked, of course).

Eight horses dead, sixteen wounded. The move took several hours. The terrain was very rough. Once upon the hill, we woRked with infantry to make formidable breastworks and two well-placed gun redoubts. Here, the enemy would pay dearly getting at us.

When I am alone, I question the need for war, especially this war. These men we fight, the enemy, are our brothers, our countrYmen. I would never tell my boys this. God knows they need a leader right now. But still, I question it.

He read it again. And a third time. The letters—had he noticed them in the first entry? He flipped back a page and scanned the first of the writings. They were there too. There was more to these cryptic messages than he thought. But what did it mean?

Sam let the notebook fall from his hands onto his lap. He was going nuts, that's what it meant. He was sure of it. What kind of a person wrote this stuff and didn't remember it? Was he scribbling it in his sleep? He wasn't even a Civil War buff. He didn't even know some of the terminology he'd written with his own hand, with his own pen. Wiping a palm across his forehead, he noticed he'd broken out in a cold sweat.

From downstairs Molly hollered, "Hon, I got the plastic. You ready?"

He had no idea. He tried to change gears and think about the window, the plastic, the gaping hole pouring cold air into the house, but he couldn't do it.

A knock, quiet and hesitant, cut through his thoughts. "Daddy?"

Sam swallowed hard and steadied his voice. "Yeah, baby girl?"

"Do you have my notebook? The one I write my stories in?"

Prickles took to Sam's arms. Her notebook. The one *he'd* been writing *his* stories in. He couldn't let her see the entries. She couldn't know what was happening to him. "Uh, yeah, I have it. Just a minute."

Ten

THE MAN DROVE HIS 1998 DODGE INTREPID WELL INTO THE night. He didn't bother noting the time. It didn't matter. These days he rarely slept anyway. His metabolism was in overdrive, causing insatiable hunger and a terrible case of insomnia. Sleep was as rare for him as a raucous nightlife was for a nun.

His destination: Gettysburg, Pennsylvania. That hallowed soil had swallowed the blood of fifty-one thousand men over three days in the summer of 1863. He tried to imagine the carnage of that battle. The ground soaked and stained red. Dead bodies piled and bloating under the summer sun. The moans and cries of the wounded. The smell of rot and decay. One of the bloodiest battles in American history. He knew his facts. He had no idea how he knew them, but the numbers were there in his head, along with an encyclopedia of other junk. Useless stuff. Stuff like the population of Fargo (ninety-three thousand), the lifespan of the common housefly (about twenty-one days), and the world's tallest tree (a Mendocino redwood in California, 364 feet).

But none of that mattered at the moment. The only thing that mattered was the target, and she was in Gettysburg.

He'd first been instructed about the target a few days ago, over the phone. The voice on the line had called him Symon, though he doubted that was his real name, his birth name. Fact was, he had few recollections earlier than a couple of months ago. They were spotty at best, like headlights whizzing by in the dark. Except these headlights were the stuff of nightmares, the kind that turned into fiery eyes above toothy jaws waiting to chomp down and eat him alive.

The male voice was familiar, though he couldn't identify it. No amount of pondering could jar that memory loose from the concrete in his head. The man gave him information, directions, and orders, and he felt compelled to obey them—like a soldier following his superior's commands.

Even as the voice kept him connected to this world, his thoughts wandered to a world of sketches and snapshots, of broken memories and lost history…

His earliest memory was of his stepfather stuffing him into a closet at the age of five. He can't remember why he'd been put there or how long he stayed, but he tasted blood, warm and metallic on his lips, and he nestled back past the coats that smelled like his mother's Miss Dior perfume. The darkness brought safety and seclusion. He tried not to focus on the line of light beneath the door. It was only as thick as his little finger, but it scared the stuffing out of him. There was no comfort in it. The light, that single line of light, reminded him of the cold world where mothers are beaten senseless and boys are locked away.

His next memory whizzed by. It was four years later. The drunk was still a drunk, maybe even worse—if that's possible—and this was the first time Symon saw the man's hands on Symon's older sister. She was sixteen and had no friends. When she walked past the drunk in the Barcalounger, she tried to steer clear, but he leaned over and got his hand on her rear. She did nothing to push it away, and their mother acted like she didn't notice. But Symon noticed, and he hated the drunk even more.

In the dark of the night, with only the dash lights to illuminate the Intrepid's interior, Symon pushed a tear from his eye. He had no idea if the drunk was still alive; that wasn't part of his flashcard memory. He did know, though, that the car was low on gas, and if he didn't get a fill soon, he'd be stranded and lose precious time.

A few miles down the road, he pulled into a twenty-four-hour convenience store and stopped alongside a gas pump. A handwritten sign said:

Please pre-pay after dark.
Thank you, Management.

When Symon inserted the nozzle into the tank and squeezed the lever, nothing happened. He squeezed again with the same result. A knock on the store window caused him to turn. A man was there, forty-something, pudgy, bald, rubbing his fingers together, making the sign of money. Symon smiled and entered the store.

"You gotta pay first, buddy," the man behind the counter said. "You didn't see the sign?" His tone called Symon an idiot. He had a high-pitched, almost squeaky Porky Pig voice that plucked at Symon's nerves.

"Guess I missed it," Symon said. "Let me get some supplies for the road first."

The place was a dump, one of those stop-and-shop jobs that were dirty, dingy, never stocked well, and rarely frequented by the locals. Symon walked down an aisle and grabbed several candy bars, a bag of chips, a few snack cakes, and three Cokes. He dropped his supplies on the counter in front of the register.

Porky chuckled. Symon hated the way it made the man's double chin quiver like a half-filled water balloon. "Got a long trip ahead of you?"

Symon didn't return the smile. "What state is this?"

The amusement disappeared from Porky's face. "You don't know? You're in Virginia, man. Just outside Lynchburg."

"How far to Gettysburg?"

"Pennsylvania?"

Symon said nothing.

"Um, well, if you get on 81, it's 'bout five hours maybe." He gave a nervous laugh. "Depends on how fast you drive, you know?"

Symon looked from the supplies to Porky. "I do."

"You some kind of Civil War buff? 'Cause we got—"

"Thirty in gas," Symon said.

"OK. Thirty it is." A thin film of sweat had formed on Porky's expansive forehead. His nervousness pleased Symon. After ringing up the supplies, the clerk said, "That'll be forty-four dollars and sixty-two cents."

Symon looked around. "You here alone tonight?"

Porky looked at his watch. His right eye twitched. "Actually, it's morning."

"Do you like working the graveyard shift?"

Porky didn't answer right away. He stuck one finger—the thing looked like a stubby hot dog—in his collar and loosened it, revealing dirt-crusted creases in his neck. "Forty-four dollars and sixty-two cents, please."

"Do I look familiar to you?"

The question obviously caught Porky off guard because he removed the finger from his collar and swallowed hard, forcing a weak smile. "No... no, sir. I've never seen you before. Never at all."

Symon leaned over the counter and drilled him with a stare. "You sure? Look closely. It really is a matter of life or death."

The sweat had increased on Porky's forehead and now beaded on his cheeks and chin. His lower lip quivered. "I, uh... well, I... maybe, I mean, I can't be sure, you know, we see a lot of customers around here, tourists moving through, people just like yourself, and, you know, so many faces it's hard to tell."

"Have you ever been robbed?" Symon had had enough of Porky's blathering. "Held at gunpoint and forced to do something you didn't want to do?"

The clerk's hand moved from the countertop to his side. His eyes were wide and buggy, and his lower lip trembled even more now. The quiver made it to his neck and jiggled the fat surrounding it. It disgusted Symon. He hated this man, this common gas station clerk. He reached into his jacket pocket, wrapped his fingers around the grip of his handgun.

In his mind he saw how it would play out. He'd put three holes in Porky's thick neck, driving the man back into the pane of glass shielding stacks of cigarettes. He would slip to the floor as crystalline rain fell around his writhing body.

Porky's eyes darted from Symon to the ceiling and then back to Symon. The security camera. He couldn't leave a trail. It would ruin his entire mission. So instead of the Beretta, Symon pulled out a money clip and handed the clerk a fifty.

With shaky hands Porky counted out the change and gave it to Symon, with no further words being exchanged between the two.

After filling the Intrepid, Symon got back on the road toward Gettysburg.

Three hours later, after consuming most of the candy bars and one and a half Cokes, he saw another memory creep toward him with its fiery eyes and toothy snarl…

He was fifteen. Angry. He hated his sister for letting the drunk use her up. He hated his mother for keeping the man around. And he hated the drunk for a variety of reasons. A montage of still images stuttered by:

His mother on the kitchen floor, crying, her jaw displaced and bleeding.

His sister near the counter, hands over her mouth and blood on her shirt.

The drunk hulking near the door, gripping a baseball bat in both hands, face twisted like a demon's.

Then motion returned to Symon's memory. He ran from the kitchen, eyes blurred with tears and hatred, as the drunk hollered something foul at him. He was in his bedroom, with the .22 he had snuck into the house and hid under his bed. He'd never used it, saving it for a time such as this. Quickly, with trembling hands, he made sure the magazine was securely in place, clicked off the safety, and stumbled down the stairs.

Back in the kitchen his mother was still crying, her whimpers muffled by her hands. His sister was screaming something incoherent, and the drunk was cursing, telling them both to shut up. Just as Symon arrived, the drunk raised the bat to bring it down on Symon's sister. In one swift motion, yelling like an idiot, Symon lifted the rifle, pointed the barrel at the bulk of the drunk's torso, and squeezed off a shot. He didn't even hear the concussion of the gun. The drunk snapped back, dropped the bat, and clawed at his gut. Symon didn't hear the boom of the next three shots, and the next three after that.

His final memory, another snapshot, was of the kitchen linoleum coated in sticky red.

Eleven

Molly awoke in the darkness with the feeling something was wrong. She'd had no nightmare, no dreams of any kind, in fact. The smoke detector wasn't screaming; there was no acrid smell of smoke in the air. Sam was next to her, asleep. Wide-eyed, she lay still on her back, hands clasped to her chest, and listened. Outside the wind howled, and she imagined a hundred long-haired, snaggle-toothed, hollow-eyed ghouls circling the house, crying a mournful dirge—an image from a recurrent childhood nightmare.

Molly heard a voice from down the hall, carrying over the baying of the wind and the occasional creaks of the house. It was Eva. On the bedside table the clock's numbers clicked from 3:01 to 3:02.

Molly's first thought was that Eva was talking in her sleep. It wouldn't be the first time. Last year she'd gone through a bout where almost every night she emerged from her room in a lazy sleepwalk, mumbling nonsensically about needing to do this or watch out for that, asking how the green water got on the sofa and where it came from. Her pediatrician said that the stresses of first grade sometimes manifested themselves in children sleepwalking and talking in their sleep. Within weeks the episodes sputtered out and never surfaced again. Until now.

Molly pushed off her covers and swung her legs over the edge of the bed. Behind her Sam grunted, then rolled over. Eva was still jabbering away, though Molly couldn't make out what she was saying. Nothing unusual.

As long as her daughter wasn't wandering the halls or navigating the steps, Molly would just tuck her in, pat her head, give a little kiss, and let her continue her harmless prattling.

Out of the bedroom and down the hallway Molly walked, shuffling her slippers so as not to stumble on one of the toys left out from the previous day of play. She stopped at Eva's closed door. Her daughter was holding quite the conversation with her sleep friends.

"...Max likes to play hide-and-seek. That's his favorite game of all time. He's really good too. His best hiding place is under the bed. And he's not even scared of the dark under there."

There was a break in the rambling, and for a moment Molly thought Eva was finished. Then she started up again.

"No, I'm not really scared of the dark. Well, sometimes I am. Not when my night-light is on, though. And not when you're here with me."

An electric static buzzed over Molly, and every inch of her skin tightened. This was not the idle chatter of sleep talk. It was too coherent, made too much sense. And as far as Molly knew, Eva had no invisible friends. She was a child with an active and colorful imagination, but she'd never taken it in that direction. Her feet had stayed firmly rooted in the soil of reality.

Molly pushed open the door and found Eva sitting Indian-style on her bed, the covers clumped at the foot of the mattress. She was holding Max in her lap and appeared wide-awake, as alert at 3:00 a.m. as she had been at 3:00 p.m.

Uneasy, Molly approached her daughter, hoping Eva's conversation was with Max the stuffed dog and no one else. "Eva? What're you doing, baby?"

Eva looked from her mother to the corner of the bedroom, causing Molly to glance back over her shoulder, but the room was empty. No uninvited visitor lurked in the corner. "Nothing," Eva said. "I couldn't sleep."

For a moment her daughter's eyes looked glassy, and Molly thought she was indeed still asleep. "Baby, are you awake?"

Eva grinned. "Yeah."

"How many fingers am I holding up?" She held her hand at face level, all five fingers splayed. This was the test she always used to determine if Eva was awake or not.

Eva's smile grew bigger. "Four... and one thumb." Molly wanted to laugh but didn't. Definitely awake. She sat next to Eva and ran her hand over her daughter's soft hair. "Who were you talking to?"

Eva glanced at the corner again. "Jacob." She pointed. "He's right over there."

The prickles were back, tickling Molly's skin like insect legs. She saw nothing but Eva's dresser in the corner.

"I don't see anyone."

Eva continued pointing. "He's right there. He's all shiny, like someone dipped him in glue and rolled him in sparkles."

OK, so maybe Eva did have an invisible friend. That was normal for kids, right? And it didn't surprise Molly one bit that Eva's friend would be sparkly, since her daughter loved anything with glitter or sequins.

Molly smoothed Eva's hair again. "All right, beautiful, but it's time to go back to sleep now. You have school in the morning. And your brain needs some rest. OK?"

Eva flopped back against her pillow. "OK, Mommy. I guess I am a little tired."

"Thatta girl." Molly stood, pulled the covers up to Eva's shoulders, and folded them back at the top. Molly thought of her own childhood. Having a father with a short fuse, she had acquired some dysfunctional ideas of what a friend should be like. And her imaginary friends hadn't always been kind.

She knelt beside the bed. "Eva, is Jacob nice to you?"

"He's the nicest grown-up I know. Besides you and Daddy. He tells me to be brave and to pray for you and Daddy all the time. You would like him."

"He's a grown-up?" Molly wasn't expecting that. She had it in her head that Jacob was a fellow seven-year-old. A child. The playmate that Eva missed by not having brothers or sisters.

"Yeah. He has really white hair."

"What else does he tell you?"

Eva shrugged. "All kinds of stuff. He tells me how special I am and how much God loves me. But mostly he tells me to pray for Daddy. I think he's worried about him."

Twelve

MORNING CAME AND WITH IT THE PADDING OF LITTLE FEET on the steps. Eva was awake. Sam heard her from his seat on a barstool at the kitchen counter, where he was watching Molly throw together some scrambled eggs and toast. Eva rounded the corner still in her pajamas, holding Max close to her chest, rubbing her eye with her other hand. Sleep lines crisscrossed one side of her face.

"Morning, baby," Molly said.

Sam tousled his daughter's hair. "Good morning, sweetness."

"Good mornin'." Eva gave Sam a hug, laying her head on his lap. "I love you, Daddy."

Eva's words from yesterday came back to Sam. The words from the strange visitor in her dream. *He told me to tell Daddy I love him every day and make sure he knows it. And he said Daddy's real scared and needs my prayers.*

"I love you too, little buddy." He rubbed her back in slow circles. These were the moments he wanted to bottle and put away on the shelf, that shelf in the root cellar of his mind, where memories were sealed and catalogued for a future time when tenderness would seem alien and sentimentalism a priceless medicine. In these moments he loved her so much that it hurt right down to his bones.

Eva looked up at him. "What's the matter, Daddy?"

He said Daddy's real scared and needs my prayers.

"Not a thing. Don't you worry about me."

"Are you scared?"

"No," Sam said, sounding as confident and nonchalant as possible. "What makes you ask that?"

Eva did not respond to his question, but the look on her face said it all: because Jacob told her he was. Instead she said, "No reason. Just making sure."

Molly filled three plates with eggs and toast. "Who's hungry?" she said.

Popping up like a jack-in-the-box, Eva shouted, "I am," and climbed onto a barstool.

Molly put a plate in front of her. "Look, chick, when you're finished with this, I want you to run upstairs and get dressed for school. Your clothes are on your dresser. We have to get going soon, all right?"

Eva nodded enthusiastically. "OK. I can hurry real fast, Mommy."

Sam smiled. Fact was, he *was* scared. And Eva knew it. Molly probably did too. He wasn't sure he would ever be able to do his carpentry work again. And if not, how would he provide for his family? The long-term disability checks were nice, but they were only a fraction of his normal income. Their savings wouldn't last forever. And what then? What happened when the money ran out? It wasn't like they had rich family to turn to. Sam was an only child now, and his mother was too busy with her own problems and taking care of his father to notice the struggles of her son. Molly had one older sister in Oregon, and her parents were in Maine, too distant geographically and emotionally to care.

Sam and Molly were alone in this nightmare. Correction: Sam and Molly *and Eva* were alone in this nightmare. And it did scare him.

"Daddy."

Sam pulled his mind back to the kitchen, his wife, his daughter. "Yes?"

"Your eggs. You're not eating them."

"Oh." He feigned surprise. "Where did they come from?" He looked up at the ceiling as if the eggs had fallen from the sky in some rare cosmic event.

"A chicken."

Sam pointed at her. "Ah, good one. You got me there."

Eva laughed. "Mommy made them. Eat 'em. They're good. She even put cheese on 'em."

Sam speared a chunk with his fork and shoveled it into his mouth. "Mmm, wow, Mommy makes wonderful scrambled baby chickens."

Eva scrunched up her face "Eww, gross. Don't say that."

"What? That's what they are."

Eva looked to her mother for confirmation.

Molly shook her head. "Don't listen to him. He's just fooling with you."

"Are they baby chickens?"

"Sort of, yes. They're baby chickens before they become baby chickens."

"That's kinda gross."

Sam tickled her side. "Maybe. But they taste so good, don't they?"

Eva opened her mouth wide and put in her last bite. "Sure do."

"OK, you rascal," Molly said. "Upstairs, and get dressed. And don't forget to brush your teeth. When you're done, bring the hair-brush and a hair tie down, and I'll fix your hair."

After gulping the rest of her milk and wiping her mouth with the back of her hand, Eva said. "'K, Mommy. I'll hurry too; don't worry."

When the sound of Eva's socked feet had made it to the top of the stairs, Molly said to Sam, "She was up really early this morning, sitting on her bed and talking to herself."

"How early?"

"Three o'clock, about. Said she was talking to Jacob, her shiny friend. She said he looks like he was dipped in glue and rolled in glitter."

Sam didn't say anything.

"Did you know this Jacob was a man?" Molly said.

"A man? I'd imagined another kid."

"So had I. Eva said he tells her to be brave and pray for you all the time."

Sam shrugged. "That's a good thing, I guess, right? It's normal for kids to have imaginary friends, especially when they've gone through a stressful time like she has."

"Did you have an imaginary friend?"

"No. But I talked to myself a lot. All the time."

"Did you ever answer yourself?"

"Of course I did. Held whole conversations with myself. How about you?"

"How 'bout me, what?"

"Did you have an imaginary friend?"

Molly's eyes twitched. She grabbed a dishtowel and started wiping the counter with small, quick circles. "Yes."

"And was she a kid or a grown-up?"

"*He* was my age."

Sam could tell there was more to the story, something hurtful Molly didn't want to talk about. He knew she'd had a rough childhood, an abusive father, an inattentive mother. Her make-believe friend must have been an escape from all that.

Molly paused. "Do you think I should have the doctor talk to Eva?"

"I don't think that's necessary. It's just her way of dealing with the stress."

"But is it healthy?"

"Is it unhealthy? It sounds like she's processing things in a positive way. I can use all the prayer I can get. And it sounds like this Jacob is telling her all the right stuff. He could be telling her to go online and hack into Bill Gates's bank account."

Sneakers clomped down the steps, and Eva rounded the kitchen corner. "I'm ready."

"Wow," Molly said. "That was fast. Did you brush your teeth good?"

"Sure did." Eva smiled wide, showing off slightly crooked but white teeth. She turned and flashed them at Sam.

Sam covered his face. "Oh, man. They're so bright they hurt my eyes. Good job with the brushing, young lady."

Molly took the hair tie from Eva, combed her hair, and pulled it back into a ponytail. Her deftness at this always impressed Sam. She was like an accomplished artist working in her favorite medium. Whenever he tried fixing Eva's hair, it looked like it had been done by a three-year-old.

Molly said, "All right, baby girl, give Daddy a kiss and let's get going."

Sam bent so Eva could reach his cheek. She gave him a peck on his stubble, then wiped her lips. "Daddy, you need to shave."

"I know, kiddo. Have fun at school, OK? I'll see you when you get home."

"OK. I love you, Daddy. A lot."

Sam's throat tightened. He used to be the one leaving for work, giving out the kisses, and saying good-bye. Eva would sit in the window, the one now covered with plastic, waving and blowing kisses as he backed out of the driveway. He called her his waver in the window. It was one of those memories he had tucked away for later. "I love you a lot too, Eva. Do your best."

Molly kissed Sam on the lips. "After dropping her off, I need to run to the store. You'll be all right here?"

He knew yesterday's incident with the gun had scared her. "I'll be fine, babe. No worries."

She *would* worry, though, and that bothered him. She shouldn't have to worry. In fact, it was his job to make sure she didn't. But lately he seemed to be stumbling along, unable to find his footing.

At the door he helped them with their jackets and gave them each another kiss. "Bye, you two. See you soon."

"Bye, Daddy."

When Sam shut the door, the house was as quiet and still as a church sanctuary midweek. Such a contrast from the hustle of the morning. If he listened real hard, he could hear the remnants of Eva's footsteps and her loving voice, as though the sound waves were trapped here, gathered in the empty corners, and stored in the plaster of the walls.

Sam walked over to the window and stared at the plastic covering it. Questions, like day-old bug bites, nagged him. Questions about his work and his ability to do it. Questions about finances and insurance and disability benefits, about his ability to care for and protect his family. Questions about Molly and Eva and her imaginary friend.

He said Daddy's real scared and needs my prayers.

Was his fear that obvious to Eva? She was an observant kid, but he thought he had done a better job of hiding it, of shielding her from his own troubles.

From the top of the stairs, from behind the study's closed door, a voice cut through Sam's thoughts.

Tommy's voice.

"Sammy."

Thirteen

Edward and Gladys Moeller were early risers. Born in Adams County—Edward in Gettysburg, and Gladys in nearby Biglerville—they'd both spent their childhoods on farms where people rose before the sun to put in a day's worth of labor and where sleep came quickly and peacefully at night. For the Moellers, married close to sixty years, life had always been simple and uncomplicated.

But they'd recently been introduced to a word neither thought they would ever hear: Alzheimer's.

It had started a year ago with Edward and his forgetfulness. Forgetting to lock the door at night. Forgetting to shut off the shower water. Absentmindedly leaving the hose running outside. Little things that could easily be explained away as preoccupation with more important things in life. Except there were no more important things. Not for the Moellers. Ever since Edward's retirement from the Gettysburg School District where he'd taught history for a few months over thirty years, they'd lived a carefree life of leisure and relative comfort. Life had been good to them, they'd worked hard, and now they were going to enjoy their golden years and reap what they'd sown.

Six months ago Gladys had noticed Edward's forgetfulness becoming more frequent and harder to explain away. He was taken to the family doctor, who sent him to a specialist. And two weeks ago the diagnosis was made: early-stage Alzheimer's. It would only get worse from here. Medication would slow its progress, but the end was inevitable. The day would come when Edward would start to wander, ramble nonsensically, forget familiar faces, even forget Gladys.

And that was what she feared, what she mourned. She'd had a good life with Edward—the best, in fact. They'd raised a family, served in their church, traveled the country in an RV, and watched many sunsets together. And in a few short years he would remember none of it. The slate of his mind would be wiped clean, and the only thing they had to hang on to, the shared memories of their wonderful life, would be gone.

Gladys tried not to think about it, but it was a pesky voice in her ear, always threatening, taunting, mocking. Many nights she cried herself to sleep.

Now, in the kitchen, she was waiting for Edward to wake up so she could start on breakfast. She heard him stir in the bedroom and hollered after him, "Ed, what would you like for breakfast?"

Edward appeared in the hallway, his pajama pants on backwards, shirt buttons off by one. "I said I wanted sausage and eggs."

"You just woke up, dear. You haven't told me what you wanted yet."

"Why, sure I did, just a few moments ago."

Gladys never knew whether to go along with Edward's dementia or try and correct it. Usually she just went along with it. No use in arguing over trivial things. "OK. Sausage and eggs it is. Scrambled, right?"

"That's what I said." Edward turned to head back to the bedroom, then paused with that look on his face, that look of bewilderment. He was staring at something in the living room. "That lamp. Where'd it come from?"

"What lamp, sweetie?"

He pointed at the brass floor lamp. "That one, the tall one."

"That's not new. We've had that lamp for thirty-some years."

He shook his head. "No, we haven't. I don't remember seeing it there before. When did you buy it?"

"Ed, we've had that lamp forever. It's always been in our living room."

Fortunately Edward didn't like to argue any more than she did. Instead of standing his ground, he simply turned, shook his head, and said, "Gladys, sometimes I think you're losing your mind."

Fourteen

The Dodge Intrepid was just about on empty when Symon pulled into the driveway. This was the correct house, the one the voice on the phone had told him about. White vinyl-sided rancher, brown shingled roof, attached garage, neatly landscaped, Pumping Station Road. The mailbox bore the correct name: Moeller. The voice said the place had been chosen because it was right down the road from the target's house, four-tenths of a mile, to be exact.

Symon lifted a photo from the dash. It was of a young girl, seven years old, blonde hair, freckles, blue eyes. She was leaving school with another girl, purple book bag slung over her shoulder, pink jacket, blue jeans. She was laughing.

Symon never laughed. At least he had no memory of doing so. Maybe he had in his childhood, but he doubted it. Those memories were not the type to inspire laughter.

After folding the photo in half, he unzipped his jacket and placed the picture in his shirt pocket. The clock on the dash said it was a little after eight. He shut off the engine and listened to the ticks of cooling metal. Another memory surfaced, whale-like, revealing only a sliver of its full mass yet refusing to be ignored…

He was in a restaurant or bar or something—it was hard to tell—eating buffalo wings while Madonna's "Material Girl" played in the background. A woman sat in the booth with him, though he had no idea who she was or what she looked like. She was laughing, an irritating sound akin to a goose's honk. She wasn't laughing with him in response to something funny he'd said but rather at him. He knew this because of the quality of the laugh and the way she pointed at him.

A man came to the table and asked him to leave. He said no way, told the man to beat it. The man ruffled Symon's hair and poked at his side. The woman laughed again. Anger and fear tasted metallic in Symon's mouth. He cursed at the man. The man cursed back, not angry, but mocking. He was a big man, thickly muscled, shaved head, tightly cropped beard, with a small but deep scar above his right eyebrow. He pinched Symon's cheek hard and made baby sounds to him. More laughter from the woman. The metallic taste grew stronger in Symon's mouth, permeated his saliva and filled every cavity, even worked its way into his sinuses.

Symon slid out of the booth and stood, reached for the glass of water on the table, took a gulp, and then in one smooth motion smashed the glass into the side of the man's head. The woman started screaming. The big man stumbled back, lifted his hand to his face. He opened his mouth, but no words came out. Between his eye and ear, a piece of skin peeled back along the cheekbone like a fold of paper, and blood gushed from the wound. The woman was still screaming. The man hit a nearby table, lost his balance, and fell to the floor. Symon was right there, landing a boot in the man's gut, then another in the man's face. The sound was that of a hole punched in a watermelon. The man howled as more blood spilled onto the floor.

That was it. Symon sat in the Intrepid, listening to the *tick-tick* of the engine, grasping at the last remnants of the memory, but that was like trying to catch a trail of smoke.

Who was the woman? The man? Why had she laughed at him? He felt a great loss not being able to remember more of his past. Scattered pieces of a puzzle, that's all his memories were, and none seemed to fit into a larger picture. He was a man with no beginning, a drifter trying to navigate a foreign landscape without a map, compass, or point of origin...only a destination, a mark, a target.

Sadness overcame him like a sudden summer storm that rolls in over the horizon, unexpected and uninvited. It was then he noticed that metallic taste in his mouth again and realized he was biting the inside of his cheek. He drew air through his nose, bringing in the aroma of snack foods and soda, then exhaled through his mouth. He continued this pattern for a full minute to calm himself.

Finally he exited the car and approached the house. It had a long porch in front with a bench and a couple of wicker chairs. A wreath of fake brown and orange flowers adorned the front door, along with a wooden sign that said *Happy Thanksgiving.* On the sign a scarecrow held two pumpkins at shoulder height, as though getting ready to smash them together. Symon had no memory of any Thanksgivings. No family gatherings, no turkey or stuffing or football.

Rather than knocking, he reached for the doorknob. To his surprise it was unlocked. The Moellers were trusting people. They felt safe in their home on Pumping Station Road in Gettysburg, Pennsylvania.

Shame on them.

He eased the door open and slipped into the house. He was in a living room, fully carpeted and neatly furnished. Everything was done in shades of beige. The TV was on, with Matt Lauer jabbering about some kid who'd saved his parents from a burglar. Good for him. No one was in sight, but sounds of cooking came from the kitchen directly ahead. The smell of eggs and sizzling bacon made his stomach grumble.

Without making a sound on the carpet, Symon walked through the living room to the kitchen. An older woman stood at the stove, facing away from him. Gladys Moeller. She was plump, with rounded back and shoulders beneath a light blue, fleece housecoat. At seventy-one years of age, her short, curled hair was dark gray and wet, as though she'd just taken a shower. She was humming a tune he didn't recognize. Reaching for a plate on the counter, she must have caught Symon's image in her periphery, because she jumped and nearly dropped her spatula.

"Oh, my goodness," she said, turning to face him. "You frightened me." She looked past him toward the living room and hallway.

"I'm sorry," Symon said, placing his hand over his heart in a gesture of sincerity. "I knocked twice, but no one answered."

Gladys lifted the spatula chest-high, the way one would hold a sword or dagger.

Symon continued, "My name is Henry Imholtz, and I'm with the Department of Labor. I need to speak with your husband, Edward."

From another part of the house a man's voice said, "Gladys, who's there?"

Symon stepped from the kitchen into the hall as an elderly man, Edward Moeller, emerged from a bedroom. He wore baggy blue jeans and a plaid shirt, which looked nice on him. His wispy white hair hadn't been combed yet and hung in strands across his forehead. He was short and pudgy like Gladys but distinguished looking, an educated man who had once held a good-paying job.

When Edward saw Symon, his eyes narrowed and suspicion tightened his face. "Hello there. Is there something we can do for you?"

Symon almost offered his hand, then decided against it. One could tell a lot about a person with a simple handshake, and though Symon knew the facts on Mr. Moeller, he did not know the man himself.

"I'm Henry Imholtz, from the Department of Labor. I need to speak with you about your pension."

Behind him Gladys said, "Can I offer you some breakfast?"

Symon smiled. He'd practiced this smile and now executed it satisfactorily. Although his stomach begged for sustenance, he said, "No, thank you. I'm not permitted to accept gifts from clients."

"Clients?" Edward took a seat at the head of the kitchen table, legs crossed.

"That's probably not the best term." Symon turned to Gladys, who was carrying two plates to the table. "Will you please have a seat too?"

"Certainly," she said. "But first, can I get you a coffee, tea?"

"No, thank you. I'm sure whatever beverage you provide would be delicious enough to be considered a gift."

Gladys smiled and sat.

"So what's this all about?" Edward said. He didn't try to hide his lack of cordiality. He was either annoyed by the intrusion or anxious to hear the answer, thinking his pension might be eliminated.

Either would've been better than the news Symon had to offer. He paused long enough that Gladys must have thought he was feeling awkward.

"Won't you sit down?" she said.

"No, Gladys. Thank you, though. I prefer to stand. It was a long drive here, and I sat the whole way." He looked from husband to wife. "Do I look at all familiar to you?"

Their blank looks, the total lack of recognition in their eyes, said it all.

"Son," Edward said, "I've never seen you before in my life. Now is this about my pension or what?"

"You're certain you've never seen me before?"

Gladys shifted in her seat. "You do look kind of familiar. Doesn't he resemble Aaron, Edward? My, they could be brothers."

"Aaron?" A spark of hope flickered in Symon. A name.

Edward shook his head. "No, Gladys. I don't see that at all."

"Who's Aaron?"

"Our grandson," Gladys said. Then, to Edward, "You don't think they have the same eyes and chin?"

"Not at all. Can we get to the pension?"

But Symon no longer cared about that. "Where does Aaron live?"

"He lives in Chicago," Gladys said. "Chicago, right, Edward? Or is it Cleveland?"

The elderly man was notably frustrated. He uncrossed his legs and leaned forward. "Chicago, I think. But it could be Cleveland."

"When did you speak with him last?" Symon said. That spark was still there, an ember of possibility.

"Oh, my." Gladys put her hand over her mouth and thought. "Was it two days ago, Edward?"

He sighed deeply. "We haven't talked to Aaron in ages. Now about my—"

"Excuse me," Symon said, "but this is very important. Was it two days ago, or ages ago, that you last spoke with Aaron?"

"Two days ago," Gladys said. "I remember the conversation well."

Edward grumbled under his breath, then said, "What is this about my pension?"

"Your pension, yes," Symon said. His hopes had been extinguished with Gladys's last bit of news. He could in no way be the Aaron she spoke of since he had never talked to her on the phone. It wasn't possible. He looked at her. "You know, I've changed my mind. May I have some of that wonderful-smelling bacon?"

A smile stretched across her face, bunching her cheeks. "Oh, yes. Coming right up." She stood with some effort and crossed the kitchen to the stove.

Without stopping to think, Symon reached into his jacket, retrieved the Beretta, pointed it at Gladys's torso, and squeezed the trigger three times. The weapon spit out three rounds, each landing not six inches apart in the woman's back. Gladys slumped forward in slow motion, as if bending toward the stove for a closer look, and her face landed in the pan on the burner. Her knees buckled, and she dropped to the floor, taking the pan with her. It rattled and clanged and spilled its contents on the linoleum. Gladys's body rested on its back by the stove. Her face, covered with partially scrambled eggs, wore a frozen expression of surprise.

Edward let out a weak grunt and twitched in his chair. Symon gave him no time to process what had taken place. He aimed the pistol and squeezed off another three rounds before the old man could raise his hands in self-defense. The shots punched Edward in the chest and sent him reeling backward, the chair toppling. His lifeless body tipped sideways with the chair and landed in the fetal position on the floor.

In the living room the local weatherman commented on what a beautiful autumn day it would be.

Symon placed the Beretta on the table. He removed and slung his jacket over one of the ladder-back chairs. Then, as if he was a friendly visitor who'd stopped by for a pleasant chat, he walked over to the stove. The bacon sat in its own grease, perfectly fried. He rooted through the drawers and cupboards for a fork and plate, then helped himself to breakfast.

When his hunger was satisfied, he placed the dishes in the sink and went to work disposing of the bodies. Between the living room and kitchen, a door accessed the staircase into the basement. He dragged Edward first (who was much heavier than he looked), then Gladys, to the top of the stairs and let their corpses tumble downward. They sprawled onto the concrete at the bottom of the steps. He shut the door and forgot about them.

Returning to the kitchen, Symon pulled out the photo of the girl. The target. She was actually a cute kid.

He thought it odd that he felt no emotion about his mission. Nor about what he'd just done to the Moellers here. He was sure they were nice people, probably parents and grandparents, model neighbors and exemplary citizens. He doubted they ever paid their taxes late and could not imagine either Edward or Gladys mouthing off to a cop. There was no sadness over their loss. No regret or even joy. Nothing. It was as if his emotional palette had been wiped clean, with nothing there to draw from.

Using a *Branson, Missouri* magnet from the refrigerator, Symon placed the girl's photo on the freezer door, front and center. There were other photos, as well. Two of a young family—mom, dad, and two kids, a boy and a girl. In the first, they were at the beach, posing like a nice family should. They looked very happy and very tan. In the second, the children, no more than six or seven, stood proudly beside a sandcastle as tall as the girl's waist. Probably the Moellers' grandchildren. Again, he wondered at his emotional void.

Tapping the target's photo, he said, "This time it's all about your daddy, sweetheart."

Fifteen

SAM STARED UP THE STAIRCASE, FEELING NUMB. TOMMY'S VOICE came again from the study, behind the closed door.

"Sammy."

He knew it wasn't real, the voice. It was just an echo from his past. Somewhere in his brain a neuron had made a bad connection, picking up signals from a memory deep in the recesses of his gray matter. A memory meant to be filed away and forgotten.

"Sammy."

The voice drew him, as if Tommy were here, crossing the threshold of time and space and hooking Sam with bait he couldn't refuse. Tommy was reeling him in. Ascending the stairs one at a time, one foot in front of the other, Sam drew closer to that blasted closed door. There was unreconciled business between him and his brother, and he needed to settle it once and for all. Tommy did too.

At the landing Sam paused, fought the hook so deeply imbedded in the flesh of his consciousness. The door to his study seemed to breathe. If he looked closely, he could almost see the wood expanding and retracting with each breath.

"Sammy."

The voice churned a memory to the surface. Those neurons were digging up images and sounds and video clips that had been archived years ago, and Sam found himself in the basement of their house in Cumberland County and...

...the stone walls always looked so cold and lifeless. Here and there, mortar had fallen out in chunks. In one corner the stones were wet, and when it rained, water trickled down the wall and puddled on the concrete.

Sam was standing at the bottom of the wooden steps, gripping the rough handrail. In the center of the basement sat "the monster," the octopus coal furnace that had been converted to gas. Here, in the middle of winter, the furnace was going full throttle. Tommy and he sometimes sneaked down here with their old action figures, tossed in a Han Solo or Greedo or C-3PO, and watched it melt. If Dad ever caught them, he would have their hides for sure.

"Sammy? That you?" Tommy's voice came out of the darkened far corner. It was just a bodiless voice.

"Yeah. What're you doin'?"

"Come here. Got something to show you."

Something about the way Tommy said "come here" raised knots of flesh up and down Sam's arms. His brother had not been himself lately, that was no secret. Dad thought he was as crazy as the Mad Hatter at high tea; Mom argued he was just going through a tough time, like teenagers do. Hormones and stuff. Sam didn't know what to think. At times Tommy was himself, laughing, joking, talking about girls and the Philadelphia 76ers and how much he hated math and Mrs. Kump. But other times Tommy got a different look—faraway, glassy, like someone had popped out his eyeballs and replaced them with shiny new marbles. Those times scared Sam. His brother was not his brother then but some sinister being with a short fuse and a hankering for violence. It had never been directed at Sam, but he'd seen it aimed at walls and doors and poor Gomer.

"Sammy." The voice again. "Come here, scaredy-cat."

Sam crossed the basement, making a wide circle around "the monster." He had the same feeling in his gut as when he entered a dark room, not knowing what may be hiding in the corner or behind the door.

When he rounded the furnace, he found Tommy in the corner on his knees, holding something against the floor. The something moved and growled.

Tommy looked up at Sam, a grin stretched across his face, and his eyes—those glassy marble eyes—flashed with excitement. "Look what I got."

"What is it?"

"A cat. A stray I caught outside. Stinkin' stray."

Tommy squeezed harder, and the cat growled again, except this time the growl was more like a moan. Tommy's eyes were wild and distant.

"What're you gonna do with it?" A part of Sam didn't want to know, wanted to turn and run for the steps and get out of that basement and away from Tommy as fast as he could, but another part forced him to stay and see what Tommy had in mind. Maybe he could stop him.

"Just you watch, Sammy boy. Just you watch."

Tommy got to his feet, holding the cat by the scruff of the neck, and Sam noticed its paws were tied together with twine. He also noticed the cat was gray and full-grown. The thing's eyes were buggy and terrified, and because of the way Tommy was holding it, it wore a goofy grin on its face.

Walking to the furnace, Tommy threw the lever on the door and swung it open. Inside, the flames licked high and fast.

Those knots of flesh were back on Sam's arms and neck. "Tommy, don't."

"Why, little brother? It's just a cat. A scaredy-cat like you. Don't you want to see what happens?" He held the thing up next to his face, and it hissed at him. "Kitty want to play a game?" Then, turning to Sam: "You remember the story of those three guys in the furnace?"

Sam's skin was crawling with bugs now. "Yes. Tommy, come on, man. Don't."

But before Sam could stop him, not that he would have been able to, Tommy swung the cat around and tossed it into the furnace. The cat howled. Tommy laughed. Sam turned and ran, tears burning his eyes and blurring his sight. He stumbled up the basement steps as Tommy called after him, "Run, you sissy. Sammy. Sammy…"

"Sammy."

For the second time in as many days, the scar running over his ear ached.

Sam looked down the hall. The study door was open now, as though it hadn't been closed all the way and a shift in the settling house had nudged it a few inches. More than a few inches, actually. It was wide open. Like someone had left it fully ajar as an invitation. Had he imagined it was closed to begin with? No way. It had been shut tight. He'd shut it himself and heard the click of the latch. He shuddered, recalling where all that business with the furnace and the cat had ended.

You did what you had to do, son.

He took one step forward. "Tommy?" There would be no answer; there never was. Nevertheless he felt compelled to make his presence known. "It's me. Sammy."

He approached the study, half-expecting to see his brother swivel around in the desk chair with a gray cat clutched to his chest. That same gray cat.

Hey, little brother, want to see something cool?

But of course the room was empty.

Sam crossed the study to the window. The sky was deep blue, mottled with cotton-ball clouds. At the end of his property, where the yard met the neighbor's field, the groundhog waddled into view. Sam knocked on the glass, and the fat little rat stopped what it was doing to look at him. It was taunting him: *Well, go on, sucker. Take your best shot.*

Without thinking, Sam retrieved his rifle from the closet, the Winchester Model 70. This time he'd be a monkey's hind end if he missed. With the rifle loaded and ready, he found the groundhog in the same place, still looking at him. He estimated it was about eighty, ninety yards off, farther than the last time.

Sam yanked up the window and screen. Cool air floated into the room. He got down on one knee and propped his left elbow on the sill to steady his arm. Against his cheek the rifle stock felt right, natural, like the weapon was a part of him, another appendage. He shut his eyes to calm his breathing.

When he opened his right eye, he centered the groundhog in the front sight and made the appropriate adjustment for distance. There wasn't enough wind to affect the bullet's trajectory. With his finger on the trigger, itching for action, he drew in a deep breath and focused on the gray-brown ball of fur at the field's edge. The groundhog stood on its hind legs, daring him to take the shot, betting he'd miss and thus prove he was indeed a sissy.

In one smooth motion Sam squeezed the trigger. The rifle discharged and recoiled into his shoulder, the end of the barrel popping up uncontrollably. Ninety yards away, the groundhog's head snapped back, and the creature hit the ground hard.

Bingo. Right in the kisser.

Sam held the rifle a little longer, pointed at the motionless groundhog. His breathing was rapid, and his pulse raced. He'd hit his mark, and it felt good.

After shutting the window and returning the rifle to the closet, Sam went outside and tossed the groundhog's carcass into the field so Eva wouldn't find it while she was playing outside. When he returned to his study, he sat at his desk and noticed a sheet of paper he didn't remember being there before. At the top, in his own handwriting, it read:

July 2, 1863, 4:00 a.m.

Sixteen

There was nothing quite like the silence of the office first thing in the morning. Stephen Lincoln sat back in his leather chair, clasped his hands behind his head, and sighed. He found the smell of paper and furniture polish comforting. Odd, yes, but not so odd for a politician. They were necessities for Lincoln's existence. His life was captured on paper—forms, documents, bills, legislation, you name it—and he had a thing for dust. Made him sneeze something awful.

Lincoln gazed at the painting of the *other* Lincoln on his wall. The sixteenth president, Lincoln, the man with whom he shared a name. No relation. At least none that he knew of.

"What do you think, Abe?" he said aloud. "What have I gotten myself into?"

One of Lincoln's legislative assistants, Taylor Blake, entered his office holding a thick, three-ring binder. She glanced at Lincoln behind the desk, then at Lincoln on the wall. "Am I interrupting something?"

Lincoln leaned forward and rested his elbows on his desk. "I was just looking for some advice."

"From the painting of a dead guy?"

"He may be dead, but his spirit is still alive."

Taylor dropped the binder on the desk. "OK, that's just creepy. You're talking to the ghost of a dead president. If the taxpayers only knew." She pointed at the binder. "That's the rough draft of the bill from Senator Michaels. He and Senator Maka want to know what you think of it...by tomorrow."

"Tomorrow?" Lincoln opened the binder and leafed through

the pages. The last was numbered 421. "I can't read it that fast. Have you read it?"

Taylor shrugged. "He didn't say anything about me reading it."

"Have you read it?"

She smiled. "I'm working on it." Then spun and left the office.

"We'll meet at four to discuss it. Tell the others," Lincoln called after her.

He flipped through the pages again. This was the most important piece of legislation in his short political career, not to mention the most controversial, and he'd have to make sure it was something he could stand behind...and maybe die for. In the political sense, of course.

To the ghost of the sixteenth president he said, "What do you think, Abe? Is this worth dying for?"

Stephen Lincoln was already in the crosshairs of some. He'd been a senator only two years, after campaigning as a moderate Democrat, leaning right on issues of fiscal responsibility and homeland security. But he'd had a recent change of heart on the hotplate issue of abortion.

Initially he'd run on a pro-choice platform. It wasn't one of his soapboxes, just part of his arsenal of campaign talking points. Every woman should have the right to choose when it came to her own body. Then, four months ago, his nineteen-year-old daughter broke the news that she'd gone and gotten herself pregnant. A month later she exercised her right, her *choice*, and had an abortion. The following week she downed a bottle of OxyContin. After a week in the hospital she was still receiving almost daily counseling.

It was bad press and bad publicity, but that was the least of Lincoln's worries. His children mattered more to him than his political career, and he'd taken a couple of weeks off to be with his family and comfort his daughter. The things she said, the fear she felt, the remorse, the guilt, the tears, the way she trembled in his arms when he held her—all were enough to make Lincoln change his mind and heart on the abortion issue.

Which was bad for him, politically speaking. At first.

Politicians weren't allowed to change their minds. It was an unwritten rule of governing the public: no flip-floppers allowed. When, during a press conference, he released the news that he was now pro-life, the Democratic Party and his constituents all but disowned him. A week later, when he announced he was changing parties, the backlash almost ended his career.

The news outlets went into a feeding frenzy, the talking heads jabbered on about the turncoat senator, and the bloggers spun all kinds of ridiculous stories. But eventually the dust settled, and people started talking about the moderate Republican from Pennsylvania who might just be able to make a bid for the White House come next election. The White House, as in the president of the United States. Something Lincoln had thought about, naturally, but never seriously.

Here, four months after the whole incident, he was an apparent front-runner to occupy the Oval Office after next year's election, the sweetheart of every talk-show host out there. People were saying he was the perfect candidate: young (though Lincoln didn't think forty-five was all that young), handsome, articulate, and politically positioned to capture the majority vote. He was just what the people wanted, just what the country needed.

Lincoln flipped through the notebook again. Written by a group of Republican senators spearheaded by Senator Humphrey Michaels from Georgia and Senator Mitch Maka from South Carolina, this bill was the first of its kind. It laid the groundwork for a constitutional amendment protecting life in the womb and provided firepower for legislation that could outlaw abortion once and for all.

Stephen Lincoln, senator from Pennsylvania and presidential hopeful, was being asked to put his name on the bill. To make history. And he was going to do it.

Seventeen

SAM STARED AT ANOTHER JOURNAL ENTRY:

Captain Samuel Whiting
Pennsylvania Independent Light Artillery, Battery E

This page, though, was not from Eva's notebook. No, he'd given that back to her after he'd torn his writings out and stuffed them under some unpaid bills in the top drawer of his desk. This entry was written on white printer paper. It lay cockeyed on the desk, begging him to read on. But Sam didn't want to read it. He wanted to tear it to shreds and never think about it again.

And yet, like the voice of a dead lover calling from the dark beyond, it beckoned him to come near and enticed him with words of urgency. He believed, in this moment, that if he didn't respond, it would read itself aloud. How crazy would that be?

Sam rolled out the chair and sat. He dared not touch the paper, but his eyes were drawn to it. He *had* to read it, just as he had to answer the call of his dead brother.

Leaning forward, elbows on the edge of the desk, he took in the words as if they were sustenance to a starving traveler.

July 2, 1863
4:00 a.m.

I was awakened and given orders to be relieved by another battery and resupply. Went to a valley of lush wheat and also a peach orchard. Two other batteries joined us there, making a total of ten field pieces of varying sizes. Our first job was to support the infantry, in case of an assault or advance.

There was some light skirmishing all day. About noon to 2:00 p.m. the booming of cannons grew louder, and then the infantry suddenly advanced well right of our position (this was a mystery to us all). Then the musketry grew to a loud roll of thunder. We could see much smoke, so I ordered, "All guns ready," as the wounded came through by the hundreds and thousands, saying they were being pushed back.

Then it happened. We saw our battle flags streaming to the rear, and finally the stars and bars of the enemy. There were thousands of them. We opened up. At first they reeled from the shower of flying lead, but within minutes our infantry support broke and ran for cover. I ordered, "Retreat by recoil." We fired and went back as the guns recoiled.

Within twenty minutes or so, we were almost out of ammunition and forced to withdraw up a slight rise. We set up again and received some rounds of ammunition. By this time the enemy was pushing steadily and easily up the rise.

At once there was a cheer, and one regiment (1st Minnesota) charged down like demons, giving us enough time to gather our forces and repel the enemy.

Losses to my battery were very heavy. Out of seventy-two men, in two days:

Dead, 16

Wounded, 27

The regiment (1st Minnesota) lost almost every man. Oh! how brave they were. Their charge saved the day. God bless them!

That night, reflection and new orders. The day

and the one past are days I will remember, but wish I would not! I curse this war and those who started it. Good men with wives and children and brothers and sisters are dying. Men who love their country and their home.

Is it necessary? Is such loss and suffering needful? My mind grows dark at the thought of continuing in this madness, and if not for my men I would abandon this war and be done with the killing. There is no light in my life now, only darkness. At times I feel I am not my own.

Again the letters were there, dropped like lost coins. He grabbed a pen and jotted them down. It didn't make sense, but then none of this did, not one word of it.

Sam scanned the words again, not believing what his eyes saw. It was his own penmanship, but he could not recall writing even one word of it. It was as foreign to him as ancient cuneiform written on stone tablets. And yet, seeing those alien words written by his own hand sent such shivers through his body that he swore he could hear his joints rattling.

Who was this Samuel Whiting? How had he gotten into Sam's head? And, the question that burned more than any other, when had he written this?

He walked through his morning again, reviewing each moment—waking, using the bathroom, sliding into his jeans and T-shirt, having coffee while Molly made breakfast, eating with Eva, seeing them out the door, then…

The voice. Tommy's voice calling to him from the study.

Sam had walked up the steps—no, he'd been *pulled* up the steps by an unseen tether—stood at the top, and had the vivid memory of his brother. That's when he'd noticed the yawning door to the study, as if someone had opened it wide. Had he blanked out? Gone into some kind of trance? Or seizure? Had he actually entered the room, grabbed the paper from the printer, and written this stuff before returning to the staircase?

He'd read some time ago about a local man who killed his dog, decapitated the poor thing, then disemboweled it and left the entrails on the kitchen counter for his wife to find when she came home from work. He claimed that he had no recollection of doing such a hideous thing, that he'd blanked out, and when he came to again, Scooter, his beloved Jack Russell, was already headless and gutted. He loved his dog almost as much as he loved his wife. Some said he was a world-class liar who hated his wife and butchered Scooter to get back at her for canceling his cable subscription. Others said he'd experienced "missing time," a common report of those abducted by aliens. They claimed men from the other side of the universe, or maybe just the other side of the neighborhood, had kidnapped the man for experiments and disassembled Scooter for fun.

The one that had made the most sense to Sam was a physician's speculation that the man suffered from dissociative fugue disorder, a psychiatric condition characterized by short-lived amnesia and often accompanied by wanderings and other activities of which the sufferer had no recollection.

Dissociative fugue disorder sounded right to Sam. Amnesia. Wanderings. Writings from 1863. He had no memory of any of it. At least he hadn't disemboweled anything yet.

He smacked the top of the desk with an open hand. He couldn't go nuts. He couldn't. But he felt he was heading that way, and there was nothing he could do about it.

Eighteen

A HALF MILE FROM HOME, WITH A CAR FULL OF GROCERIES and Johnny Cash coming through the speakers, Molly spotted the smoke. It reached above the distant treetops, like an arthritic finger pointing at the heavens, where there was no more suffering, no more morning stiffness.

Molly's breath caught in her chest, as it always did at the sight of smoke. When she was nine, her family had returned from a visit to Aunt Elaine's to find their house nothing but charcoal and matchsticks. Her mom had left the stove on, and the pot of boiling water had burned dry. Or so said the fire chief, a large, round man with a pencil-thin mustache and only four fingers on his right hand. Molly remembered him well. She had rummaged through the ruins for hours, sifting through their blackened possessions, salvaging what she could (which didn't amount to much), and listening to her father curse at her mom the whole time.

As she neared her own home now, she realized it was just the burn barrel belching smoke, and the tension behind her ribs eased. Since Sam's accident they had depended on the meager income from his long-term disability, and they—or rather, *she*—had decided to discontinue the garbage service to save themselves the four hundred dollars a year and instead burn the trash in a barrel at the end of the yard, where lawn met field.

Sam must have started the fire while she was gone. Not like him. Lately, disposing of the accumulating refuse outside the back door was the last thing on his mind, along with every other household chore she had to direct him to do.

She steered the Ford Explorer into their driveway, stopped

beside the sidewalk, and beeped the horn twice. Within seconds Sam emerged from the house, hands in the pockets of his jeans.

"Hey, mind helping me unload these groceries?" she said.

"Sure."

"Saw you started the burn barrel. Thanks."

Sam hesitated, and Molly noted the shadow of irritation that passed over his face. "Yeah. The garbage was piling up, and the smell was coming into the house."

She opened the back hatch and handed Sam a bag. "Everything go OK with it?" She handed him another.

"'Course it went OK. Why wouldn't it?" His voice was edged with annoyance.

"I'm just asking, honey. No need to get snippy."

"Why do feel you even need to ask? I'm not allowed to start a fire without my mommy around?"

She stopped, holding a bag in each hand. His sarcasm always reminded her of her father and sent alternating waves of anger and frustration through her. She lowered her voice, tried to calm herself. "That's not what I said. I was just wondering, is all. No need for you to get all irritated about it." And with that she walked past him and into the house.

The rest of the groceries were unloaded and dumped on the kitchen counter in silence. When the last bag was removed from the Explorer and the hatch closed, Molly mumbled thanks to Sam as he disappeared upstairs. She heard the study door shut, the desk chair roll against the wood floor.

Then she let the tears come, curtains of them. She hated arguing with him. It brought to memory the countless battles she'd had with her dad, battles he always won, even when he was dead wrong.

Thirty minutes later, eyes still blurry, lump still in her throat, Molly put the last of the groceries away. When new food went into the refrigerator, the old leftovers were removed. She dumped them into a paper bag, then headed out the back door to toss them in the burn barrel before the fire died. If she left a bag of spoiled food outside, it would be an invitation to every raccoon, opossum, and stray cat within a mile radius. Feast at the Travis house.

Walking across the yard, she realized the grass would need one more mowing before winter arrived. She'd get the riding mower out Saturday and do it. Beyond the barrel, a rusted and burnt fifty-gallon drum, a couple of vultures picked at something in the field, not more than ten yards beyond the property line. They flapped their massive wings and took flight as she neared the barrel. They circled, silent but watchful, as if warning her not to mess with their find.

After dropping the bag in the barrel, Molly walked to the line where lawn met witchgrass. The carcass in the field had not yet bloated, so it couldn't have been there long. The fur looked like that of a—

A groundhog.

For the second time that day Molly's breath caught in her chest. She edged closer and confirmed that it was indeed a groundhog.

The vultures still wheeled overhead, occasionally swooping dangerously close. Molly was moving in on their territory, on their meal.

But curiosity drew her closer to the carcass. She noticed part of the beast's head was missing, not pecked away by the beak of a very large bird, rather carved away by the slug of a high-powered rifle.

Sam.

She turned her head and located his study window on the second floor. He was standing there, behind the glass, watching her.

Nineteen

Trash littered the passenger's side of the Dodge Intrepid. Soda cans, cake wrappers, and foil bags spilled off the seat and almost filled the leg space to the dash, but Symon didn't care one bit. Outside the weather couldn't be better—midsixties, clear sky, light breeze—but Symon didn't care one bit. From across a quiet street and down the block came the noise of children at play in the schoolyard—giggling, screaming, hollering—but about this Symon didn't care one bit either.

There was only one thing he cared about, one thing that caught his eye and held it captive: the target. The girl. He had no need of the photo; that could remain on the refrigerator back at the Moeller's place. Her image was stained on his memory like one of those inkblots the shrinks had you look at. Whenever he shut his eyes, she was there, on the insides of his lids, a perfect ghostly negative of her face.

But she wasn't in this group of recessing children.

He watched as one of the adults, a young slender woman with a fine build, blew a whistle, and the children assembled in a line, single-file. What good little kids.

One boy, a big-headed, pudgy kid with shaggy hair, stepped out of line and hit another boy in the arm. Symon could tell the smaller boy was hurt and trying desperately not to cry. Crying was a sign of weakness, even in the social structure of elementary school. A girl hollered at Shaggy, and the woman with the nice figure said something and motioned him to the back of the line. He obeyed, but not before giving the woman a very adult hand gesture behind her back.

Symon had half a mind to walk over there and teach Shaggy some respect. But he refrained; he had to stay focused.

The line began to move like a segmented worm, disappearing into the school through double glass doors. Shaggy shoved the boy in front of him as they stepped into the darkness of the building. Minutes later another line wormed out through the same doorway. As soon as the children hit the blacktop, the line disintegrated and kids scattered like bugs under a rock at the first glimpse of sunlight. Somewhere among this group was the target. Earlier the voice had supplied him with all the information he would need to complete the mission. And Symon never forgot a detail.

He lifted the binoculars from the passenger seat and aimed them at the playground. It took him only a few seconds to locate her. She was on the swings, kicking her feet, trying to generate momentum. She looked exactly as she did in the photo.

A memory, like a gunshot, exploded in Symon's mind, causing him to drop the binoculars on the seat...

He remembered a girl, about the age of the target. Brown, curly hair, and an upturned nose. Brown eyes too. She was laughing, talking to him, pulling on his hand and telling him to follow her. They were in a park or clearing of some kind. In the distance a tree line marked the edge of shadow-filled woods. The leafless trees loomed like an army of the walking dead, and it scared him. In contrast, the girl's voice was musical, and the feel of her hand in his angelic. He resisted at first, fighting his fear, yet wanting to give in to her urging. Eventually courage won out, and he let her lead him toward the tree line.

And that's where it ended. That was it. He tried to coax more from his mind, replaying the scene over again, hoping it would lead to more. But it didn't. Just as quickly as it had surfaced, it vanished and left so many questions unanswered. Who was the girl? Where were those woods? Why did it frighten him so?

On the playground the target was going higher in the swing now, and Symon wondered if he had a daughter. He didn't know what kind of life he'd had before...before what? Of course, it no longer mattered. The only thing that mattered was the target.

Again he pressed the binoculars against his eyes and watched the target at play.

A knock on the car door startled him. He swung his head around and found an older man, sixties maybe, bent at the waist in a blue jogging suit.

"Mister, what are you doing?" the man said. His words were clipped and tight.

Symon smiled politely. "Just watching my daughter. She's on the swings. I'm on my lunch break from work, and thought I'd stop by. Don't get to see her much, except on weekends."

The man looked toward the playground. He stood like that for several seconds, eyes moving back and forth. A few streets over, a horn honked and tires screeched.

"She's the one with brown hair on the swings," Symon said. "She loves the swings."

The man fixed his eyes on Symon again. They were steel blue and deep set. He looked like a man who once wielded a good bit of authority and was used to peering into men's souls. "She's a cutie," he said and tapped the door. "You enjoy your day now. It's a beauty."

"Sure is. Enjoy your walk."

Symon watched the man stroll out of sight, showing no sign of age in his gait, then returned to watching the target.

Twenty

At his desk Sam Travis stared at his handwriting on the paper. The words, so foreign and strange, seemed to swim on the white background, and it made him dizzy to look at them too long. Molly had found the groundhog, and she knew he'd shot it. Her look said it all. He would hear about it sooner or later. She'd question him and tell him that she didn't like him shooting small animals in the backyard, that it wasn't safe. She had no confidence in him anymore. She no longer respected him, no longer looked to him for answers or comfort or protection. He was nothing more than a burden or, at best, an extra child she had to mother.

He perused the paper, the handwriting, the words.

> *My mind grows dark at the thought of continuing in this madness.*

It was as if this Samuel Whiting had once again braved the threshold of time and read Samuel Travis's mind. Sam didn't know how much longer he could keep going like this. His madness was growing, and no matter how hard he resisted, how hard he fought, its pull was relentless. But the other words had struck him hardest.

> *There is no light in my life now, only darkness. At times I feel I am not my own.*

These were Sam's words, written by his own hand. Since two nights ago, when he'd heard Tommy's voice and followed it downstairs, when he heard the sounds of battle as if they were in his own front yard, when he fell asleep on the couch and awoke to find the first of the Samuel Whiting entries, when the window shattered, he had not felt like himself. Uninvited guests had taken up residence within him, and their names were darkness and despair.

At times I feel I am not my own.

He ran his finger over the words. He studied the letters, the way the double *e*'s looped together, the way the *m*'s looked like *n*'s. There was no mistaking—and he wished with all his heart he was mistaken—that the entry had been penned by his hand. His eyes could not be fooled.

It was as if this Samuel Whiting were communicating with him, whispering over a great gulf, centuries wide. Like they were becoming one…maybe already were one.

But who was Samuel Whiting? And what was the Pennsylvania Independent Artillery? Should he know this stuff?

Turning in his chair, Sam grabbed the computer mouse, and the monitor's screen sprang to life. His fingers danced across the keyboard. He googled "Pennsylvania Independent Artillery Battery E" and got a few results that looked interesting. The first listed battles in which the battery was engaged. There was Manassas, Antietam, and Harper's Ferry, in 1862. In 1863, they were at Chancellorsville, then…

There it was. July 1 through 3, the Battle of Gettysburg.

He went back to the search screen and added "Battle of Gettysburg" to his inquiry. More sites popped up. Clicking on one, he found a concise history of the battery during the Gettysburg campaign. Two memorials commemorated the battery, one at the summit of Culp's Hill and one on Power's Hill. The article also said the battery had been commanded by a Lieutenant Charles A. Atwell. No mention of Samuel Whiting at all.

He ran a search of "Samuel Whiting." There was a doctor in San Antonio, a Massachusetts clergyman who died in 1679, a Texas newspaper publisher who died in 1862, and a photographer who lived during the Civil War era but resided in England. None were his Samuel Whiting.

Downstairs, dishes clattered and the microwave beeped four times. Seconds later Molly hollered up at him. "Lunch is ready, Sam. You hungry?"

He wasn't, but if he didn't go down, she'd be suspicious and prod him with more questions. He scolded himself for thinking so negatively of her. She was a good woman. For the past six months she'd taken on the brunt of the housework and cooking, of helping Eva with her homework and keeping up with the yard, and rarely if ever complained.

"Yeah. I'll be right down."

He shut off the computer and headed to the kitchen for lunch.

Twenty-One

Molly heard the clomping of Sam's feet on the steps before she saw him. She'd made grilled cheese sandwiches and tomato soup, one of his all-time favorite lunches, and set their plates on the counter that had the barstools. She was still shaken by finding the groundhog. She knew it killed Sam not being able to work and that he danced with depression daily. Maybe his way of dealing with the emotions was to dig that rifle out of the closet and gain back control in one part of his life. Shooting was something he could do, and apparently do well. Besides, those groundhogs were pesky. She was glad to be rid of one.

Sam entered the kitchen, hands in his pockets, a guilty look of pleasure or satisfaction on his face. Like he wanted her to understand he didn't care if she knew about the groundhog.

"Hey," Molly said. "What do you want to drink?"

"Diet Coke," Sam said. "Where's the paper?"

She pointed to it on the table.

After retrieving the paper, Sam sat on a barstool and picked up his sandwich.

"We don't pray before eating anymore?" Molly knew she'd let her irritation show and immediately regretted it.

Sam bowed his head, closed his eyes for thirty or so seconds, then opened them and took a bite.

Trying to change the subject and the mood, Molly said, "What are you up to, up there?"

Sam chewed, swallowed, shrugged. "Nothing much."

"Working on your writing?" She noticed the shift in his eyes. He was uncomfortable with this subject.

"A little."

"Mind sharing what you're working on?"

More chewing. He swallowed, then rested his elbows on the counter and laced his fingers in front of his face. "Thought I'd try a Civil War piece."

"That's great, babe. Mind if I read it when you get some done?"

Except it wasn't great. It was odd. Despite living in Gettysburg, the largest national military park in the country and arguably the best-known location of all the Civil War battles, Sam had never shown an interest in it. History wasn't his thing and, the way he told it, never had been. So why this sudden fascination with the War Between the States?

Sam shrugged again. "Sure."

The silence between them grew for a good five minutes while they ate. It was a wall built higher and thicker with each second that passed, and Molly felt the tension mounting as each new brick was laid. She dipped her sandwich in her soup, something she enjoyed but Sam found revolting. He hated soggy bread and crumbs in his soup. Eva took after Molly in this, and the two of them teased him about being picky. But Molly could tell he was in no mood to be teased today.

Finally she broached the subject that had niggled at her since seeing the vultures circle above the dead animal. "Sam, I found the groundhog."

"I know."

"Want to talk about it?"

"What's there to talk about?"

His avoidance tactics annoyed her. It was the same thing her dad used to do when he stumbled in after midnight, glassy-eyed and thick-tongued, and her mom questioned him about his whereabouts. Molly would stay up, making sure he got home safely, then listen as her parents argued about his nocturnal activities.

"How about the fact that as long as I've known you, Sam, you've never fired a gun, let alone shot at anything living? I've heard stories of what a great shot you were when you were a kid, but you've never even liked talking about it. I feel like there are whole pieces of your past, your life, that I don't even know about."

"You don't want to know. You don't need to."

"Yes, I do."

He looked at her with something in his eyes she hadn't ever seen before, something dark, something frightening. "You don't."

She'd had enough. "Fine. So what? All of a sudden, you dig your rifle out and start taking shots at groundhogs from your window. Where did this come from?"

Sam dropped the remainder of his sandwich and pushed the plate away. It clanked against the bowl, which spilled some tomato soup onto the counter. "Why's it matter where it came from? Maybe I just got bored and felt like doing it." He stood quickly, knocking the barstool over. "Do you know what it's like to sit home all day and do nothing?" He grabbed the newspaper, then the car keys from the hook over the counter.

Molly watched him with a certain level of disbelief. "What are you doing?" He hadn't driven since the accident, the fall, the brain injury.

"I'm going for a drive. What? Are you gonna take my car keys away too?" He turned to leave.

"But you're not supposed—"

"You don't know that." Sam spun around, and Molly saw the aggravation, maybe even anger, in his face. The tightness of his brow. The tension in his jaw. "The doctor cleared me to drive two weeks ago. I haven't because I knew you didn't want me to. But now I want to go for a drive. I need some freedom, Moll. Can you understand that? I need to be able to *do* something I want to do, to pick up and go when I want, without you worrying or firing a million questions at me. Isn't that OK?"

She knew she wouldn't be able to stop him. He was doing it to spite her now. To prove he could and that he no longer needed her to mother him. Maybe he needed to get out. Hopefully the freedom would start him on the road back to work. She forced a smile and knew it looked weak. "I'm sorry, babe. Go for a drive. Go clear your mind."

Without another word Sam left the house, closing the door behind him a little harder than necessary. Molly listened as the car started, the wheels turned on the driveway, the engine revved, and her husband drove off to who-knew-where.

God, keep him safe.

Twenty-Two

Sam pressed the Explorer down Pumping Station Road faster than the posted forty-five mile per hour speed limit. The faded asphalt uncurled before him like the gray tongue of a dragon that had held him prisoner within massive jaws behind dagger-like teeth.

He was free.

Driving came back so naturally, even after six months. The feel of the steering wheel, the touch of the brakes, the acceleration, the handling—it was as if he'd driven just yesterday. And the vehicle took the gradual turns and rises and falls of the road without complaining. It was a good purchase. They'd saved almost three years for it.

But Sam's mind wasn't on the quality of the Explorer or on the road or on how right it felt to be behind the wheel again. His thoughts were on Molly. He understood, of course, her concern. Part of that was just her personality. She liked to dote on people, to care for them. She would have made a wonderful nurse. But growing up with parents who never encouraged her to do anything worthwhile had dampened any initiative. She could have gone to college with the right kind of support, could have made something great of herself. Instead she finished high school, took a job as a clerk at a Gettysburg gift shop, and soon after met and married Sam.

Her mistake.

Sam slowed the Explorer at a stop sign, crossed Steinwehr Avenue, and entered the battlefield. Monuments and cannons lined the roadway, reminding him of the sounds from the other night. The blasts of cannon fire. The successive pops of rifles. The screams and hollers of men in the throes of warfare. It was so real, so vivid, so close.

He passed an elderly couple driving the other way. The man waved politely, but Sam did not return it. He parked the Explorer in a gravel lot, shifted it into park, lowered the windows, and cut the engine.

The world around him, the killing fields of Gettysburg, were silent. No cannons, no rifles, no hollers or sounds of boots marching or wagon wheels turning. Only the occasional singing of a bird or creaking of old branches in the breeze. There were witness trees around him, over a hundred and fifty years old, that had watched as the battle raged and as bloodshed bathed their roots. To his left, large, pocked rocks jutted from a field like cavity-laden teeth. The grass had been freshly mown and lay in clumps here and there. The field sloped gradually then took a steep turn for the sky, where it was topped by a fortress of granite rocks: Little Round Top. And to his right, Devil's Den, a striking setting of rocky outcroppings and rounded boulders. He suddenly wished he knew more about the area.

Sam picked up the *Gettysburg Times* from the passenger seat and unfolded it. The front-page headline read "Senator Lincoln to Address Nation From Famous Gettysburg Location." He scanned the article. He wasn't one to keep a close eye on current political affairs, but he knew enough to recognize the name of Stephen Lincoln, the senator from Pennsylvania who'd recently taken a stand against abortion and switched party allegiances. Apparently this Lincoln was part of a movement to amend the Constitution to outlaw abortion once and for all. And from the way the article read, his bill was gaining momentum. His change in political convictions, though initially unpopular, was now rallying and strengthening the conservative movement throughout the country. Senator Lincoln was coming next week to deliver a speech from the very spot where Abraham Lincoln gave his Gettysburg Address.

Big deal. Sam wasn't impressed. Politicians came and went all the time, offering this and promising that and delivering on none of it. This guy was no doubt just another slick, snake-oil salesman, getting everyone tied up in knots over some amendment that would never see the dawn of day. He was a liar like the rest of them.

From his left Sam heard the muffled crack of a dry branch and the rustle of grass. He lowered the newspaper and snapped his head toward the sound.

Tommy was standing there, not twenty yards from the Explorer.

It wasn't the seventeen-year-old Tommy that Sam had so often imagined, but a younger version, thinner, smaller, maybe fourteen or fifteen. Head and face still intact. He stared at Sam, arms hanging at his sides, right hand grasping the end of a broom handle, left hand wrapped in something. Hair tousled by the breeze, he wore that black AC/DC shirt he had liked so much and faded, torn jeans.

Sam broke out in goose bumps. The scar on his head took to aching again, that dull ache as from a stiff joint.

Could this really be? Of course it couldn't; he knew that. But Tommy looked so real, so *now.* He was betrayed, though, by the dark haze that surrounded him, a glow but not a glow...an *anti*-glow. The haze seemed to suck the light from the atmosphere around Tommy, and it shimmered when he moved.

Tommy shifted his weight from one leg to the other and lifted the stick high over head. He grinned like a mangy old hyena.

Sam knew this part. No, please no. Not this.

His older brother—his *dead* older brother—opened his mouth to speak...

"Hey, Sammy." He was standing in the field behind their house, on the other side of the small rise that blocked their view of the first-floor windows. In his right hand he held a broken broom handle; a long leather leash was wrapped tightly around the knuckles on his left. At the end of the leash was Gomer, the family dog. Good old Gomer.

Gomer was crouched low to the ground, ears laid back against his head, watching Tommy from the tops of his eyes.

"Hey, Sammy, wanna have some fun?"

Sam knew what Tommy had in mind, no question about it. He'd grown tired of cats and moved on to dogs. To Gomer. Feelings of both fear and pity overcame Sam, and he almost started to cry. "Tommy, don't. Just let him go. It's Gomer."

"Oh, don't be a sissy. He deserves it anyway."

"What'd he do?"

Tommy motioned to the field behind with the stick. "I found him out there, rolling against some carcass, told him to knock it off, and he tried to bite me." He looked at Gomer, made a threatening move. The dog flinched, then growled deep in his throat. "I'm gonna show him who's boss."

Sam's mind churned and locked, churned and locked. He knew Tommy was lying. They'd had Gomer since he was a pup, and he'd never tried to bite anyone. If he had tried to bite, Tommy had it coming. "He was probably just scared. You probably scared him."

Tommy turned and glared, the stick held waist high. "What? You siding with Gomer, little brother? The dog? You think he had a right to bite me?"

"No, I…"

"I should beat you with this stick after I'm done with your buddy Gomer here. How would you like that?" He paused to see Sam's reaction, then broke into a wide smile. "I'm just kidding, sissy."

He started wrapping the leash tighter around his hand, drawing Gomer closer, like a deep-sea fisherman reeling in the big catch. Gomer tried to resist, digging his feet into the soil and letting out a deep guttural growl, but it was useless. He was no match for Tommy's strength.

"Just let him go, Tommy, please." Sam hoped his plea would flip a switch in his brother's brain. Hoped it would wake him from the madness he was about to do.

Without taking his eyes off Gomer, Tommy strained against the dog's resistance and said to Sam, "Shut up, sissy. I thought you'd want to help, but if you're scared, you can just leave."

Anger boiled in Sam's chest. He clenched his fists and pressed his molars together. Gomer was now within Tommy's striking distance. He was hunched on his hindquarters, pressing his forelegs into the ground and trying to backpedal, twisting his head side to side so violently that Sam was afraid he'd break his neck before Tommy could take a crack at him. Half of Sam wished Gomer would break his neck and bring the end quickly, thereby escaping Tommy's maliciousness.

At last Tommy struck. He raised the stick above his head and brought it down on Gomer. Gomer flinched and ducked, but the stick landed against his shoulder, drawing out a sharp yelp. Gomer cowered and bared his teeth, snarled and growled. Again Tommy brought the stick down. And again.

Sam could take no more. He rushed his brother and reached him in five steps. He had no idea what he would do. Tommy was two years older and at least thirty pounds heavier. Tommy saw him coming. He whipped the stick around and caught Sam in the chest, knocking him off his feet so that he landed on his butt in the dirt. The blow momentarily stunned Sam and knocked the breath from his chest. He sputtered and gasped and coughed until he found air again. His chest burned, and his eyes blurred with tears.

"Get lost, Sammy," Tommy yelled. There was hatred in his eyes, a malevolent look more intense than Sam had ever seen from him.

Gomer seized this moment to lunge and take his captor's ankle in his teeth. Tommy cursed and crashed the stick down on Gomer's head. Gomer released his grip immediately and stumbled back, dazed.

Sam climbed to his feet and started his own retreat. He wanted no part of this. Whatever Tommy was going to do was between him and God now.

Tommy hit Gomer again, hard. The dog let out a weak holler. With a grunt his brother landed another blow. Then another, and another, and another, until Gomer no longer resisted and lay still and silent.

But Tommy didn't stop. He kept beating, grunting, swearing.

That's when Sam turned and bolted.

Twenty-Three

STEPHEN LINCOLN SAT AT HIS MAHOGANY DESK, STUDYING the Gettysburg Address. November 19, 1863. He never tired of reading it.

Four score and seven years ago our forefathers brought forth, on this continent, a new nation…

Outside his office his staff busied themselves with the duties of the day, other senators made deals in their offices or returned phone calls or mulled over pages and pages of legislation, and the citizens of the United States of America went about their lives, working, shopping, relaxing, laughing, crying. And they were all oblivious to the battle, the civil war, raging within Stephen Lincoln.

…conceived in liberty and dedicated to the proposition that all men are created equal….

He was going to define himself with this next speech; he was going to set himself apart from the other presidential hopefuls and take that proverbial road less traveled.

Now we are engaged in a great civil war, testing whether that nation, or any nation so conceived, and so dedicated, can long endure….

He had to do it. It was a risk; he knew it was. His advisors told him if he went through with it, his career was as good as dead. All the momentum he'd managed, all the ground gained, the capital earned, would be lost. But if he did not, he would forever despise his own image in the mirror.

The world will little note, nor long remember what we say here, but it can never forget what they did here….

Stephen Lincoln aimed to be a man of honor, a family man, a

patriot. He had one life to live, and if his lot was to run for president of the United States, then he would do so on his convictions and with honor. He would not run as a politician. Besides, the American people were wise to the game played in Washington—the promises, the lies, the talking points, the mudslinging—and they deserved more.

It is for us, the living, rather to be dedicated here to the unfinished work which they who fought here have thus far so nobly advanced....

The world thought he was going to speak on the abortion issue, and he would, but his speech would be so much more than that. For at the heart of that issue stood the sanctity of life and the inherent right of liberty and freedom for all.

It is rather for us to be here dedicated to the great task remaining before us...

Lincoln was convinced America was a troubled nation, deeply wounded and broken. Government had grown too big and the people too powerless. She needed to return to her roots, to the principles she once embraced and upon which she was founded.

...that from these honored dead we take increased devotion to that cause for which they gave the last full measure of devotion...

She had strayed, and he saw it as not only his duty but also his passion—and dare he say, his responsibility, maybe even calling—to bring her back. His speech, delivered in Gettysburg on the same date in November that the other Lincoln delivered his, would kick off his campaign to restore America...and quite possibly be political suicide.

...that we here highly resolve that these dead shall not have died in vain...

A knock sounded on the office door.

"Come in."

Jeremy Pitts, his prematurely balding, bespectacled speechwriter, entered. He set a packet of papers on Lincoln's desk. "Here's the first draft of your Gettysburg speech."

Lincoln leafed through it. "Thanks, Jer. I'll read over it right now and get back to you."

"Good enough." Jeremy exited the office, closing the door behind him.

Fifty-two pages.

Lincoln ran his thumb over the edges of the papers. It would have to lose a few pages. He didn't want to bore the people with a superfluity of words. The message would get lost in the muddle. No, he had to keep this short. The other Lincoln's was the model. He had spoken for two minutes, and his speech far outweighed the two-hour monotony of that day's other speaker, Edward Everett.

Lincoln turned to the computer screen and read the Address again. That final sentence captured the essence of his own message.

...that this nation, under God, shall have a new birth of freedom, and that this government of the people, by the people, and for the people, shall not perish from this earth.

Twenty-Four

Symon waited. The school was quiet from the outside. It was almost two thirty, and a few parents had arrived early to wait in line for their little ones.

Symon watched patiently from across the street, from the Intrepid, enjoying the sunshine and cool air. The few trees on the school's property, nearly barren of leaves, cast long jagged shadows across the lawn. The days were getting shorter, bringing darkness sooner. Symon liked the darkness, found it comforting and safe. The memory of being in the closet, smelling his mother's Miss Dior while his stepfather used her as a punching bag, surely had something to do with it.

He had no recollections of school, though. He figured he must've gone because he knew things. A lot of things. And since he was now in Gettysburg, he tested himself.

He knew the battle had taken place between July 1 and 3, 1863. He knew ninety-five thousand Union troops and seventy-five thousand Confederate troops had clashed, with over fifty-one thousand casualties. He knew about Devil's Den and Pickett's Charge and Jennie Wade. Abraham Lincoln, the sixteenth president of the United States, had given his famed address here. And Symon could recite the entire thing.

He also knew Senator Stephen Lincoln of Pennsylvania would be giving *his* Gettysburg Address here on November 19.

That turned his attention back to the school and the target. The clock on the dash said 2:42. The kiddies would be emerging soon, and she would be with them.

Twenty-Five

Molly Travis checked the driveway for the twenty-first time. Yes, she was counting. Sam had been gone over three hours, with no word, and she was past the point of worrying. Almost two hours ago she had tried calling his cell phone and heard the familiar ring tone upstairs in the bedroom; he'd forgotten it. Shortly after she heard a distant siren and nearly panicked.

She opened the phonebook and found Gettysburg Hospital, but she resisted dialing the number. She was overreacting. She needed to relax, give Sam some space. And trust. But that didn't stop her from checking the driveway one more time.

And it didn't stop her from worrying. It couldn't. She worried by nature. Sam was always telling her to stop fussing over things and just let them happen. Things had a way of working themselves out, he would say. But she knew he worried too. She knew he fretted constantly about his health and their finances and Eva's teeth that the dentist was already saying would need braces in a few years and making the mortgage payment and keeping in touch with clients and on and on, around and around.

He was under so much pressure. And what was she doing to alleviate it?

She looked out the window at the empty driveway one more time.

Oh, Sam. I'm sorry for smothering you. Please come home soon.

The phone in the kitchen rang, and Molly jumped. She'd heard about this, the "phone call." *"Ma'am, I'm sorry to inform you that…"*

Please, God, no. Please don't let it be about Sam.

It rang again. Maybe she'd let the answering machine get it. If it was important, then she'd pick up.

Another ring. No, she needed to answer it, even if it was what she feared most.

Running to the kitchen, she grabbed the receiver from the wall on the fourth ring. The plastic was cold in her hand. "Hello?" She held her breath, anticipating the response of an unfamiliar yet professional voice on the other end: *"Is this Mrs. Travis?"*

Instead it was a familiar voice.

"Molly, it's Beth."

Relief eased over Molly, and she almost started to cry. "Hey."

"Eva was in school today, right?" Beth's voice sounded slightly panicked.

Whatever relief Molly had felt was short-lived. Now the cool winds of fear blew over her and put the prickles down her back. "Yes. What's wrong?"

The moment's pause gave Molly time to conjure all sorts of bad scenarios.

"Um, I'm here at the school, and no one seems to know where she is."

"What do you mean they don't know where she is?"

"When I got here to pick up Eva and Lucy, she wasn't here. Miss Stambaugh said she was—"

"Wasn't there? What do you mean?"

"Miss Stambaugh said Eva was with the class when they left to go to the carpool line, but when I got there she was gone."

Molly pressed the phone so hard against her ear it hurt. She loosened her grip and took a deep breath. "What's the school doing now?"

"Well..." Beth hesitated. "The principal called the police."

"Oh—" Molly pressed her left fist against her mouth to stop the sobs that pushed themselves up from her throat. Her eyes burned. This couldn't be happening.

"They're on their way. Molly, Miss Stambaugh is sure Eva never left the school. She swears she was with the class right up to the car-pool line. She must have gone back into the building."

Molly felt no consolation. The words were hollow, without meaning or substance. Her baby was missing. "I'm coming. I'll be there in a few minutes."

She clicked off the phone and let the tears flow. But there was no time for crying. She had to go. She thought of Sam, but she had no way to contact him. Sam! She let out a scream of frustration and grabbed the keys to his work truck.

The school was only minutes away, and when Molly arrived, a police officer was already there. He stood at the school's main entry, talking to Beth and Miss Stambaugh. Getting out of the truck, Molly felt as though her surroundings had shrunk. The sky, with its criss-crossed contrails and wispy clouds, was like a giant hand pressing down. The school's trees loomed close, their bony arms seeming to form a cage around her. The sidewalk appeared to writhe and slither under her feet.

Mr. Godin met Molly on the walkway. "Mrs. Travis, we're sure she's in the school somewhere." He was a small man with a narrow head and pointy face. A man Molly never cared for much.

"How could this happen? How could you let a little girl out of your sight?" Politeness was the last thing on her mind at the moment.

She hustled up to the officer, a bulky middle-aged man.

"Mrs. Travis?"

"Has anyone checked in the school yet?" Molly looked from the officer to Eva's teacher.

Beth stepped alongside and put her arm around Molly's shoulders. "All the teachers are looking now. Officer Richardson just got here."

"We're sure she's inside," Mr. Godin said again.

Molly pulled away from Beth and pushed past the officer into the building. The smell of the empty school hit her, and she thought of other times she'd been here with Eva. Book fairs, school plays, talent shows, assemblies. The place was usually buzzing with children. She'd never seen it this desolate, and it made her all the more nervous. The silence mocked her. If everyone was so sure Eva was in here, why was the place so quiet, so vacant?

A woman's voice called Eva's name. Molly hurried down the hall toward the sound, classrooms on either side, her sneakers chirping on the tile floor. Rounding a corner, she ran into Kristy Krakowski, the newly married first-grade teacher.

"Mrs. Travis, I'm so sorry this has happened, but she has to be in here, she has to be somewhere. I saw her just minutes before they left the classroom with Joan." Tears glimmered in Kristy's eyes. "We'll find her. I know we will. She has to be OK."

Molly didn't say anything and kept walking. She saw one of the fourth-grade teachers step out of a classroom. His eyes widened, and a shadow of empathy moved over his face.

"Oh, hi, Mrs. Travis. We'll find her." And he was off to the next classroom.

The whole experience was unreal, like walking through a dream. Eva's name being called through the rooms and hallways. Teachers and janitors here and there, looking and talking in hushed tones. Doors opening and closing. Heels clicking on the tile. Cell phones ringing.

"Eva!" Molly called.

Suddenly there she was.

Eva. Her daughter. Her little girl. The blonde hair pulled back in a ponytail with loose strands at the temples. The freckles. Those big cerulean eyes. At the sound of her mother's voice, she had emerged from a utility closet and stood in the doorway, shoulders slumped, eyes fixed on Molly.

"Eva." Saying her baby's name brought tears that blurred Molly's vision. She wiped at them and ran to her daughter. Picking her up, she held her close and cried into her hair. "I found her!" she hollered. "She's here."

Within seconds the hallway was packed with people chattering amongst themselves. Molly held Eva and wouldn't let go. Beth was there, her hand on Molly's back. She was crying too.

At last Molly released Eva, wiped her tears again, and knelt before her little girl. "Eva, baby, why didn't you go with Miss Beth? What were you doing?"

Eva looked from Molly to Beth and back. There was no fear in her eyes, only a childlike innocence. "I'm sorry, Mommy. Jacob told me not to. He told me if I did, that something bad would happen."

Twenty-Six

When Sam pulled into the driveway, he noticed his work truck had been moved. He glanced at the dashboard clock. 4:12 p.m. He'd totally lost track of time. Was it Molly's day to pick up Eva and Lucy from school? If so, she'd had to take the truck and wouldn't be happy. He thought about backing out and leaving, just driving away and never coming back. But that wasn't an option. He loved Eva and Molly too much. Yes, Molly and he had their differences. She was too mothering and he was too stubborn. But they loved each other and, for the most part, overlooked those character flaws. It's what had kept them together for thirteen years.

Lately, though, he'd grown more and more irritable and restless. Ever since the night he heard Tommy's voice. It was as though his brother had returned and brought all the rotten memories with him. Those memories now haunted Sam, reaching out of the past and digging spidery fingers into his head.

Steeling himself for Molly's wrath, he killed the engine and exited the Explorer. He would be the next thing killed if he didn't handle this right. He'd apologize and tell her he was a jerk. And now that he'd proven he could drive, he would volunteer to help with the carpool.

Sam stepped up onto the front porch. Opened the door.

Molly came at him from the kitchen. "Where've you been?" She held a dishtowel in hand like a horsewhip, and her face said she was mad.

Sam wondered if she'd chosen the best murder weapon. Flogged to death by dishtowel lacked a certain ring. Regardless, he raised both hands in defense. "Hold it, Molly, just hold it. Before you lay into me, I'm sorry I got home so late and you had to take the truck to get the girls. I lost track of time."

She twisted her face into a question mark. "What? Do you know what happened while you were gone?"

"No. How could I?"

"Right, how could you? Your phone was upstairs the whole time. I got a call from Beth saying Eva wasn't there when she went to pick her up."

"Not there? Is…is she OK? Is she here?"

"She's fine. She was hiding in the janitor's closet."

"What? Did something happen? Did she get scared?" He couldn't help thinking the worst. There were male teachers in that school and… He pushed away the thought.

Molly shook her head. "No. Nothing like that. At least, not that she's saying."

Not that she's saying. Kids usually didn't say anything. Anger coursed into Sam's blood; the room felt like it had grown ten degrees warmer. "But we don't know for sure."

Molly looked to the top of the staircase then back at Sam. She lowered her voice. "Eva says Jacob told her not to go with Beth. He said if she did, something bad would happen."

Sam ran his fingers through his hair. "Oh, man. That's crazy. This Jacob thing is getting out of control. Is that normal?"

"Does it sound normal?"

"Is she in her room?"

Molly nodded. "Don't be hard on her. I don't think she even realizes she did anything wrong."

Sam walked past his wife and up the steps. Of course he wouldn't be hard on Eva.

When he entered her room, she was seated Indian-style on the floor, playing with her dollhouse, arranging miniature furniture and accessories and the family. Her eyes widened when she saw him. A smile stretched across her face, bunching her cheeks.

"Daddy!" She jumped up and ran to him.

"Hey, baby girl. How's it going?"

Arms still wrapped around his waist, she looked up and said, "My people are having a yard sale. Wanna buy something?"

"Sure." He sat on the floor next to the house. "Let's see what they have that I could use."

Eva plopped beside him and reached for a tiny water basin and pitcher. "You could use this to wash your face after you shave." Then she giggled. "But it wouldn't hold enough water."

"Hey, are you saying I have a big face?"

"Daddy. You know what I mean."

"I'll take it anyway. How much?"

"Um." She put her finger on her chin and pretended to think. "Five dollars."

"Ha! A bargain," Sam said. "Sold." And he gave her five pretend dollars.

"Thank you, sir." Eva put the imaginary money in her pocket. "I hope you like it."

"Oh, I love it. How was your day at school today?"

Eva sighed. "I know, Daddy. Mommy already talked to me about it."

"About what?"

"About hiding in the closet and not going home with Miss Beth."

"Yeah, she told me. Wanna talk about it?"

"Not really. I don't know why everyone was so scared."

He pretended to pour water from the pitcher into the basin. "You weren't where you should have been, and they didn't know where you were. They thought you were lost or that maybe someone had taken you."

"But Jacob told me not to go with Miss Beth. He said something bad would happen if I did, and I thought everyone would be more scared if that happened."

Downstairs a cupboard door opened and pots clanged. Molly was starting dinner.

"Well, that was very considerate of you. Do you do everything Jacob tells you to?"

"He's my friend. He would never tell me to do something bad."

Sam leaned sideways so he could meet Eva's eyes. "Even if it goes against what Mommy and Daddy tell you to do? Like to go home with Miss Beth?"

She seemed to think about that one. She didn't answer.

He put his hand on Eva's head and stroked her hair. "Sweetie, is there a reason you didn't want to get in the car with Miss Beth?"

"I said, Jacob told me not to. He said if—"

"Eva, Jacob is just an imaginary friend—"

"No, Daddy, he's not. He's real."

"He's imaginary. Pretend. Like the water in this pitcher." He held up the miniature pitcher and turned it upside down.

Eva's eyes filled with tears. "You don't know. He's real, and he tells me to do stuff, good stuff. He's worried about you, Daddy. Why is he so worried? Is something wrong?"

A knot twisted in Sam's throat. "Baby, there's no need to worry about me. I'm getting better and better all the time." A twinge of guilt stabbed at him. He wasn't getting better; he was losing his mind.

Twenty-Seven

Ned Coleman's suspicions had been stirred. An hour and a half before his shift started, he'd been informed by Chrystal at the 911 Center of a call made by Lou Godin over at Lincoln Elementary School. She thought he'd like to know that a little girl, Eva Travis, had gone missing for almost an hour after school. The mother's name was Molly. Molly Travis. The name from his residential call the other night.

Yes, that was information he wanted. First an alleged home shooting, then the daughter went missing at school. Something was beginning to smell.

Almost time for his shift, the graveyard. After brushing his teeth and throwing on jeans and a pullover, Ned dialed the Gettysburg station. "Hi, Lynette, this is Ned Coleman. How're you this evening?"

"Just fine, Ned. What can I do for you?" Lynette, the secretary, was a middle-aged grandmother who sounded tired over the phone.

"Who was the responding officer at Lincoln El today? The missing Travis girl."

"Well, hang on there just a minute and I'll see." There was a short pause. "Looks like it was Glenn."

Glenn Richardson. Good, Ned liked him. He wasn't one of those cocky young Gettysburg guys that Ned butted heads with. "Thanks, Lynette. Is he still on?"

"Uh, yes. His shift ends at eleven."

"Thanks again." *And thanks for not calling it a "ride."*

He reset the phone and punched the buttons. Two rings later Officer Richardson picked up.

"Hey, Glenn, Ned Coleman here."

"Coleman. I shoulda known you'd be calling me right before my shift ended. You better not ruin it for me." Richardson's voice was gruff, but it didn't match his personality.

"Actually, I was hoping to meet you at the tracks for some late-night chatter. Want to ask you about the missing Travis girl."

"She wasn't missing at all. They found her hiding in the utility closet."

"Hiding? Sounds like a story there. Can we meet in, say, fifteen, and you can fill me in? I may have something of interest for you too."

"Fifteen at the tracks?"

"Yeah."

"I can do that."

Twenty-Eight

"At the tracks" was police talk for the Lincoln Diner, a local gathering place for cops and blue-collar types. It wasn't much to look at, just a no-frills, nothing fancy, railcar diner, but it served great food and treated cops right.

When Ned arrived, Richardson was already sipping coffee in a booth that faced the door. He saw Ned and nodded.

Ned approached. "You're quick. What, you live here or something?"

"Pretty much. I don't even have to order. Claudia over there just serves up the coffee and keeps it coming. How 'bout you? You want a cup?"

Ned figured Richardson to be at least fifty, but he'd managed to stay in decent shape, unlike some of the other local uniforms. Ned was amused, however, by the man's mustache, one of those Wyatt Earp jobs that had grown so long it covered his entire mouth.

"Sure."

Richardson waved at Claudia, the busty waitress who usually worked the evenings. "Coffee for Coleman here." Then he turned to Ned. "Glad to see you still drink the real stuff. Lotta the young guys drink that Red Bull battery acid. Gets 'em all hopped up like a buck in season."

Ned shrugged. "We all do what we gotta do to stay alert."

Claudia set the coffee in front of Ned. "Creamer?"

"No, thanks. Just black." He watched her leave, then scanned the clientele. The place was more than half full, mostly locals he recognized. The smell of cooked grease thickened the air. "Man, I can feel my arteries hardening just sitting here. I'm gonna have to take another shower when I leave. The Stinkin' Lincoln—you know that's what they call this place, right?"

"I've heard it," Richardson said. "Hey, the food is good, the price is right, and the staff is friendly. I'm not complaining. So, what is it you want to know about the Travis girl?"

"How 'bout what happened. From the top."

"Sure." Richardson took a sip of coffee, then swirled the black liquid in the cup. "I got a call saying a second-grader was missing. Teachers didn't think she'd left the school, but when they lined up for the carpool, she wasn't there. By the time I got there, they had cleared the building and were searching each room. The mother arrived shortly after I did and found the kid hiding in a utility closet."

Ned thought for a moment. He remembered the girl sitting on the house steps. Blonde hair, freckles. Cute kid. Quiet too. Didn't seem like the type to cause trouble. "Kid say why she was hiding there?"

Richardson's frown dropped his mustache almost to his chin. "That's where things get kinda weird. She said Jacob told her to hide. Said Jacob told her if she went home with the carpool mother, Beth Fisher, something bad would happen."

"Who's this Jacob? A friend? Please don't say a teacher."

"Nope," Richardson said. He snuck another sip of coffee and wiped his mustache with a napkin. "Mom says he's an imaginary friend. Something little Eva just started."

"So this imaginary friend tells her not to go home because something bad will happen if she does, and she hides in a closet."

"Not to go home with 'Miss Beth.' She was very specific about that."

"Did you check Miss Beth out?"

"Yep. She's clean as a new car. Been friends with the family for some ten years."

"And any Jacobs at the school? Any teachers?"

"One kid, Jacob Burnah. Fourth-grader. Swears he's never even talked to Eva Travis."

OK, so the kid had an imaginary playmate. Not that unusual. What was a bit disconcerting, though, were the things this friend was telling her. Ned was no psychologist, but his instincts told him that if Eva was hiding in broom closets to avoid going home, she must have a good reason. What was going on in that Travis house?

"Why the interest?" Richardson said.

Ned took a long draw of coffee. "Two days ago I get called out to a residential shooting. Man says he woke up, went downstairs, opened the front door, and heard a gunshot. The front window explodes. The man? Samuel Travis. Little Eva's dad. Both mother and daughter were sleeping when it happened. Both said they heard the glass shatter but not the shot."

"Not that unusual. 'Specially if the shooter was some ways away. Anyone could sleep through a distant shot, small caliber, doesn't make that much noise."

Ned shook his head. "Travis said the shot and the glass were instantaneous, boom-boom. Had to be a close shot. And in the country like that, minus the sounds of the town? It'd be loud enough, even a twenty-two."

Richardson's eyebrows arched, and the corners of his mouth dipped. His Wyatt Earp went with them.

"Wait, there's more. When I get there, I see glass everywhere in the living room. But no entry point. No slug. Nothing disturbed on the opposite wall or side walls. Like the bullet hit the window then just disappeared. Poof."

"Or there was no bullet. No gunshot."

"Bingo."

Richardson ran a thumb along the rim of his mug. His nail was partially torn, exposing some of the pink nail bed underneath. He took a sip, wiped his mouth. "Anything else that struck you as strange? The girl's behavior? Travis's relationship with his wife or kid?"

"Not that I noticed. They all were obviously shaken, nothing out of the ordinary. I think I'll pay them another visit tomorrow. I work a turnaround."

"Let me know what comes of it, OK?"

"Of course."

Twenty-Nine

THAT NIGHT SAM DREAMED OF WAR. SLEEP CAME IN FITS, disturbed by images of the maimed and dying. Men pleading for death, calling for their mommas. Sounds of battle haunted him, and more than once he cried out in his sleep.

Finally he climbed from his bed and stumbled down the hallway to Eva's room. She was sleeping soundly on her stomach, covers at her waist. The night-light cast the room in a moody glow, like a dusting of snow. He smoothed her hair from her face, pulled the comforter to her shoulders, and tiptoed out. Downstairs the house was quiet. No voices beckoning from the grave.

Into the study he went. He crossed the darkened room to the window and peered out.

The groundhog. The shot. It *was* a good shot. And it felt right. The rifle felt like it used to in his hands. Natural, comfortable.

Outside the world was dark and lonely. The sky, starless. The leafless maple stood in the backyard, silhouetted like the raised makeshift weapons of an angry horde of peasants. Pitchforks and rakes and sickles of all sizes.

The floor, the ground itself, began to shake under Sam. Disoriented, he grabbed the windowsill to steady himself and watched in horror as the earth at the base of the house split and crumbled away in huge chunks. His mind reeled, thinking an earthquake—which was most unlikely—had struck the Gettysburg area. But then he noticed something pushing its way through the dirt.

A giant hand emerged, at least the size of the Explorer, clawing upward, bent and curled. At the fingertips, long, broken nails were crusted in black soil. The hand stopped level with the window. Sam, paralyzed with fear, dug his own nails into the sill. He told himself to run, run from the room, gather his wife and child and beat it out of the house, but his feet were stuck to the floor. His heart banged hard and fast within its bony cage.

The hand uncurled to reveal a bloody and dirt-smeared palm. Sam noticed a series of cuts in the skin and, looking closer, realized they formed letters. A capitalized *K* here, an *I* there, an *L*, an *N*, and others. His mind assembled the letters into words.

Two words: KILL LINCOLN.

Sam awoke with a start. He was sitting in his study, both arms crossed on the desktop, his head resting between them. Drool connected his mouth to a sheet of paper. He lifted his head, wiped at his lips, and found a pen in his hand.

How had he gotten here?

The dream. The hand. Kill Lincoln. It *was* a dream, wasn't it?

Still muddled with sleep fog, he dropped the pen and rubbed his eyes. Through the window he saw the sunrise lighting the sky. The maple was there, twisted branches reminding him of that hand, that awful hand. The rest of the house was quiet. Molly and Eva were still sleeping.

Sam Travis looked down at his desk. "Oh, c'mon," he mumbled.

A piece of paper lay there, filled with writing. His writing.

About 10:00 p.m. some fighting from Culp's Hill broke out. General Greene held them. It's not likely the enemy will attack here tomorrow, but we wish they would! We are ready and will belch death their way.

The cries of the wounded are sickening. Thousands of men are now mangled, twisted, crying beings asking death to take them!

Took better stock of my battery. Lost a lot of good men, young and old, today. I was lucky or with grace. One slight scratch on my neck, about three inches long.

I have two guns left out of four. The third was

left but spIked, the fourth cracked its barrel from the work we did.

Forty men, twenty horses, full load of ammunition. God bless these men. I do love them all!

Tired. Must get some rest.

John M. Baker III lost his life in the service. Let it be said that there was no braver man on earth. My dear John went down while pulling a double canister. This gave us time, a precious fifteen to twenty seconds, during which we stalLed the enemy and saved the day. I will put him in for a medal for his family.

He was my friend!

I curse this war more every moment. The dead and dying are testimony to its evil. Good men lost, and for what? They could be living lives of contentment and happiness, home with their famiLies. And yet they are here, dying meaningless deaths. Horrible deaths.

I can no longer support this effort. I will fight for my men and for them only, and to return to my dear Emma, but I can no longer support President Lincoln and his bloodthirsty government.

In fact, right or not, God forgive me, if that man were across the line from me, I would not hesitate to point my weapon his way. I am fully aware it is treason to even write such words, but given the opportunity I would kill him for all the lives lost on his watch. I am drowning in darkness. It is swallowing me, and I would take him with me.

I would kill Lincoln.

I would kill Lincoln.

Kill Lincoln

Kill Lincoln

Kill Lincoln

Thirty

Sam stared dumbly at the paper. The beginnings of a killer headache throbbed behind his eyes. What was happening to him? He felt himself slipping, losing ground, sliding into the abyss that Samuel Whiting had entered and written about.

No, that *he* had written about.

Gradually, like a tide creeping up the beach, his mood changed. A great shadow moved over him, and Sam Travis felt the weight of despair. It wouldn't be long before he had completely lost it, and that would be bad, very bad. Whether the brain injury was to blame or the feelings of uselessness or these cursed writings, he did not know. But it was happening. That dark tide's undercurrent gathered him in its powerful arms, dragging him toward a watery death. All he had to do was let go and let it have its way. And he wanted to. Oh, how he wanted to. He was tired of fighting it. Tired of resisting.

Now that he thought of it, he realized he'd been dealing with this since before that night of Tommy's voice and the sounds of battle outside his home. This had been going on for weeks. The darkness had been stealing its way toward him, like the night overtaking daylight, inch by inch, minute by minute. And now it had reached him. He was half in, half out, and had a decision to make. Would he retreat into the light and only prolong the inevitable, or would he allow the darkness to overcome him as it had Samuel Whiting?

For Sam, it should not have been a difficult decision. He had Molly and Eva to think about. Especially Eva. She needed her daddy. But he was so tired of running. And where had it gotten him? The darkness had still wormed its tentacles into his mind.

In the same way, it had engulfed Tommy. His had also been

a slow descent. He'd grown weary of resisting—and look at the outcome.

You did what you had to do, son.

Sam shoved the paper across the desk and pressed his hands against his temples. A headache was beginning. He needed to talk to someone. Needed to bounce this off another man. He opened the desk drawer and retrieved the other writings. He would take them to Thad Lewis for his take on the whole thing. Thad always shot straight with him.

Quietly, so as not to disturb his sleeping wife, Sam crept back into the bedroom, slipped out of his sweatpants and into some jeans, the old ones with the hole in the right knee. The ones Molly kept telling him to get rid of. He grabbed his sneakers and left the room, easing the door shut behind him.

Downstairs the kitchen was bathed in honey-colored sunlight, the stainless steel appliances tipped with gold. He got a Coke from the refrigerator and a granola bar from the pantry. His headache was worsening. Molly kept Motrin in the drawer next to the stove. He downed one and gulped half a glass of water.

Sam snatched the truck keys from the hook and looked at the clock on the microwave: 6:37. Thad would be up now. He was an early riser. Careful to avoid the creaky floorboards, Sam moved toward the front door and reached for the dead bolt.

"Where're you going?"

Molly.

Sam turned and found her at the top of the steps, robe wrapped tightly, sleep still smudged across her face.

"I'm going out."

"I can see that," Molly said. If she was trying to keep her voice to a whisper, she wasn't being very successful. "Where?"

"I just need to get out for a little bit. Got some things to do."

"At six in the morning?"

"Six thirty."

"OK, six thirty."

"Yeah. I guess. So what?"

Molly ran her hand through her hair, pushing it out of her face. "What's that in your hand?"

The manila folder containing the writings.

"Nothing," Sam said. "I'm just going out. I won't be long."

He swung open the door and was about to step over the threshold when a different voice stopped him.

"Momma, where's Daddy going?"

Eva had joined Molly on the landing. Molly's hand was on Eva's shoulder.

"Where are you going, Daddy?"

"Nowhere, sweetie. I'll be back soon."

"Before I go to school?"

"I don't know. Maybe, maybe not." He regretted the harsh tone he'd used.

"Be careful. Jacob told me—"

"Eva, please," he said. "No more about Jacob, OK? He's gotten you into enough trouble." He could see the hurt on her face, the hurt he'd caused with his sharp words.

"I love you, Daddy. Be careful."

Sam hesitated, one hand on the doorknob. He couldn't look either his wife or daughter in the eyes. He needed to get away, get out of the house. For himself, yes—he felt he couldn't stand being trapped between those four walls any longer—but more importantly, for them, for Molly and Eva. If he stayed, he'd only hurt them more.

"I gotta go," he said and walked out, pulling the door shut behind him.

Thirty-One

Thad Lewis lived in an early-model mobile home tucked into a corner of his parents' farm. It sat at the end of a dusty dirt lane lined with knee-high patches of witchgrass and ragweed. It wasn't much to look at. The siding had long ago faded to a pasty stone color, the roof was rusting along the edges, and the skirting was gone, revealing the cinder blocks that supported the structure.

Sam parked his truck alongside Thad's custom van. A long wooden ramp carried him up two switchbacks to the flimsy foam-core door on which he knocked.

A voice from the inside shouted, "Yeah, it's open."

He stuck his head in. The place reeked of cigarettes and beer. "Hey, it's Sam…"

From somewhere in the back of the trailer Thad called out, "Hey, Sam. Come on in, man. I'm in the bedroom."

The lights were dim, the shades pulled, and Sam gave his eyes a moment to adjust to the hazy interior. Stacks of newspapers, magazines, appliance boxes, As Seen On TV gizmos, and a couple of guitar cases lined the walls and occupied the sofa. A big-screen TV sat in one corner, an overstuffed, worn-in-the-armrests recliner opposite it. On the nicotine-stained wall above the sofa a painting of a Civil War battle showed soldiers in gray uniforms clashing with those in blue. Thad had told him it was a depiction of Pickett's Charge.

"Follow the hallway back," Thad said.

Sam moved past a bathroom on the left and into the bedroom. Thad was in his wheelchair, facing a flat computer monitor. He spun the chair around, removed the cigarette from his lips, and grinned. "Hey, man. What's cookin'? Long time no see."

Thad was a double amputee. He had worked in a machine shop, cutting open a steel drum with a blowtorch, when the gases in the drum ignited and took off both legs above the knees. That was two years ago. He'd lived in the wheelchair since. Said he could never get the hang of prosthetic limbs.

Sam shook his hand. "Yeah, it's been too long."

"How're things comin' with your...?" Thad pointed at Sam's head and wiggled his finger.

Thad was a holdover from the 1970s. Sam guessed the man was in his early forties, though his leathered skin made him look older. He had shoulder-length hair, thinning on top, and a thick, handlebar mustache. He wore a faded Lynyrd Skynyrd T-shirt and cutoff jeans tied at the end of each stump.

"They're coming," Sam said. "Slowly, but coming."

"You back at work yet?"

Sam shook his head. "Not yet. Just... not yet."

"I gotcha, man. And how's the fam?"

Thad had met Molly and Eva once at a reenactment in town, and every time he saw Sam, he asked how they were doing.

Sam shrugged. "They're great. You done any reenactments lately?"

The Civil War was Thad's obsession. He lived off his disability income and what little he'd won in a lawsuit, and he spent his time either reading about the war or reenacting battles up and down the East Coast. Thad's claim to fame was being the Union infantryman who gets his legs blown off by a mortar shell. He had a whole system he'd designed, complete with an exploding pair of legs, which made it look quite authentic.

"Yeah, man. In September I did Antietam, and the end of this month we head down to Chattanooga."

"Keeps you busy, huh?"

Thad turned both palms up. "It's a life. Know what I mean?"

"Sure do." Sam pulled the manila folder from under his arm and opened it. "Hey, you got a minute to look at something?"

"Man, I got all the time in the world. I ain't doin' nothin'."

Sam handed over the papers, the ones with his writing on them.

"Wait a sec," Thad said. He snatched a pair of oval, wire-rimmed glasses from the desk. "OK, let's see whatcha got here."

Sam stood, arms crossed, and watched his friend's eyes rove over the paper.

Midway through the first page Thad peered over the top of his glasses. "You gonna stand there and stare at me the whole time?"

"I was planning on it, yeah," Sam said, smiling.

Thad motioned to a folding chair along the wall. "You can have a seat, you know."

Sam sat, and Thad went back to reading.

It took him no more than five minutes to get through all four entries. When he finished, he handed the papers back. "Cool stuff. You wrote it?"

Sam nodded. "Yeah."

"Thought you didn't dig the war?"

"I don't. Never been into it."

Thad set his glasses back on the desk. "Man, you're losing me." He pointed at the papers in Sam's hand. "That was written by someone who understands the war, who digs what it was like to be on either side, behind a wall of gunfire."

"That's why I wanted you to read it," Sam said.

He wasn't sure if he should dump the truth on Thad or not. He'd only known him a short time. They had met while Sam was doing some work for Thad's parents, and for reasons beyond either of them, they'd immediately connected. After Sam's accident, Thad visited him in the rehab center several times, and a bond of sorts, maybe the mutual respect of the disabled, formed. Sam had come here to unload, to get an honest opinion. No backing off now.

He shook the papers. "I don't understand a bit of this. Over the past few days I've written this stuff in my sleep."

"Man, you're like, givin' me the creepies here. What're you talking about?"

"I don't remember. I either fall asleep or black out, and when I come to, this stuff is sitting in front of me."

Thad raised both hands and leaned back in his chair. "Whoa, now you're scaring me."

"Scaring myself. I don't know who this Samuel Whiting is, I know nothing about the First Minnesota, and I have no idea what spiking a cannon is. None of it makes any sense to me." He omitted the parts about the voice of his deceased brother visiting him in the still of the night and the increasing despair taking up residence in his mind. Thad didn't need to know everything.

"That's some freaky stuff, man." Thad crossed his arms. "Well, for starters, they'd spike a cannon and leave it behind when they retreated, most of the time because a wheel was busted or something like that. They'd drive a nail or anything else they could find into the vent hole to put the cannon out of commission. That way the enemy couldn't turn it on them and light up their butts with their own gun."

"How would I even know that?" Sam said. "I've never heard that term in my life. How could I write about it?"

"In your sleep, no less."

"Exactly."

"Weird, man. Just weird. You sure you didn't read about this guy somewhere or watch a movie? You ever see the *Gettysburg* flick? Something that would sit in your subconscious and maybe, with all that's happened in your head, manifest itself this way?"

"No. I've never seen the movie, never read the book, never watched any sort of documentary. Nothing."

"And you call yourself an American? And live in Gettysburg, no less?"

"That's low, man. Low."

Thad smiled and smoothed his mustache. "What about high school? You had to learn something about the battle then."

Sam tilted his head. "Really? High school? That was twenty years ago. I remember there was a battle that took place in Gettysburg, and that's it."

"Dude, something's going on here. You shootin' straight with me?"

Sam looked at the writings. Save the familiarity of his own handwriting, they were still so foreign to him. Like seeing his hands attached to someone else's arms. "Yeah, I'm shooting straight. What else can you tell me? What about this First Minnesota?"

Thad smiled wide, and excitement sparked in his eyes. "Oh man, now you're talkin'. The First Minnesota were some bad dudes. They were crazy warriors. OK, here's the situation. You know where Cemetery Ridge is, right?"

"Of course. I do live in Gettysburg."

"Hey, I don't know what you know and what you don't know. Look, on the second day of fighting, the rebels advanced against the ridge. See, if they could knock the Union troops off that ridge, they could swing in around their rear and shut 'em down, take the town, and wham-o, battle over. Now there was one section along the ridge where the Union troops were thin, and that's where the rebs concentrated their force. Sickles, a Union general, called in reinforcements, but it'd be a good five minutes before they could get there. They needed five minutes. So Hancock ordered the First Minnesota to advance on the rebs. Now, you talk about being outnumbered. This was two hundred sixty-two Minnesotans against almost eleven thousand rebs. It was suicide, and everyone knew it, but it had to be done or the battle would be lost. No doubt about it. So they did it, and you know what? Mission accomplished. They held 'em for ten full minutes." Thad paused and thinned his lips. "But at a cost. Of the two hundred sixty-two men that charged the rebs, you know how many survived to fight again?"

"Not a clue," Sam said. He'd never heard this story before.

"Forty-seven. That's an eighty-three percent casualty rate, highest in the history of American warfare. But their action saved the battle. Those were some bad dudes."

"Thanks for the history lesson. It's all very interesting, but I still don't know what it has to do with me. Why am I writing about it? How do I even know about it?"

Thad snorted. "Man, I'm not a shrink, just a history buff. If you came looking for a sofa and free advice, you picked the wrong joint, but if you're looking to find out what that"—he pointed at the papers in Sam's hand—"means, I can do that. As for the whys and hows, beats me. You must be drinkin' some freaky juice."

Freaky juice was right. Sam's realization that he had written about actual Civil War events made the journal entries all the more sinister, all the more cryptic. "Can you at least tell me who Samuel Whiting was?"

"Nope. Never heard of him. I doubt he was with the PA battery, though."

"Why?"

"Because Atwell was the lieutenant of the battery during Gettysburg. Now, it's possible Whiting was with another battery, got separated, and joined up with the PA Independent. That wasn't unheard of. I'll do some investigating and see if I can dig up anything."

Sam shook his friend's hand. "Thanks, Thad. For your time and the history lesson. Really."

Thad pointed again. "You mind if I make a quick copy of those?"

"Not at all." Sam gave him the writings.

Thad scanned them into his computer before returning them. "I hope you find what it is you're lookin' for, man. I'm here for you, you know that, right?"

"Sure. Thanks."

And then Sam left the trailer, but not to go home.

Thirty-Two

It was near lunchtime when Sam pulled his truck onto Hancock Avenue and rolled down the windows. This late in November there weren't many tourists around, so the road was all but abandoned. A navy Suburban with Virginia plates was parked up ahead. On either side of the road sat granite and concrete monuments and lines of restored cannons. This was Cemetery Ridge, where the fighting had taken place, where the 1st Minnesota had committed their suicide charge to save the battle and probably the war. They were crazy warriors.

Stopping the truck in front of a large monument with the word "Minnesota" on it, Sam cut the engine and breathed in the fresh air. On top of the marker a statue depicted a running Union soldier, an infantryman from the 1st Minnesota, rifle held at his waist, bayonet in place. Down the road a few hundred yards stood the huge, four-columned memorial for the Pennsylvania troops. A kid on the steps, a teenager, appeared to be looking Sam's way. Probably at the Minnesotan in full stride.

Sam got out of the truck and gazed up at the monument. It stood fifteen, twenty feet high, and towered over the area. He wondered what it must have been like to make that charge. The adrenaline-laced fear, the anger, the rage, even the pride those men no doubt felt. They had to have known they were making their last charge, their last stand. That was it for them. They would never kiss their wives again, never hold their children. What made a man willingly do such a thing? Bravery? Fear? Insanity? Dumb obedience? His thoughts turned to Samuel Whiting, the mystery man. In the latest journal entry, Whiting was fed up with the war and blamed the whole thing on Lincoln. Why not point a finger at the most powerful man in the country, the man responsible for the conflict, the man who had ripped the nation apart and pitted brother against brother?

Sam stopped himself there. He was thinking like a crazy man, thinking like this Samuel Whiting was a real person and these writings were really his journal entries. They weren't. They were a hiccup in Sam's brain, a misfire between neurons. Nothing more. He must have read something in the past about the war. Thad was right; he'd certainly learned about it in high school. His less-than-healthy brain was concocting scenarios and playing games with his memories. Digging deep, finding information long buried and forgotten.

He probably should see a shrink.

Another thought entered his mind: what if the country broke out in war now? A modern-day civil war over one of the hot-button issues. Sam was no political junkie, but he read the newspaper and watched the evening news. He knew what was hot and controversial. And he knew this Stephen Lincoln was the latest lightning rod to hit the political scene.

Some said he was a front-runner for the next presidential election. Some hated him. The papers reported that he'd cosponsored a bill to amend the Constitution, outlawing abortions once and for all. Those on the left cried foul and warned that if he got away with this and won the presidency he wouldn't stop there. They said the country would be divided, ripped right down the middle.

How many lives would have been saved if someone had assassinated Lincoln before the war rather than after?

Sam had no idea where that thought came from.

He pushed it from his mind. It was nonsense anyway.

He walked around the monument and noticed the kid on the steps of the Pennsylvania memorial still looking in his direction. The teen was tall and lanky, with a head of shaggy brown hair. His round-shouldered posture reminded him of…

Sam's breath caught in his throat, and he coughed once. It

couldn't be. It was impossible, ridiculous. Then again, much of what had happened in the past two days was impossible, and yet it had happened. He took three steps toward the memorial and stopped. The kid raised a hand to shoulder height and waved it back and forth. And that's when Sam noticed the black, shimmery, anti-glow surrounding him.

Goose bumps ran up and down Sam's arm and tightened the flesh on the back of his neck. A sick feeling cramped his stomach. The scar, the blasted scar, began aching again. He ran his fingers along its length.

He knew that wave, that dark halo.

It was Tommy. No doubt about it. His brother. His *dead* brother.

Sam shoved both his hands into his pockets lest he be tempted to wave back. There was no one else around. The Suburban was gone. He was alone. He looked back and saw Tommy still standing on the steps. He looked about seventeen, the age he was the last time Sam saw him. The time he…

You did what you had to do, son.

In the distance, in town, a car horn squawked. But here, in the midst of these stone memorials, in the midst of death, the silence resonated. Sam and the Tommy-image stared at each other like two gunfighters in the Old West.

"Why are you back?" Sam said, not nearly loud enough for a person at Tommy's distance to hear. That did it. He was certifiably insane, talking to a hallucination, a trick his brain was playing on his optic nerves.

Regardless, he said it again, louder this time. "Why are you back?"

"You're the one, Sammy." It was Tommy's voice, close, as if he were standing just feet away instead of a hundred yards or more, and having a casual conversation.

You're the one, Sammy.

Those words rushed back from the past like a winter wind, buckling Sam's knees. He went down, head buried in his hands. The grass was cool and the ground hard. He shut his eyes and plugged his ears. He wanted no part of this, no part of his past, no part of Tommy, no part of Samuel Whiting. But, unbidden, the memory came back. He was in his bedroom in the old farmhouse and…

Mom and Dad started yelling downstairs. They were at it again, and once again it was about Tommy. Something had happened at school. Something bad.

Mom had that tight voice that meant she was crying. She always cried when they argued about Tommy. "We can put him in a special school," she said.

"A special school ain't gonna help him." Dad's voice was loud and deep. "He could go to jail this time."

"They can't put him in jail."

"Then one of those juvie schools, where the bad apples go."

Mom let out a wail. She was notorious for drama. "But it wasn't his fault. He was provoked."

"Gloria, a kid's in the hospital because of what your son—"

*"*Our *son, James. Don't you excuse yourself of this responsibility."*

"Fine. Because of what our *son did to him. Fighting is one thing, and defending yourself is another. But there's a point when you stop beatin' on the kid, and Tommy didn't stop."*

Sam stood next to the door in his bedroom. There was no need to put his head against the wood; their voices were plenty loud enough to carry up the stairs.

"Will he be OK? The other boy?" Mom asked. She sounded scared.

A moment of silence followed. A chair scraped across the wooden floor, probably Dad pulling one out from the dining room table to sit down. "I don't know." His voice was lower now and more somber. "Tommy beat him good. Busted up his face and broke his skull. Broke a few ribs, and one went into the lung. He really did it this time."

Mom said something, but her voice was too low to make out. Sam got down on his hands and knees and pressed his ear to the gap between the floor and the bottom of the door. He caught Mom's final words.

"Sometimes I'm scared of him."

Part of Sam was revolted by that—no mother should be scared of her own son—and part of him was relieved that he wasn't the only one.

He rolled to his back and stared up at the ceiling. A crack in the plaster, like a jagged fault line, ran the entire length of the room.

Soft footsteps in the hallway caused him to turn his head toward the door again. They stopped right outside his room. Tommy's Reeboks were visible under the door, and Sam's heart stuttered. A gentle knock came at the door. Sam didn't say anything, didn't move. The knock came again. Then a whisper.

"Sammy."

Sam still didn't answer. He looked up at the doorknob, and yes, it was locked. Maybe Tommy would just go away.

"Sammy. Open up. I need your help with something."

Tommy's voice sounded...normal, like the old Tommy. But slightly panicked.

"Sammy, c'mon, bro. Open up. Please. You gotta help me."

Although later Sam would question his decision, he got up and unlocked the door. The knob turned from the outside, and the door creaked open. Tommy stood there with his rifle, the military one with the shoulder sling. He had a look in his eyes that was scared, maybe even desperate, but not dangerous. In fact, it was the most lucid Sam had seen him in weeks.

Tommy surrendered the rifle to Sam. "Here. You take this. I need you to do something." He turned to leave. "Come with me."

Down the hall they went, into their parents' bedroom. The window over the front porch was open, and Tommy climbed through it. From the porch roof, he stuck his head back in, and said, "C'mon bro. Can't let Mom and Dad know we're doing this. I need you to do something for me."

Legs first, Sam climbed out the window and onto the rooftop. From there he and his brother shimmied down the latticework along the porch, Sam with the rifle slung over his shoulder.

When they were both on the ground, Tommy said, "Follow me to the north field."

They walked in silence, Tommy slightly ahead. It took a good fifteen minutes to reach the other side of the north field, beyond the tree line that blocked the view of the house.

"What's this about, Tommy?" Sam asked. He had the gun, yet he felt very anxious, like he did right before giving a speech in English class.

"I need you to shoot me," Tommy said.

Sam forced a laugh. "Yeah, right. C'mon, really."

But Tommy wasn't joking. His eyes were clear and sharp. This was the real Tommy speaking. "Really, Sammy. No joke. Something's happening to me. I'm changing and . . . " He looked Sam right in the eyes, and Sam detected the fear there. "I'm scaring myself. What I did to Eddie, I couldn't stop myself. I wanted to, but I couldn't. Once I saw the blood, I had to keep kicking." He turned and faced the other direction. "There's a darkness in me, bro, and it's growing."

Sam's anxiety was gone. Now he was just scared. "I don't understand. Mom and Dad can get you help."

Tommy spun around. His hair was in his eyes now. "There is no help for me. Don't you get it? This darkness is taking over me, changing me. You gotta kill me. You're the one, Sammy."

Those words. They still rang in Sam's ears. Tommy had told Sam to move back a hundred yards so that he wouldn't have to see his eyes, then to drop him from there, but Sam refused, threw the rifle, and ran home. A few days later—and every day since—he wished he had taken the shot when he had the opportunity.

"Mister." A hand rested on Sam's back. "Mister, are you OK?"

He looked up and found an elderly lady bending over him. A man, most likely her husband, stood a few feet back, hands in his jacket pockets, eyes narrowed.

"Are you all right? Do you need help?" the woman asked.

Sam straightened up. "No. No, thank you. I'm fine."

"Are you sure?" she said. "You don't look fine."

The woman's husband eyed Sam as if he were a criminal.

"Yeah. My, uh, great-grandfather fought for the...for the Minnesota, and I was just...you know."

She patted his shoulder. "I know. It's OK. They were all heroes, weren't they?"

Sam nodded and got to his feet. "They were. Thanks." He nodded again at the woman and her husband, then headed to his truck.

At the driver's door he shot one last look at the Pennsylvania memorial and found it empty. He slid in behind the wheel, fired up the engine. Something on the passenger seat caught his eye, and he went numb.

Carefully placed blades of cut grass spelled two words: KILL LINCOLN.

Thirty-Three

THAD LEWIS WHEELED HIS CHAIR TO THE BOOKSHELF AND retrieved a massive volume of Civil War information. He'd done a cursory Internet search for Samuel Whiting and came up with nothing. No problem, though. Computers were great and the Internet was an amazing tool, but there was something to be said for doing the research the traditional way. In spite of all technology could do, he still loved the weight of a real book in his hands, the smell of old paper and ink, the feel of the pages as he flipped through them. Call him old-fashioned, call him a throwback. Thad Lewis was both—and proud of it.

Back at the desk he opened the book to the index and slid his finger down the page.

"C'mon, c'mon. Where are you?"

Yes, there he was. *Whiting, Jefferson Samuel. Pages 798–799.* Ah, that's why Thad couldn't find him on the Internet. Whiting's first name was Jefferson.

He turned back to the entry on Captain Jefferson Samuel Whiting and skimmed the text. Nothing out of the ordinary. He'd started the war with Battery G of the 4th US Artillery, and sometime during the Gettysburg campaign found himself with the PA Independent. Thad read on.

"Wait a minute. Wait a country minute. What's this?"

At the end of the entry, a single paragraph stated that in November of 1863, one day before Lincoln's address from Gettysburg, Whiting was arrested for conspiring to assassinate the president. Six months later he was tried and found guilty of treason. Two months after that he was hanged as a traitor.

"Oh, Sam, what are you up to, man?"

Sam Travis's claim that he knew nothing of the pages he himself wrote just didn't sit right. He'd come across as sincere, but that was some weird prose to be spitting out in your sleep.

Thad leaned back in his chair and rubbed his eyes. He then read over the scanned copies of Sam's writings again. Sam obviously knew something of Whiting and his conspiratorial ideas. People just didn't pull this stuff out of their heads and have no clue how it got there in the first place. But…

"Whoa, whoa, whoa. What's this?"

The journal entries. He spread all four of them across the desk. Yes, why hadn't he noticed that the first time through? He grabbed a pen and started writing as his finger traced the words of each entry.

"Sam, my man, what have you gone and gotten yourself tangled in?"

Thad dialed his friend's phone number.

Down the hall the trailer's front door opened and closed. No knock had preceded the intrusion.

Thad shut off the phone. "Yeah? Who's there?"

Thirty-Four

SYMON HAD NO PROBLEM FINDING THE TRAILER. AS ALWAYS, THE voice had given him excellent directions and more than enough information. When he arrived, he knew exactly where the cripple would be. It was almost too easy. The trailer was secluded, the door unlocked. Inside, though, Symon met something he hadn't expected. A memory…

He lay on a sofa in a living room, in a trailer just like this one. Same worn furniture, same clutter, same nicotine-stained walls. The lights were dim, the place hazy with greenish smoke. Canned laughter from the television mixed with the annoying fake laugh of the woman seated across the room from him on another sofa. It was one of those nervous laughs that miserable people force to convince others, and maybe themselves, that they really are enjoying life.

The door opened, and a slab of smoky daylight fell across the room. A man entered and kissed the woman. Really kissed her. She giggled, and Symon's fists clenched. The man sat next to her on the sofa, said something to Symon. He was large, with a long gray ponytail and a goatee. He had beady eyes above an enormous, hooked nose. The facial hair was probably meant to hide some of that beak.

The man said something again to Symon. His words were long forgotten, but not the anger they ignited. Symon swore at the man and made some kind of threat.

The man with the hooked nose reached behind his back, fishing for something. He produced a pistol and pointed it at Symon. It shook a little in his hand.

The woman put her hand on the man's arm. "Alan, don't."

Yes, that's right. Alan. Alan Kosovich.

Alan's eyes darkened, and his mouth hung open. Symon could see his tongue in there, moving side to side the way a slug squirms when you put salt on it.

Symon moved toward the trailer door. Before leaving, he turned and cursed at Alan and the woman... Vicki, yes. Alan jumped to his feet, Vicki hanging on his arm. The pistol was still pointed at Symon and still shaking in Alan's hand.

Alan pulled the trigger. Symon saw only the first two flashes.

Here now, in this trailer, Symon paused to collect himself. The memory had produced no response other than anger. He felt his chest and the three tender spots capped with thick scar tissue.

"Hey," the cripple called from down the hall. "What's your business, man?"

Symon felt the pistol in his jacket pocket as he headed that direction. The light from the bedroom filtered onto the hall carpet and illuminated the filth on it.

The cripple, Thad, was in his chair, facing the doorway. The sight of the legless man turned Symon's stomach, revolted him.

"Hey, what's up? What's the—"

"Sorry to bother you." Symon clasped his hands in front of his chest and bowed a little. He tried to avert his eyes from the two stumps. "I'm doing a survey and wondered if I could ask you a few questions."

Thad looked confused. His eyes darted between Symon and the hallway, seeming to doubt that someone would find their way down a dirt lane and into a run-down mobile home to do a survey. What survey could be that important?

"Uh, well—"

"Please, it'll only take a moment of your time. I promise."

Thad hesitated, glanced at his watch. "All right, man, but just a moment. I'm kinda in the middle of something, know what I mean?"

Symon smiled. "Sure I do. It'll only take a moment." He paused for effect, then said, "Do I look at all familiar to you?"

"Is this a joke?" Thad laughed.

It angered Symon. That laugh reminded him of Alan's. Despite the cool November temperature, beads of sweat formed on Symon's forehead. "No joke." His voice broke a little. "Do I look familiar to you?"

"Should you?"

Symon didn't answer.

Thad shifted in his chair, moved his eyes to the hallway again. "Man, I ain't never seen you before. What's your name?"

"Alan," Symon said. Truth was, he still had no idea what his real name was. "Alan Jackson."

"Like the country singer? 'Cause he's the only Alan Jackson I ever heard of. Sorry, man."

Symon closed the short distance between them and placed his hands on the armrests of Thad's wheelchair. He didn't like this cripple one bit, and being this close brought the taste of bile to his mouth. Regardless, he leaned forward till their faces were no more than twelve inches apart. "Look closer, *man*, and see if you find a resemblance to anyone you know from your past."

Pushing back, Thad said, "Whoa, you're kinda in my personal space here. I said I never seen you before. You got that familiar-face thing going on, but I don't know you. Never have."

Symon jerked upright and put his hand in his jacket pocket. "You sure about that?"

"Man, I'm sure. This is your survey? Do you look familiar? I'm gonna have to ask you to leave."

In one smooth and casual motion, like he'd done it a hundred times, a thousand maybe, though he remembered only two, Symon pulled the pistol from his pocket and pointed it at Thad, the cripple.

Thad's eyes widened to the size of walnuts, and his hands went up reflexively. "You gotta be kidding me."

Symon pulled the trigger three times. The cripple wrenched upright then slumped over in his wheelchair. In seemingly slow motion, his body doubled over at the waist and tumbled onto the floor. Symon let it lie there and left the trailer. He felt no remorse, no guilt, no sorrow. He felt nothing.

Thirty-Five

SAM HAD ONE PLACE LEFT TO GO: THE OLD FARMHOUSE UP IN Cumberland County. But first he had to talk to his mother.

Since that final incident with Tommy, Sam's parents had abandoned the farmhouse, leaving it to the forces of nature and whims of time. Mom believed it was possessed, but she didn't want to vacate the premises completely. Instead, they moved into a rancher on the farm's edge, near Route 187, a quarter mile over a rise from their previous dwelling. Mom was convinced that if she could see the farmhouse it would worm its way into her head and control her, like it had Tommy. Irrational, maybe, but nobody wanted to argue with her. Nor could they.

Sam turned off the road onto a short asphalt driveway that led to the rancher's garage. He parked his truck and got out. Not much had changed in the past twenty-one years. Mom had leased their property to other local farmers for growing corn and soy. The Murphys still lived across the road a hundred yards down or so, with the same Buick in their driveway that had been there when Sam left home. Nothing but farmland and rolling hills stretched in the other direction.

Sam rounded the garage to the back of the house. Mom was already outside, hanging laundry.

"Samuel? What are you doing here?" She looked past his shoulder. "Where's Molly and Eva?"

"Hey, Mom. Boy, it's good to see you too. Eva's in school, and Molly's home."

"You drove yourself here? Is everything OK?" In the two months or so since Sam had seen his mother, she had aged a lot.

She looked much older than her sixty-three years. Especially when she wore that light green housecoat.

"Yeah, everything's fine. The doctor gave me the OK to drive again."

She hugged him and gave him a dry peck on the cheek. "You sure you're up to driving? I don't want you doing anything you're not ready to do. It's no rush, you know. You could—"

"Mom, I'm fine. Man, you sound like Molly now." Sam regretted not seeing his mother more, but the memories that surfaced when he did were ones he tried not to visit more than a few times a year.

She took his hand. "Well, come inside. I'll get you a drink. Are you thirsty?"

"Parched as a sun-burnt cow patty."

She laughed. "Your grandfather used to say that all the time."

"I remember." And he did. Being back here, even if only on the edge of the farm, brought back a rush of childhood memories. Some welcome, some very unwelcome.

Inside, the house smelled like tomato sauce and garlic.

"I'm making a batch of spaghetti for dinner," Mom said. "Can you stay?"

As much as Sam was tempted, he knew he shouldn't. He needed to get over to the farmhouse. "No. How's Dad?"

Mom poured him a glass of instant iced tea. "The usual. Good days and bad days. Lately, more of the bad it seems." She glanced toward the bedroom where Sam's father spent most of his time. "Sometimes it seems as though…I don't know. We're managing."

"Seems as though what?"

She shook her head. "Nothing. He's just going through another tough spell, is all. They come and go."

Sam drank down half the glass of tea. He used to have this tea every day. Dad would buy a huge tub of it, and Mom would keep it coming all summer long.

"Is it OK to go back and see him?"

Mom looked up, shocked he would feel the need to make such a request. "Of course it is. Might do him some good to see you."

When Sam entered the bedroom, his father didn't even lift his gaze. Dad was propped on the edge of a single bed. His plaid pajama bottoms and Penn State sweatshirt were wrinkled and covered with lint balls. His wispy white hair was plastered to one side of his head. His hands were on his knees, a blank expression on his face, mouth slightly ajar, a thin line of saliva gathered at the corner.

Sam sat next to him on the bed. "Hey, Dad, how are you?"

Dad turned his head. There was a disinterested look in his eyes, the gloss of complacency and confusion. "Are you the 'lectric man?"

"No, Dad. It's Sam."

Recognition dawned. "Oh, Sammy. My son. How's the farm?"

Twenty-one years ago Dad had suffered brain injuries of his own and never recovered. His was a slow, steady decline into a faraway land of make-believe and mental trickery. A place Sam was afraid he too was headed.

"Everything's fine," Sam said. "How have you been?"

Dad shrugged. "Can't complain. Was in Chicago last week. My plane was late, though. The mechanic came up to me, and he says, 'Buddy'—he always calls me Buddy—'you got a bad time of it. Hope you're not in a hurry.' I told him I needed to get to Idaho for a convention, and he laughed. I don't think he knew the plane was mine."

"Sounds like you had a quite a time," Sam said. "Hey, I'm gonna go out and talk to Mom, OK?"

Dad leaned in close and lowered his voice. His breath smelled like rotting meat. "Don't mention the Buick. She gets real upset when you talk about the Buick."

"I'll keep that in mind." Sam started for the door, but Dad stopped him.

"Sammy, how's Tommy? He still playing the trombone?"

Tommy had played the trombone for the school orchestra in fourth and fifth grade. But two years were all he could endure, and against Mom and Dad's wishes, he quit and turned in his instrument.

"No, he's not."

Dad looked disappointed. "Oh, he was good, y'know. Used to play marches for me. Make sure you take his dinner down to him."

His dinner down to him. Boy, that stirred memories Sam would rather forget. But they were never really forgotten, were they? "Sure, Dad. No problem."

Sam returned to the kitchen. Mom was busy at the sink peeling onions.

"Mom, you ever think of Tommy?"

The question caused her to jerk, as though slapped by an unseen hand. "'Course I do. Every day. What kind of fool question is that?"

Sam hesitated. He rotated the glass in his hands. "You ever think you hear his voice or even see him?"

She grabbed a dishrag from the sink and began wiping the countertop. "'Course not. Thomas is gone. You know that."

The way she said "You know that" hit Sam in the chest. She still hadn't moved on; she still blamed him. But it wasn't his fault.

You did what you had to do, son.

"How about dreams? You ever dream about him?"

Mom stopped and looked at Sam. Her lips were tight and eyes narrow. He knew that look, had seen it a thousand times growing up. "Samuel, if it's all the same to you, I'd rather not talk about this anymore. It serves no purpose at all. Now, why did you come here? It wasn't just to visit your mother and say hi to your father."

"I need the key to the old house."

Two decades ago a wall had been erected between him and his mother, and it had never been torn down. He'd lived with her and his father in the rancher until he was nineteen, then left to get a place of his own. During those four years he lived at home after Tommy's death, he and Mom rarely spoke and mostly stayed out of each other's way. Mom got a job as a telephone operator for a direct-marketing company, and he landscaped part-time until going full-time with a construction crew after his graduation from high school.

She looked at him as if he'd just asked her to exhume Grandpa. "Absolutely not. You're not going anywhere near that place."

But Sam knew where the key was. She kept it in the drawer next to the silverware, the junk drawer.

"I need to, Mom. I need to see the place again."

"Why, Samuel? Why would you want to go back there?"

"Why not? It was my house too." He paused and collected himself. He was surprised by the emotions—anger, frustration, confusion, fear—scratching their way to the surface. "I need to settle a few things. Work a few things out in my head."

Mom dropped her gaze to the counter, and her hands trembled. "Please, Samuel. You're all I have left. Please don't. That place..." She raised her eyes to meet his. There were tears in them. "It's evil. I know it. It caused our family so much pain. I can't take no more of it."

"Mom, what happened to—"

"Hush!" She pointed a finger directly at Sam's face. "Don't you mention it. That house...that cursed house got to him. It wasn't his fault."

"I know it wasn't his fault," Sam said. And he did know it. What'd happened to Tommy was nobody's fault. It just happened.

"Your father loved him to the end, you know. And I did too."

"I did too."

Mom scrunched her face up as if she'd just sucked on a lemon, and Sam knew she didn't believe him. She would never believe him.

"Mom, I need the key, and I'm taking it." He walked around the counter to the drawer.

"It's not in there anymore," she said. "I moved it."

"Why? Where?"

After releasing a labored sigh, Mom said, "'Bout a year ago, I guess it was. I got itching to go down the lane and see the house again. It'd been a good five or so years since I last laid eyes on it. I just wanted to see how bad the weather had been to it." She glanced out the window in the farmhouse's direction. "You know how I used to keep the place up."

"It was always immaculate. The gardens, the painting, the windows."

"It was my pride. I was shocked to see how worn and old it looked. Kinda like me, I guess." She looked up with fear in her gray eyes. "I coulda sworn it was calling to me, Samuel. Like it was alive and wanted me. I don't know if it was my imagination or if it really was calling to me, but I felt like a fish on the end of a line with a big old hook in my mouth. And I know, I just know, that if I'd a-gone to that place, it would have eaten me up and spit me out, and I wouldn't be sitting here today."

A heavy feeling settled in Sam's stomach. "Mom, it was probably your imagination." But was it? Was Tommy's voice only his imagination? Was seeing Tommy at the memorial his imagination? Were the grass letters on the seat of his truck his imagination? *Kill Lincoln.* "Your mind was playing tricks on you. I mean, after what happened there." He stopped. He didn't want to go any further, and he knew she didn't want him to either. "Where's the key, Mom?"

She wrung her hands and let out a mournful whimper. "I buried it in the backyard. Out by the maple."

"Is it marked? The spot?"

She shook her head. "No, but it's right in front of the trunk. There's a root sticking up from the ground, and I dug a hole between it and the trunk. You'll see. There's a trowel in the garage, on the wall with the garden tools."

He knew the spot. He rested his hand over his mother's. It was cold, so thin and frail. "Thanks, Mom. And don't worry, OK?"

She looked away. "'Don't worry,' he tells me."

"I won't be long," Sam said. "Just want to take a look around."

Thirty-Six

THE KEY WAS RIGHT WHERE HIS MOTHER SAID IT WOULD BE, buried about four inches down in a metal key box.

The house was nothing like Sam remembered. Mom was right; she and Dad had always kept the place immaculate. The paint was never chipping, the flower beds never infested with weeds. The picket fence around the front yard was whitewashed every spring, and the windows always sparkled.

What stood before Sam, though, as he crested the rise in the lane, was a beaten and weary old home, one that had suffered years of neglect and simply given up the fight. The paint was chipped and curled and worn off in some areas, revealing the gray clapboard siding. The porch roof sagged in the middle, which made the house appear to be smiling, but not with a smile of joy. Covered with two decades of grime and residue, the windows were lifeless, hollow eyes. And waist-high weeds and witchgrass filled the flower beds.

The sight of the farmhouse, so tired and weathered, put a knot in Sam's throat. Memories of summers filled with painting and clipping and mowing and digging rushed through his mind like a fast-moving train. All that work, and for what?

He approached the house and pushed through the gate. It opened smoothly and latched again on its own. The sidewalk, though overgrown with grass, was still in good shape. The porch was not. Sam skipped the three steps and sidestepped a few sagging boards on his way to the front door. The key still fit perfectly and turned without a hitch. The dead bolt clicked, and the doorknob twisted easily.

When the door opened, Sam wished he had brought along a

flashlight. The interior was darkened, but enough muted light filtered through the windows to illuminate the rooms. The place reminded him of a sarcophagus—empty, musty, lifeless. To his left was the living room. One three-legged sofa table leaned on its side, but other than that the room was bare. The rest of the first floor was no different. Dust and cobwebs were the only occupants.

Sam moved through the living room and came out into the hallway again. The staircase rose in front of him. It was still solid and sturdy, but the boards were creakier than he remembered. At the top of the stairs was Sam's old room. Tommy had stood there with the rifle, the one he had wanted Sam to shoot him with. The door was closed.

As Sam reached for the knob, metal clanged down in the cellar. He knew that sound. He'd spent many nights fighting sleeplessness, listening to that sound.

■■■

Somewhere on Sam's way down the staircase, the clanging stopped. He stood at the cellar door feeling short of breath and weak. He didn't want to go down there; he knew what he would find. And yet he felt he had no choice. He drew open the door and flipped the switch at the top of stairs, but of course the power had been turned off years ago. There was enough light, though, coming through the windows below to keep the cellar from being totally dark.

One step at a time Sam descended into the underworld of the house. Halfway down his head cleared the ceiling, and he saw the crate. It looked the same as it had the day Dad built it, with the exception of the broken boards on one side.

Unwilling to go closer, Sam sat on the step. That crate, that horrible crate. He thought of his brother, so long ago. Tommy's condition had worsened until he was unfit to be around the family. His outbursts became more frequent, his violent tendencies more belligerent. He was no longer Tommy Travis; he was a creature that only resembled Tommy. His eyes seemed to grow darker and sink further into his skull. His lips thinned, and his cheekbones became more prominent. He dropped pounds by the day, which may have explained the changes—or it may have been something else.

Afraid of what others would say should Tommy be placed in an asylum, Dad built the basement crate. It was large, twelve-by-twelve, with a cot in one corner and a toilet basin in the other. The little door in the front could be slid up and down to push plates of food through. It was Sam's job to feed his brother. But Tommy wanted none of any of it. He sat in the corner, smeared with his own feces, and hurled insults and curses the three times a day that Sam delivered the meals.

It was a Thursday when it happened. The plate was still in the crate after all these years. Sam remembered sitting on these same steps with...

...a metal plate of Mom's fried chicken and stewed carrots on his lap. He was always afraid to go down past the seventh step. It was the halfway point, the point of no return should something happen. Dad had built the crate out of thick, knotty oak, but Tommy's strength seemed to increase with his hatred. And if he ever got out of there—

"Hey, sissy boy," Tommy said from inside the crate. "You gonna come down here or not? Maybe I can eat you."

Sam stayed put, trying to muster his courage. He was fifteen, too young to deal with this kind of fear. He hated his parents for making him endure his brother's insanity.

"Yeah, I'm talkin' to you, sissy boy. You too scared to come any closer? You too scared? What a sissy you are, a pathetic little sissy. A momma's boy. Why don't you come over here and bend over and let me spank your sissy butt? Momma's 'little precious.'"

This was how it always went, and Sam told himself each time to just do it quickly. Descend stairs, cross room, open door, slide in the plate, get out of there. Easy enough. But each time he stopped, afraid to go closer, and endured the insults and taunting.

And Tommy was relentless. "I bet you never even kissed a girl, sissy. You're too much like one. It'd be like girl-on-girl with you.

Why don't you come over here so I can give you a kiss, a big sloppy one right on the lips, show you how it's done."

Enough. Sam gathered his courage, descended the rest of the stairs, and crossed the cellar.

"Oh, oh, look, he's comin'," Tommy said. "The sissy grew a backbone."

Dad had built the crate with the two-by-four slats six inches apart, enough for an arm to fit through, and every time Sam brought the plate, Tommy reached through and tried to snag Sam's arm or hand. Sam had to be quick or get caught, and if he ever got caught, well…

He threw open the little door and slid in the plate, just as Tommy's hand shot out. "Come here, ya little sissy, you girl. I'll rip your arm off and eat it in front of you."

Sam kicked the door closed and fled upstairs, chased by his brother's curses. He didn't stop on the first floor. He ran all the way to his bedroom. Even from there he could hear Tommy hollering and carrying on and banging the metal cup against the plate.

The clanging.

Eventually the clanging stopped, and the thudding began. Sam knew immediately that Tommy was throwing himself against the two-by-fours, trying to bust loose. That possibility puckered the skin on Sam's arms. He turned the key in his door to lock it. Not that it would stop a raging Tommy-thing, but it offered some comfort for the time being.

After fifteen minutes of the thudding, Sam heard splintering wood and an animal-like bellow that resonated up through the floorboards.

Tommy was loose…

Now, on the seventh step, Sam clenched fistfuls of hair and let the tears come. But this was not a healing cry, far from it. Instead, the memory opened a gate to the darkness in the cellar, and Sam felt it pressing in, begging for entrance, for control. It was the same darkness that had enshrouded Tommy and Samuel Whiting before him. And now it wanted Sam Travis.

For what purpose?

Kill Lincoln.

The voice came as if someone were sitting on the step next to him.

Kill Lincoln.

It was Tommy's voice. His brother. The one they'd caged and treated like an animal. The one who had become an animal.

Sam looked across the cellar and shivered. Tommy was there in the far corner behind the furnace. He stepped from the shadows and approached the steps, but the darkness seemed to cling to and surround him with that anti-glow. Sam wanted to get up and bolt. He wanted no part of this apparition, yet something held him there, whether fear or curiosity or guilt, he couldn't tell. Midway between the furnace and the staircase Tommy stopped. His face was still obscured, but there was no mistaking the shape of his body, outlined by that lightless haze.

"Kill Lincoln." It was Tommy's voice, but different, deeper, more guttural.

Sam said nothing. His fingers dug into the wooden step, his heart thrummed like a motor in his chest, and sweat popped out on his forehead.

Tommy sniffed. "Look at you, crying like a sissy. Once a sissy, always a sissy."

"I'm not." Sam found his voice, wiped the tears from his cheek. "I'm not a sissy."

"Once a sissy... always a sissy."

"Why are you back?" Sam felt crazy talking to this hallucination, but he needed to know.

"I've been gone a long time, little brother. Little *traitor*."

"I had to do it. You know that. You wanted me to."

Tommy growled, then mocked Sam. "'You wanted me to.'"

"Why are you back?"

"Kill Lincoln, little brother. Grow a backbone."

"I don't know what you mean."

Tommy took a step backward. "'Course you don't. Sissy. But you will. Give it some time." After three more steps backward, he stopped and said, "Once a sissy, always a sissy."

The figure retreated quickly now, moving behind the furnace.

Sam's blood went hot. "You shut up, you hear," he hollered. "You shut up."

Back into the darkness Tommy went, vanishing from sight.

With tears streaming again from his eyes, Sam stood and climbed the steps two at a time. He had to get out of here. Had to get out of this house.

Thirty-Seven

SAM STEERED THE TRUCK INTO THE DRIVEWAY AND HAD AN eerie feeling of déjà vu. Hadn't he just done this yesterday? The arriving home, with Molly not knowing where he'd been. The questions, the arguing. He was in no mood for that again. His visit to the old house had left him shaken and irritable.

For a second, the briefest of moments, he considered telling Molly everything. Spilling his guts to her. Recounting the auditory hallucinations, the visions, the memories, the writings, the grass KILL LINCOLN on the seat, the cage in the basement, his weird confrontation with Tommy, everything. But he decided against it.

There would only be more questions. She'd want him to see a shrink. The shrink would probably want to dump him in some asylum where he'd be labeled a kook and signed up for group therapy and forced to share a room with a guy who thought he was Frank Sinatra. No way. He could handle this on his own. He knew the difference between reality and fantasy, and he'd just ignore the fantasy part.

Sam gathered his manila folder and exited the truck.

Molly was standing on the front porch, arms crossed over her chest, head cocked to one side. "Nice of you to finally come home," she said. Her tone was anything but friendly and welcoming.

He blew right by her and into the house.

She followed him. "Mind telling me where you've been all day?"

"Out and about," he said over his shoulder, as he headed for the kitchen.

"Out and about. Good answer. Very forthcoming. Thanks for including me so much in your plans."

Sam dropped his keys on the counter. The kitchen smelled clean, like lemons. She'd been doing housework. He didn't look at her when he said, "I went to Thad's to do a little research for my writing. Then I went to the battlefield to check out some of the monuments and just...to just think. I visited my parents too."

Molly was quiet for several seconds. When she spoke, her voice had lost its edge. "Sam, why are you pushing me away?"

He turned to face her. There were tears in her eyes. Great. The tears. He hated the tears. "Pushing you away? I'm not pushing you away. Why is it that I can't go out and do things without feeling like I'm going to be interrogated when I come home? Do I ask you a million questions after you go shopping or running errands? I just wanted to get out of the house and do some things. Why is that such a crime all of a sudden?"

"It's not a crime," she said. The tears flowed freely, and she hid her face with her hand. "I feel like I don't know you anymore. First, this new interest in writing, then the whole gun thing, now you're running around and not telling me where you're going or where you've been. Visiting your parents? When's the last time you visited your parents on impulse?"

"I just told you where I was. Thad's, the battlefield, my parents, in that order. And so what if I'm writing again? I would think you'd be happy about that. How 'bout a little 'Hey, babe, I'm really glad to see you're writing again'?"

Molly wiped away the tears, but more came. "I am happy for you. I think it's great. I just wish you'd include me more."

It was no use. Arguing with Molly was like arguing with a rock. "Fine. From now on I'll give you my itinerary every morning so you know exactly where I'll be each minute of the day. Will that make you happy?" He knew he'd crossed the line.

She walked past him, bumping him with her shoulder. "You're a jerk."

A flash of anger seized him, and he grabbed her arm. "Don't talk to me that way."

She pulled away and stared poison at him. Tears made long

tracks down her cheeks. Her lips tightened and turned white, trembling. “Don’t ever touch me like that again.”

Sam turned to punch the cupboard, focusing his rage there rather than on Molly, but was stopped by a knock on the front door. He and Molly exchanged looks. Her eyes were puffy and rimmed in red, her cheeks wet.

“Don’t answer it,” he said.

The knock came again, harder this time.

A few seconds passed, then from outside: “Mr. and Mrs. Travis, it’s Officer Coleman, state police.”

Molly looked at Sam. “Get the door,” she said, wiping at her eyes. She went to the sink and wetted a paper towel.

“I’m not getting it,” Sam said. “He’ll go away.”

“Sam, it’s the police. He probably heard us arguing. He knows we’re home. Get it.”

Reluctantly Sam opened the door to the cop from the other morning. He didn’t try to hide his irritation over the unexpected visit. “Officer Coleman.”

Coleman looked past Sam into the house. “Is this an OK time to ask you a few more questions about the gunshot, Mr. Travis?”

“Uh, sure, I guess.” He leaned against the doorjamb, blocking the way into the house. “Did you find anything else out?”

“Well, unfortunately, no, but—”

“Hello, Officer Coleman.” Molly came up behind her husband.

Sam looked at her and held his breath. Her eyes, while not as red as before, were puffier than usual. It was obvious she’d been crying.

“You OK, Mrs. Travis?” Coleman said, glancing between Molly and Sam.

Sam thought he saw something condemning in the cop’s eyes, and that voice was there again in his head, telling him to get rid of the cop, nothing good would come of this little drop-in.

Molly waved off the cop’s concern. “I’m fine. Really. I was, uh, cutting onions.”

Oh, that's great, Sam thought. He'll buy that one for sure.

Coleman hesitated, eyeing both of them. "I, uh, I just wanted to run down the sequence of events from the other morning again, if that's OK with you. Make sure I have everything right."

"Sure," Molly said. "What do you need to know?"

Coleman pulled out a steno pad and pointed a pen at Sam. "Mr. Travis, you woke up at what time?"

"'Bout four thirty, five, somewhere in there. I had to use the bathroom, then couldn't get back to sleep."

"So you came downstairs."

"And lay on the sofa. Fell back asleep."

Coleman made some notes. "And, Mrs. Travis, did you know he was missing from bed?"

Molly shook her head. "I heard him get up but fell right back to sleep. Since his accident Sam has had trouble sleeping. He often gets out of bed during the night. I'm a light sleeper. I guess it's a mommy thing."

"What accident was that?"

"Six months ago," Sam said. "I fell off a roof and landed on my head."

"He had six contusions on his brain and a blood clot they had to do surgery to remove," Molly said. "He was in a coma for four weeks."

Coleman looked at Sam. "And how are you now?"

He shrugged. "Fine. I'm not back at work yet, but I'm getting there."

More writing from Coleman. "OK, so you fell asleep on the sofa, and then what time did you wake up again?"

"Six fifteen or so, I guess. I don't know. Just before sunrise."

Through the window Sam saw a Ford Mustang race by and blare its horn.

Coleman seemed unfazed. "And what happened then?" he said.

"I opened the front door for some fresh air," Sam said. "Nice morning too. Heard the gunshot, then the window shattered."

Turning to Molly, Coleman said, "And what did you hear?"

"The glass woke me up. Eva too. At first I thought a bird had flown into the window. When I got downstairs, Sam said it was a gunshot."

"Sam said it was a gunshot."

Sam didn't like the tone of Coleman's voice.

From the upstairs bathroom Eva called for Molly.

"I better see what she needs," Molly said. "Excuse me." She shut the door behind her as she went back into the house.

Thirty-Eight

Molly found Eva on the toilet. "What's wrong, baby?"

"Mommy, who's that downstairs?"

"It's the police officer that was here the other morning, after the window broke."

Eva looked away and rested her elbows on her thighs.

"What is it?" Molly said. Eva obviously had something on her mind, and she normally wasn't one to hold back.

"It's just like Jacob said."

Jacob again. Molly's shoulders tensed. "What did he say?" She never wanted to discourage her daughter's imagination, but this Jacob stuff was getting tiresome. And just weird.

"He said a policeman would come to talk to you and Daddy. He said it would upset you, and I'm supposed to make sure I tell you that I love you and that Jesus loves you too." She paused and interlaced her fingers. "Does Daddy know Jesus loves him?"

Before the accident Sam had never been outspoken about his beliefs; his was a quiet faith, but Molly was sure it was real. The evidence was there. Lately, though, she was beginning to wonder. He was becoming more and more volatile, more and more like her father. "Of course he does, honey." The words sounded hollow, lifeless, but she hoped her daughter hadn't picked up on it.

"Mommy?"

"Yes?"

"Do you know Jesus loves you?"

Molly wrapped her arms around Eva's shoulders and hugged her tight. It was all she could do to fight back the tears. She didn't want to cry in front of Eva. "Yes, baby, I do. I know He loves me very much."

"And do you know I love you?"

It was pointless. The tears came, not in any kind of barrage like they had in times past, but in a steady stream, like a morning springtime rain. "Yes." Her voice was strained and tight. "And I love you too. Very, very much."

Releasing Eva, she wiped her tears, kissed her daughter on the forehead, and said, "Now you finish up here and go play in your room, OK? Daddy and I need to finish talking to the policeman, and then I'll start dinner. Maybe you can help me, all right?"

Eva reached up and dashed a stray tear on Molly's cheek. "OK, Mommy. But I need to tell Daddy too. Jacob said."

"I know, baby. You can when the policeman leaves."

She left the bathroom and shut the door behind her. Downstairs Coleman said something she didn't catch.

Sam said, "I can only tell you what I know."

Molly detected his agitation.

"It's just, if the gunshot and window breaking were almost simultaneous," Coleman said, "the shot had to be close, which meant it would be loud, louder than glass breaking, and yet your wife and daughter both say they never heard it."

Sam didn't say anything. Molly had wondered about that too.

Coleman continued. "And then there's the fact that we found no entry point in the house. What do you think happened to the bullet after it entered?"

"How should I know?" Sam said. "It's gotta be there somewhere. You probably just didn't find it."

"Possibly." There were a few seconds of silence. Molly could hear the toilet paper rolling in the bathroom. "Just seems odd to me. Something doesn't fit. You're sure it was a gunshot you heard."

"Yes, yes, and yes again. I grew up on a farm shooting guns. I know what they sound like."

"Well," Coleman said, "thank you, Mr. Travis, and please thank Mrs. Travis too. Sorry for all the questions, but I need to make sure we have the story right. If there's someone out there shooting at homes or poaching, the more information we have—the more *accurate* information we have—the better."

"Right." Sam sounded annoyed but relieved the conversation was over. "Have a good day, sir."

Molly heard the door open and click closed. Eva came out of the bathroom, struggling with the button on her pants. "Honey," Molly said, bending over to offer some help, "I have to ask you a question. The other morning when the window broke, did you hear a gun shoot?"

Eva shook her head. Her ponytails flipped side to side. "I already told you. No. But I heard the window break. It scared me."

"You're sure you didn't hear a gun?"

"I'm sure, Mommy. I heard the window break, and it woke me up. I was having a good dream too."

"OK, baby. Thanks. Go play for a little bit. I just need to talk to Daddy about something."

Eva kissed her on the cheek. "OK. I'm playing ponies."

"Good. You have fun."

Molly went downstairs and found Sam seated on the sofa, elbows on knees, head in his hands. She sat in a plaid wingback chair and crossed her legs. "You know, I've been asking myself that same question. Why didn't I hear the gunshot? Why didn't Eva? It had to have been loud."

Sam didn't say anything, didn't even look at her.

"Did you lie to the cop?"

Sam's head shot up. "What? Why would you even ask that?"

She saw his defenses rising. It was the same look she'd seen in her father's eyes so many times, and it made her uneasy. "Did you?"

"Absolutely not. I know what I heard."

Molly searched her husband's eyes. She could usually tell right away when he was lying, but she found nothing to indicate he was this time.

"What do you think happened?" he said.

"I don't know, Sam. But I do know the two other people in this house never heard a shot, and there was no entry point. No bullet. I've looked; believe me, I've combed that living room. Nothing. And with the way you've been acting lately, I'm beginning to wonder."

"Wonder what?"

She didn't say anything. He knew what she was implying.

He stood. "This is ridiculous," he said and stormed up the stairs.

Thirty-Nine

At the top of the steps Sam saw the hurt in Eva's eyes but brushed past her.

"Daddy—"

"Not now, Eva." Though he heard himself say the words, it didn't sound like him. Not to his own ears, anyway.

She followed him to his study. "But Daddy—"

He turned at the doorway. "Eva, not now, OK?"

Her gaze found the floor, and her shoulders slumped. "I—"

Sam closed the door and paced the room like the grizzly bear they'd seen last year at the zoo. Last year. Life was easier then—simpler, happier. He was whole and content. Now...now he felt shrouded in darkness, lost in a cave, hearing Molly and Eva calling to him, beckoning him home, but unable to find a way out. The harder he tried, the more lost he seemed to get.

Eva's voice reached him again. "Daddy, I love you."

Sam did not answer. He leaned against the wall, combed both hands through his hair and tugged on it. If Tommy didn't claw his way back from the grave and kill Sam, doing this to his family surely would. But Sam had to do it. He had to shield them from this path he was on. He knew where it led, and it was no place for his wife and daughter. No place for his Eva.

"I love you." She said it again. Louder. "I love you, Daddy."

Still Sam said nothing. He pressed his eyes closed, grinding his molars.

"I love you." She was practically shouting now, and Sam could tell she was crying too. Then she began to sing, her voice soft and broken. "Jesus loves you, this I know..."

She was right on the other side of the door.

"...for the Bible tells me so..."

Sam turned and placed his hand on the wood. He was mere inches away from Eva. Her singing, while innocent, pierced him like so many arrows.

Footsteps climbed the stairs. Molly was coming. "C'mon, baby. Let's leave Daddy alone and go downstairs."

"Daddy."

Molly again. "Eva, c'mon. Help me make dinner."

"No, Mommy. He has to know. I have to tell him. You said I could."

"He can hear you, baby girl. Daddy knows you love him."

Sam went to the window and gripped the molding with both hands. He contemplated throwing himself out and falling to the ground below, but doubted it would kill him. He couldn't do this anymore. For his family's sake he had to put a stop to it.

"He does know," Molly said. "I promise you. He knows."

The rifle in the closet. That would do it.

"Daddy. Please." Eva sounded panicked now. Frantic. "Jesus loves you. Do you know that?"

"Eva Grace." Molly put on her stern voice. "Come downstairs with me right now."

Sam pictured Molly picking her up and Eva burying her face in her mommy's shoulder. There was only one set of footsteps now. They approached the door and stopped. Paused. He tensed, waiting for Molly's rebuke, but it never came. The footsteps padded down to the first floor. He was alone again.

He walked to the closet, opened the door, and retrieved the rifle.

■■■

The wood stock felt cool and smooth in his hands. Sam sat at his desk, snapped a clip into place, did the bolt action, and chambered a round. Letting the rifle rest between his legs, barrel pointing up, he sat back and tented his hands. This was something he felt he needed to do. Sure, it had briefly entered his mind from time to time, but it had always been washed away by the waters of hope.

This time there was no hope, only despair.

Was this how Tommy felt when he appeared at Sam's door, rifle in his outstretched hand?

You're the one, Sammy.

Was this how Samuel Whiting felt when he admitted to being overcome with darkness?

Sam lifted the rifle now, weighing it in his hands. Downstairs a pot clanged and the range tick-tick-ticked until the flame ignited—the sounds of his wife and daughter living life without him. He could end it all right now. But instead his mind returned to that old farmhouse and the basement and the sounds of Tommy…

…tearing up the place. Nails moaned and creaked as they were pried from wood. Two-by-fours chunked off the walls and concrete floor. On the first floor Dad shouted something about blocking the basement door, but it was too late. Footsteps pounded up the wooden stairs, then Tommy crashed through the door. He howled and screamed and cursed like a demon-possessed man. His words were mostly unintelligible. Dad ordered Mom out of the house. Glass broke. A plate or a drinking glass.

Tommy wailed like a woman in labor. "TEEJ YEEW TO LUG MA WUP LOKIN DUG!" He was speaking nonsense.

"Get outta here!" Dad yelled at him. "Before I hafta kill ya."

More glass shattered, and something heavy hit the floor. Dad grunted. Mom screamed. Tommy spit barely intelligible vulgarities like bullets. Then a cacophony of sounds: splintering wood, breaking glass, hollers, screams, curses.

Dad: "I'll get…watch it."

Tommy: "AW KEEL YA!"

Mom: "James…no."

Dad grunted again, a sound of pain not effort.

Mom cursed, which meant things were serious. Mom never,

ever cursed. "Oh, aw, look at his eyes, James." Her voice was almost a shriek. "Look at his…"

Sam never knew what she saw in his brother's eyes and never mustered the nerve to ask. Partly he didn't want to know. Whatever it was, it was a warning of what was yet to come. And a warning, Sam thought, of what was to come for him too.

He was still holding the rifle. He thought about doing it. It would be quick and painless. Behind his ribs his heart pistoned. His palms got sweaty, chest tightened. The longer he dragged it out, the harder it would get. He needed to do it. He needed to get it over…

Without further contemplation Sam leaned back in the chair, shoved the end of the barrel into his mouth, and pulled the trigger.

Forty

He jerked and sat up straight in the chair. Sweat dotted his forehead and cheeks, matted his hair to his head. His hands quivered like the last leaves of autumn buffeted by a stiff November wind. The rifle was between his legs, stock on the floor, barrel pointed skyward.

What had just happened? He'd gone through with it, hadn't he? He'd pulled the trigger; he knew he had. The feel of the barrel knocking against the roof of his mouth was still there. As was the taste of gun metal and oil. And the feel of the trigger against the pad of his finger.

But the barrel wasn't even warm.

Had he fallen asleep and dreamed the whole thing? Had he suffered a dissociative fugue like that guy who dismembered his Jack Russell?

Molly's voice, soft and even, carried up from the kitchen through the flooring. If he'd fired the gun, she would have come running. It had to have been a fugue of some sort. He'd probably put the gun in his mouth, then imagined pulling the trigger.

But it didn't make sense. He'd had the argument with Molly. He'd come up the stairs and encountered Eva—*Daddy, Jesus loves you. Do you know that?* And finally he'd thought about Tommy, that awful memory, and decided to end it. If instead he'd had a fugue, when?

As Sam lifted the rifle to check the safety, he spotted the paper on top of his desk. His handwriting was all over it. He tried to swallow, but his mouth was too dry. With a trembling hand, he took hold of the page and read:

July 3, 1863

Still hot. Mercifully some much-needed water and some hard tack and salted pork. Not much of a breakfast, but it tasted delicious.

This morning I awoke to a lot of activity to our front. The enemy was pulling out field pieces. There must have been thousands of men and approximately two hundred pieces. Then it started, the duel. For hours we hammered at each other. Most of their rounds went over our heads but destroyed a lot of our ammunition. So orders came to slow fire and save. "Canisters only."

Silence. Then out they came, hundreds of battle flags. What a magnificent and fearsome sight. Bugles sounded. Drummers beat the march. On they came. Thousands, a mile long.

"Fire!" I shouted, and a hundred and fifty of us opened on them. At first we could see no holes in their ranks. On they came to the first line of fencing. We had marked the range. Now we saw the holes. Large ones. Time to load canisters. Our guns were hot! They had to cool.

500 yards now.

Our infantry opened up at 400 yards, and rows of them dropped at once. But on they came, then with a yell. They came at us on the run.

FIRE!

200 yards.

Smoke. Choking from it. Could not see. Surely they would not reach us. Gaps were filled within seconds.

Boom. Boom. Boom!

Smoke, screams, yells, foul language of every type.

Then the smoke lifted for a split second.

50 yards.

Their lines were much thinned, but on they came. This is not possible, I thought. We saw a general with his hat on his sword leading his men over a wall.

One last shot at 15 yards. PulLed it and BOOM! Our guns belched forth double canisters and cracked the barrel. But they were all gone. The general with the hat was down, and masses of men fought, hand-to-hand, using muskets as clubs, knives, bayonets. HORRIBLE!

Twisted screams of men in death's grip!

As they were withdrawing, a cry of "Hurrah!" went up and "Fredericksburg!" as this was their Fredericksburg.

The sight now was most grievous. The fields in front and back and all arouNd us were like maggots squirming. The ground was moving with the wounded.

The cost was brutal.

U.S. 1,000 to 3,000

C.S.A. 5,000 to 7,000

My poor battery.

One general left, nine killed, sixteen wounded, two missing.

Over three days, sixty out of seventy-two. Only twelve left.

Michael Hentz (Mike). Six years my friend. I will miss you. Every drill, every battle, he was there. Always strong. He did his work without equal. I will make sure he receives the honor due him. Good-bye, Mike.

But we gave more death than we received. How did I suffer only scratches, not life-threatening at all?

My men, my beautiful men! How I miss them. Brave lads, all. I wish it were me. To save just one I would give my own life willingly. Oh, how I curse this war and the warmonger who started it. Surely he must die. I am drowned in despair. My destiny is unfolding before me.

Time to rest. Tired. Very tired.

Night. July 3rd,

Woke to screams of every kind. The smell is becoming sickening. Starting to rain now. The enemy guns are very quiet. We can hear sounds of infantry on the move and artillery rolling slowly in the rain. They are moving away. Our fine army is exhausted from three days of battle. We must regroup, especially in our minds, for there is a lot of work to be done.

And for me, there is more than that. The darkness beckons my soul, bids me come near and drink of its foul water. I am so tired of resisting. I have fought a good fight, but it has finally overcome me. I fear I no longer have a choice. This is my destiny, my call. Whether it is the right thing to do or not, I am unsure. But it is what I must do. I am compelled. Drawn. Driven.

Sam opened the top drawer of the desk and grabbed the manila folder, the one containing the other writings. He sifted through it, finding the first page he'd written, which was actually the last one penned by Samuel Whiting:

My feet have been positioned, my couRse has been set, and I am compelled to follow. Darkness, he is my commander now.

Sam's eyes dropped a few lines.

It desires death, his death (the president), and I am beginning to understand why. He must die. He deserves nothing more than death.

Sam's pulse thumped through his carotids.

He was going to kill Lincoln. Whiting was going to assassinate Lincoln.

Kill Lincoln.

He read this entry again. The letters—the messages within the messages—were clear.

Sam gathered the papers, shoved them back into the folder, and returned it to the drawer. The morning newspaper caught his eye. A front-page article said Senator Stephen Lincoln was to address the nation from the rostrum in Gettysburg National Cemetery on November 19, the same date that Abraham Lincoln gave his famous address.

Sam knew what he would do, what he was compelled to do, driven to do.

You're the one, Sammy.

He was the one.

Forty-One

Stephen Lincoln waited at his desk, hands folded on his lap, one foot propped on the bottom drawer. Seated across from him, John Lipsik, his chief of staff, was reading over the speech Lincoln would give in two days. The revised version. John's expression was like poured concrete. He had always held his own at the poker table.

"What do you think?"

John moved his gaze to the portrait of the other Lincoln on the wall, back to the speech, then to his boss. "You sure you want to hear this?"

Lincoln knew his right-hand man would discourage such a bold, right-wing speech. Lincoln's recent conversion and shift in political views had already cost him half his Democratic base. This speech could cost him the other half.

"Of course," Lincoln said. "I wouldn't ask your opinion if I didn't."

John studied the paper again. He leaned forward and placed it on the desk. "Well, it's a risk."

"I know it is. I need more than that from you, John."

John sighed. "Look, Steve. I've always been honest with you, right?"

"I assume you have. It's one of the things I admire most about you."

Lincoln had hired John Lipsik five years ago as his campaign manager during his race for mayor of Harrisburg. John was fifteen years his elder, but the two got along famously and John's loyalty was unrivaled. When Lincoln ran for senator, he would have no one else manage his campaign, and when he won the seat, John was his only choice for chief of staff.

"Steve, the public just doesn't know what to make of you anymore. Yes, your party change and your new spin on things are popular with the Right, but I fear much of it is nothing more than media hype. You know how they are."

Lincoln did know. But it gave him a much-needed platform for getting his message out. "Of course," he said.

"You've lost a lot of support on our…on the Democratic side. Longtime supporters. Financial supporters. Heavy-hitters. They're just not sure what to make of you. A lot of them think you've gone over the edge. They think you've betrayed them."

Lincoln perused the words of the speech. Some were the writer's, but many were his own, written from his heart. "John, it's been a busy couple months, and you and I haven't had time to really talk about this yet. About my conversion and my faith. For me it's not about politics anymore, not about taking sides—our side, their side—or party affiliation, not about betraying people. I never meant to betray anyone. That's not what I'm about. But I have to govern by my convictions now, not by what's hot or what's going to get me the votes come primary time. It's that simple. I have to do the right thing. I didn't ask for this presidential-bid thing; you know that better than anyone. Back in Harrisburg, did I ever mention that I'd like to be president someday?"

John shook his head. "No, never."

"When I became a senator, did I ever mention anything about shooting for the White House?"

"No."

"This whole thing has just happened, and I see it as the leading of God. I know you're not fully onboard with a lot of the changes that have taken place lately, and I appreciate that. I also know your loyalty is beyond compare, and I appreciate that even more. But this is the course that has been set before me, and regardless of what the polls say, for better or worse, I have to do what I know is right. I have to do what honors God."

John didn't say anything for several seconds. Then he looked at the speech on the desk. "You know there've been threats."

"Of course. There're always threats."

"Not like these. At least not for you. This is a first."

Lincoln thought of his wife and daughter. He wasn't so much afraid for himself; fear would cause him to govern defensively, and he wasn't about to do that. But Emily and Becka…if anything happened to them… "Security is on it?"

"Absolutely. Most of the threats are nut-jobs mouthing off, but there are a few we're taking seriously. I normally wouldn't tell you this, but—"

"No. It's OK. I need to know."

"Just be careful, Steve. While you're making a lot of new fans and winning over new supporters, you're also making plenty of enemies."

"I'm sure. Regardless, I need you to understand that I must follow where God leads. My faith demands that of me. And I believe, I truly believe, God has pointed me down this road, and I have to walk it true and straight."

John stood and smoothed his shirt over his belly. "Well, it'll be interesting to see what comes of all this."

"Do I still have your loyalty?"

Lincoln didn't miss the brief delay before John's reply. "Of course. I'm with you all the way to the White House." Then John turned and left the office.

Forty-Two

Officer Ned Coleman eased his cruiser down Pumping Station Road for the third time in as many days. This time he wasn't going to number 456, the Travis home, and he wasn't responding to shots fired at a residence. He was headed to 512, home of the Moellers. A concerned neighbor had reported a "suspicious car" parked in the driveway, one he'd never seen before, and an "odd character" coming and going. What made the car so suspicious or its driver so odd was part of the mystery Ned hoped to unravel.

When he arrived, a Buick LeSabre was parked in the driveway beside an early-model Dodge Intrepid with a Wisconsin plate. The Intrepid's hood was faded and peeling in places, the windshield cracked down the center. He ran the plates of both cars. The LeSabre was the Moellers', but the Intrepid was unregistered.

Ned spoke into his radio. "Gettys Nine."

Nancy was the police communication officer on duty. "Gettys Nine, bye."

"On scene. I'm going to check things out."

"Ten-four."

Exiting his car, he noted that the nearest neighbor's house was at least two hundred yards away on the other side of the street. The guy who called this in must have been observing the Moellers through binoculars.

Ned rang the doorbell. No answer. He rang it again, heard it chiming inside the house. Still no answer, so he radioed in to Nancy.

"Gettys Nine."

"Gettys Nine, bye."

"I'm not getting an answer. Can you try calling the residence?"

"Ten-four."

While he waited, he walked the perimeter of the house. Nothing seemed unusual or out of place. No broken windows. The flower beds were undisturbed.

Nancy came on over the radio. "Gettys Nine, copy."

"Gettys Nine, bye."

"I tried the listed number but received no answer."

"OK." Ned tried the front doorknob. "The door is open. I'm going in."

"Ten-four."

He entered a living room. Nothing looked out of place, but the house smelled liked rotten food, like the Moellers had gone on vacation and forgotten to take out the garbage beforehand. Maybe the odd character with the suspicious car was a house sitter, a relative from Wisconsin who'd forgotten to take out the trash. But his hunch was that this was not the absentmindedness of an out-of-state visitor.

"Mr. Moeller?" His own voice sounded hollow in the quiet house.

Making his way through the living room, Ned noticed a dark stain about the size of a dinner plate on the hall carpet. He peeked into the kitchen. By the stove another dark stain had been smeared a good three feet across the floor. There was no doubt now. He needed to call for backup.

Ned was reaching for his radio and unsnapping his holster when something hit him hard in the back of his shoulder and spun him around. Searing pain radiated from the point of impact. The room spun, and before he could focus on his assailant, he was hit again, this time along the left side of the face.

The lights went out.

Forty-Three

THE COP WAS OUT COLD ON THE FLOOR. HIS SHOULDER WAS bleeding from the gunshot, but not too badly. His badge said *Coleman*. Symon stood over him, admiring the state trooper uniform.

After offing the cripple, Symon had returned to the Moeller residence. This was his base camp of sorts, and he hadn't received orders to move on yet. He hadn't expected a cop to show up. But he was not opposed to surprises.

"Well, Officer Coleman, guess you didn't see that coming, did you?"

After removing the sidearm, pepper spray, Taser, baton, and flashlight from Coleman's utility belt and tossing them onto the sofa, Symon dragged the limp body into the kitchen. The cop was heavier than he looked. Symon hoisted him into a chair and propped him against the table, his head lulled to one side, chin resting on his chest.

Symon took a seat across the table and rested his pistol in front of him. He wondered if he'd ever had any run-ins with cops. He wondered if Coleman here would know who he was, maybe recognize his mug from a wanted poster or something. He had no memory of anything like that, but of course that meant nothing.

"Officer, wake up, sleepyhead."

Coleman's radio made Symon jump. "Gettys Nine."

He vaulted from the chair, tipping it over backward, and ran to Coleman.

"Gettys Nine." It was a woman's voice.

He grabbed the radio from the unconscious man's shirt.

Depressing the talk button, he imitated Coleman's voice as best he could. "Gettys Nine. Everything OK here."

"Do you need assistance?"

"Uh, negative. Everything's OK."

There was a brief pause, and he knew he had about ten minutes to get out of the house.

The woman's voice came on. "Ten-four."

Symon released the radio and gave the trooper a good smack across the cheek.

Forty-Four

The first thing Ned Coleman felt as he came to was the vicelike pain in his right shoulder. The second thing was the throbbing in his head. He tried to move his shoulder, to lift his arm, but it was paralyzed. Even making a fist was a chore and sent pain running along his arm. He raised his head, which only increased the throbbing behind his eyes. He was in a kitchen, in a chair, propped against a table.

The Moellers... yes, he'd come here on a call, seen the blood on the floor, then... something had hit him.

"Wakey, wakey, sunshine."

The voice snapped Ned fully alert, and he focused on a man seated across from him. Lean build. Short, dark hair, and one of those soul patches under his lower lip. Beady eyes. Thin, straight lips. Thirty-something.

"Hello, sunshine," the man said. His voice was nasally.

"Whaddya doon?" Ned's jaw wasn't working right. That explained the throbbing in his head. This dude had busted his jaw and—Ned craned for a look—shot him in the shoulder, clean through. Just missed the Kevlar. He righted himself and reached with his left hand for his Taser, knowing he couldn't lift his other arm to find his weapon on that side.

"It's not there," the man said. His smile was wide and thin and flat. He looked at his watch, then lifted a pistol—a Beretta equipped with a silencer—and pointed it at Ned. "We don't have much time, so we'll have to make our chat time quick."

Ned knew if he didn't check in with Nancy soon, she'd be radioing him. She may have already tried. If so, backup would be on its way. He needed to stall only a few minutes. Every movement of his jaw sent percussive pain through his head, but he had to ignore it and keep this guy talking.

"Wha's you num?"

"You tell me." The man leaned in.

A little closer and Ned thought he might have a chance at lunging for the gun.

"Do I look familiar to you?" The man turned his head to the left, to the right. There were flecks of dry skin in his eyebrows.

Ned had never seen him before in his life. He was good with faces, so-so with names. With a mug like that, this guy would be hard to forget. He shook his head slowly and looked around. "No. Wher's da Moelluhs?"

"Look at me!" the man said, jabbing the gun at Ned. Red blotches covered his face and neck. He checked his watch again, seeming to realize backup was en route. "Have you seen my face before? On a poster, a bulletin board, the computer? Anywhere?"

Ned nodded. "Compootuh." It was what the guy wanted to hear.

The man's face brightened. Either he was a wannabe serial looking for recognition, or he was totally whacked in the head and talking nonsense. For now it didn't matter. Ned just needed to keep his mind off that watch.

"Where? When?" the man said.

"Last wik. Ef-bee-eye must wuhntid." That should keep him going. Every serial nut-job wanted to be on the FBI's Most Wanted List.

A smile stretched the man's lips, but he quickly recomposed himself. "What's my name?"

It was a test to see if Ned was lying. He said nothing.

"What's my name?" More emphatic this time.

Ned's attempt at a shrug was punished by a jolt of pain in his right shoulder. Best to just play it dumb. Backup had to be arriving any minute.

After another look at his watch, the man grunted and jabbed the pistol at Ned's chest. "Out of time, sunshine. Sorry you couldn't be more helpful." He pointed the barrel directly at Ned's face. "Nothing personal."

Ned heard only the first shot.

Forty-Five

Soft crying woke Molly Travis from a light sleep. She lay in the darkness of the bedroom, one foot in reality, one still in dreamland. In her dream Sam's mother had presented her with an attractive apple pie with flaky golden crust, but when Molly cut into it, she discovered it was filled not with slices of golden apple but with balls of plastic wrap. An argument followed, hollering, blaming, tears. It was not a pleasant dream, and she was thankful to escape it, only to awaken to the sounds of crying. The crying of her daughter.

Eva didn't sound panicked, at least.

Sam was next to Molly, on his side, still fast asleep. They hadn't spoken more than five words to each other all evening. In fact, she'd barely seen him except for the fifteen minutes he took to throw down his dinner, then it was back to the study for him. She'd gone to bed at eleven and felt him climb in beside her well after midnight.

She lifted her head and looked at the clock on his side of the bed: 3:07. She nudged her husband. "Sam, Eva's crying."

He grunted and nuzzled his pillow.

"Sam. You gonna get her?"

No answer. Not even a grunt this time.

"Fine. I'll get her." She pushed back the covers, slid her legs off the side of the bed, and sat, letting her head reorient itself. Bright moonlight filtered through the windows, casting the bedroom in a bluish lunar glow. They were calling for a storm front to move in during the early morning hours, and steady rain was forecast for the daytime.

Molly rubbed her face, tucked her hair behind her ears, and said again, "I'll get her," hoping Sam would awaken and offer to do it himself as he used to do. With the way he'd been acting, she wasn't surprised when he remained asleep, oblivious.

Down the hall Molly found Eva curled in her bed, pillow over her head muffling her crying. She sat next to her little girl and put a hand on her shoulder. "Hey, baby girl, it's OK. I'm here. Mommy's here."

Eva rolled onto her back and wiped at her eyes.

"What is it, baby? What's wrong?"

Eva hitched a breath and wiped at her eyes again with her sheet. "I had a scary dream."

Molly smoothed hair from Eva's face. "Sweetie, dreams aren't real. You know that, right? Just a bunch of memories and stuff your brain mixes all together and uses to make a movie. That's all."

"Can I tell you about it?"

"Of course you can."

Eva looked at Molly with tearstained eyes and wet cheeks. "It was about Daddy. We were at the store, and he was lost. We didn't know where he was. We called for him and looked for him, but we couldn't find him. I was scared. Then we did find him, but he didn't know who we were. I hugged him and told him he was my daddy, but he pushed me away. Jacob was there too. He was trying to help Daddy remember us. He was showing Daddy pictures of things we did together. Pictures of our vacation to the beach and our picnic in the park and hiking and riding bikes. But Daddy still didn't remember. Then he left. We all tried, but even Jacob couldn't stop him." She paused and sniffed. "That's when I woke up."

Molly swung her legs up in the bed and lay next to Eva. "Sweetheart, it was just a dream. That's all. Try not to think about it anymore. Let's think of funny things, OK?"

Eva nodded.

"All right, what's first? What makes you laugh?"

"Mr. Curtis at school does," Eva said. Mr. Curtis was her music teacher. "He sings silly songs with us and does silly dances. And he makes funny googly eyes at us. He's really weird."

"Googly eyes, huh? I don't think I've ever seen them. Show me."

Eva opened her eyes wide so that the whites showed all around her irises, then moved them in big circles, clockwise, counterclockwise.

Molly laughed. "Hey, look. I can do it too."

Eva watched and giggled, taking Molly's hand in hers. Her finger traced a vein on the back of her mother's hand. "What makes you laugh, Mommy?"

The question was innocent, of course it was, but it bit at Molly. When was the last time she had laughed, really laughed from the belly? She couldn't remember. "Well, you do, when you do one of your shows with your stuffed animals. I love them. They're very funny. And you just made me laugh with your googly eyes."

"Yeah." Eva turned on her side and looked at Molly. "Do you think Daddy is starting to forget us?"

It was no arbitrary question. Molly knew this was something Eva had been thinking about for a while now. Long enough that it'd found its way into her dreams.

"No, sweetie. Absolutely not. How could he ever forget us?"

Eva looked away then back at Molly. "Mommy?"

"Yes."

"There's something else too."

"What is it?"

"Jacob said Daddy needs us to pray for him."

Jacob again. "I know, baby; you said that before."

"No, it's different this time. He said Daddy needs us to really pray for him. He said..."

Eva's hesitation put a foreboding feeling in Molly's gut, and she waited, not wanting to encourage the whole Jacob thing.

Eva continued. "He said Daddy's going to do something really bad."

A chill poured over Molly's skin. She stroked her daughter's hair again. "It was just a dream, Eva."

"No, Mommy. This wasn't part of the dream. This was after I woke up."

Forty-Six

Sam slipped noiselessly out of bed before the alarm went off. Molly didn't stir. A plan was formulating in his mind, a plan that would work, that only he could pull off. He was the one.

You're the one, Sammy.

His sleep had been restless, disturbed more than once by voices feeding him details and timelines. Today he had to make arrangements, and tomorrow he would satisfy the darkness. That's what this was all about really—satisfying the darkness, appeasing it, giving it what it wanted. It was the only way to ease the burden and relieve the pressure. The darkness would have its way; he was sure of that. And he could resist it no longer.

Outside, rain pattered against the window like an old woman tapping her thin fingers. The sun had yet to rise, and a ghostly haze filled the room. Sam looked at the sleeping Molly and thought, for the briefest of moments, of taking his pillow and placing it over her face.

The suggestion did not arise from within himself—he loved Molly—but rather from the darkness. It wanted death, fed on it, celebrated it. And death it would have.

Kill Lincoln.

Sam crossed the room as silently as dusk moves across a lawn, opened his dresser drawer with only a slight scraping sound, and retrieved a pair of jeans and a sweatshirt. He changed his clothes in the bathroom and left his sweatpants on the floor in a heap. Without stopping to look in on Eva, something he'd done every morning since she was born, Sam tiptoed downstairs, avoiding the noisy steps, and donned his jacket. He needed to get out before

Molly and Eva awoke, before he did something he would forever regret, something horrible and vile.

Sam stepped through the back door into the cool, damp morning and felt a surge of energy. At least his wife and daughter were safely behind him. Now his task lay ahead. Was this how Samuel Whiting felt once he resolved to follow the course before him?

Ignoring the raindrops that plinked at his head and face, Sam walked across the backyard and through the field. He was headed for the woods a couple hundred yards behind the house. He would wait there.

It took him no more than five minutes to reach the first trees, and as he passed from field to woods, a sense of power came over him. He was calling the shots now. No longer would he be told what he could and could not do. No longer would he be treated like an invalid. He was in charge. Again, Samuel Whiting came to mind. He must have felt so helpless watching enemy lead slaughter his men. And later he must have felt so powerful knowing he would be the one standing over life and death.

Ten feet into the woods Sam found a fallen tree to sit on. Overhead most of the leaves had let go of their branches, leaving no canopy to block the falling rain. Never mind. From here he could see the house and driveway. He would know the second Molly left to take Eva to school.

Sitting in the woods, watching his home, Sam felt memories stir, but the one his mind fixated on was the sound of Mom…

…screaming like a poltergeist. Furniture scraped in the dining room and crashed on the first floor of the house, glass broke, Dad grunted and cursed, Tommy continued his garbled rant, and through it all, Mom screamed. In his room, crouched by the door, Sam kept thinking that Mom had to run out of air soon. And then what?

Dad's heavy footsteps stomped to the bottom of the stairs. He was wearing his work boots.

Sam threw open his bedroom door and dashed for the top of the stairs. He needed to see that Dad had things under control, that

Tommy would be subdued and returned to his cage in the basement. That the nightmare unfolding on the first floor would end and all would be back to normal.

Sam looked down the staircase and saw Dad standing there, one bloodied hand on the banister. Sweat matted his hair to his forehead in an odd, swirled pattern. His face was tight and shiny. He set himself, then launched out of view. Mom screamed again and said something like lookowjim *right before the sickening wet thud that sounded like a pumpkin dropped from the barn loft.*

Dad stumbled back into view, the left side of his head dented and moist with blood. Tommy appeared, holding a hammer in his right hand. Where had he gotten hold of a hammer? He raised it over his shoulder. Dad flinched and lifted an arm to protect himself, but Tommy was too quick and brought the hammer down on Dad's head again. Dad dropped to one knee, let out a pitiful moan. Mom's screams turned to whimpers.

That's when Tommy swiveled his gaze up the steps. What Sam saw in his eyes was anything but human. Hunger was there, and hatred and fire, but not one speck of remorse or one plea for help. For a second Sam thought Tommy would charge the stairs and come after him with the hammer, but instead Tommy turned and disappeared again.

Mom screeched.

Sam rushed into his room to grab the rifle from his closet, but he tripped and toppled to the floor, banging his knee hard. Downstairs Tommy wailed, "YEEW NECK," and something big crashed to the floor. It couldn't have been Mom; please, not Mom. Scrambling to his feet, Sam threw open the closet door and reached for his rifle, only it wasn't there. Oh, yes, it was under his bed. He'd hidden it there from Tommy. He dropped to the floor, forgetting the pain in his right knee, and snatched the rifle. It was already loaded. He always kept one round in the chamber, just in case. Out of his room and down the hall he went, to Mom and Dad's room, then out the…

…window. In the house, the bedroom light flicked on, illuminating the glass.

Forty-Seven

Senator Stephen Lincoln was pondering his speech before the day's events unfolded and the office suite became a hub of activity. He enjoyed this early stillness of the Capitol building. It gave him pause to think about the others who had occupied these halls, these rooms, before him. Some great men, some not so great. And what separated the two? The great ones knew their convictions and stuck to them, unwavering in the face of opposition. They showed resolve.

Lincoln didn't know if he'd ever be counted among the great men, but he would stand by his convictions regardless. He couldn't govern out of fear or even ambition. Fear crippled conviction; ambition blurred it. Whether he was ever considered great or not was in God's hands; he knew that much.

Outside his office, in the suite's foyer, a door opened and closed. Lincoln heard the whispers of two men, signaling that the suite was waking up, and seconds later John Lipsik and Tony Wu, head of the Capitol police, entered his office.

Lincoln looked up. "Good morning, guys."

John glanced at Tony then at Lincoln. "Mornin', Steve. We have a situation in Gettysburg."

"What kind of a situation?"

John nodded at Tony, who put his hands behind his back and spoke. "In the last three days, four people have been murdered, one of them a state trooper."

Lincoln's chest tightened, and he had to take a breath. He sat back in his chair.

Tony continued. "We don't think this has anything to do with you, but it is creating quite a strain on law enforcement, and we're concerned your visit will strain them even more. We'll have our own details in place, of course, but we still rely rather heavily on local law enforcement as well."

"Have you asked them how they feel about us continuing with the visit?"

Tony nodded. "I have. And they're confident they can deliver."

"Do they think the murders are connected to each other?"

Tony nodded. "They do. All four victims suffered three gunshots. The first two were homeowners doing their morning routines, the third was a single man shot in his trailer, and the last, the trooper, was responding to a call at one of the homes after a neighbor reported a suspicious car in the driveway."

Lincoln looked down and noticed his white-knuckled grip on the armrest. "So what's the connection?"

"They don't know yet. It appears there's one perp but no connection between the victims, no motive."

John cleared his throat. "Steve, we need to know if you want to go through with the visit or reschedule it."

"What do you think?"

John clasped his hands behind his back. "Well, under the circumstances I think it might be prudent to reschedule. Things are a little stressed in Gettysburg right now, and your visit would only add more strain. Not to mention the risks to your own safety."

Lincoln turned to the head of Capitol police. "And what do you think?"

"Sir, I can only work from the facts. My men are ready; there's no issue there. And if Gettysburg and state law enforcement say they can handle this visit, I have to take them at their word. With that, I defer to the judgment of you and Mr. Lipsik."

"Spoken like a politician, Tony. I think you're in the wrong line of work."

Tony smiled. "Not in a million years. I enjoy what I do, sir."

"I know you do." Lincoln paused, sat forward, and rested his elbows on his desk. "I want to go through with this. Let's stay on schedule, as planned."

"You sure, Steve?" John said. "I'm concerned about your safety."

"I'm not. We have the best on the job."

"Agreed." John nodded at Tony. "We proceed as scheduled."

As they left, Lincoln dialed the number for his wife. She needed to know about this too.

Forty-Eight

Molly was in the kitchen making breakfast, hash browns and bacon, when she heard the *clip-clop* of Eva's shoes on the stairs, then in the hallway. She turned and found her daughter in the doorway, sleepy-eyed and slump-shouldered.

"Good morning, darling. How did you do after going back to sleep last night?"

Eva shrugged and climbed up on a barstool.

"You look like you're still tired." Molly also saw a fleeting shadow of fear in her eyes.

"Where's Daddy?" Eva said.

Molly put two strips of bacon on a plate. "I don't know." She'd awakened to no sign of Sam, no message or trace of where he'd gone. His truck was still in the driveway; so was the Explorer. "Maybe he went out."

"Out where?"

She set the plate in front of Eva. "You need to eat your breakfast so we can get you to school."

"Is he coming back?"

"Of course he's coming back. He probably went for a jog or a walk." Sam had run a lot in the mornings before the accident, often up and out the door before dawn.

Eva tilted her head and screwed up her face. "It's raining, Mommy. He wouldn't run in the rain."

"I don't know," Molly said, trying to remain lighthearted. "Your dad's been known to do some pretty crazy things, and running in the rain just so happens to be one of them."

"He's not coming back, is he?" Eva speared some egg with her fork.

"Eva. Don't you even think that. Of course he's coming back."

"We need to find him, Mom." Suddenly there was desperation in her voice. Calling Molly "Mom" instead of "Mommy" meant Eva was as serious as she got.

"He'll come back on his own."

"Mom, we have to find him now." She dropped her fork, on the verge of panic.

"Why, Eva? Why do we have to find him right now?"

"'Cause Jacob said he's gonna do something bad. We can't let him."

Molly leaned on the counter opposite Eva and looked her straight in the eyes. "Baby, I'm going to tell you this one more time, and then I want you to drop it, you hear? Jacob isn't real. He's part of your imagination. I don't mind you having an imaginary friend, but you have to know the difference between real and make-believe. Daddy is just fine, and he's coming back home. I promise." Truth was, though, she had no idea where he was, if he was fine, or if he was coming home again.

Eva's eyes filled with tears and her chin quivered. "Jacob *is* real, Mommy. You don't know 'cause he doesn't show himself to you, but he is. He is. He said I have to pray for Daddy, and you should too."

"I do," Molly said, taking Eva's little hand in hers. "I pray for him all the time."

"Then why won't you believe me?" And with that she slipped off the stool and ran from the kitchen.

Molly gave her a few minutes to settle herself then went after her.

Forty-Nine

FROM HIS PERCH IN THE WOODS, HIS CLOTHES NEARLY soaked through, Sam Travis watched his wife and daughter leave the house in the Explorer. He waited until the vehicle disappeared over a rise before emerging from the woods and making his way back across the field and his yard. The back door was locked, the front door too. No worries, though. He found the spare key under the clay planter, just where Molly had hidden it months ago.

Inside, the house was quiet. He'd gotten used to being home alone, but for some reason this time it felt...foreign, like he was breaking into a stranger's house to see what valuables they may have concealed in their underwear drawers.

"Molly. Eva."

He had no idea why he said their names out loud. He'd just seen them drive off. Still, he made one sweep of the first floor just to make sure. Then it was up to the second floor. He checked the bedrooms, the bathroom, found no one hiding under any beds or in any closets. He was alone.

He stuffed a duffel bag with two pairs of pants, two long sleeve T-shirts, a sweatshirt, socks, underwear, and his old sneakers. He would only be gone one night. After zipping the bag, he went to the study and got his rifle. The ammo magazine was in the top drawer of his dresser. The scope was in there as well. He put the scope in the duffel bag, the magazine in his pocket, and balanced the rifle in his hands. It felt good, like holding the hand of an old sweetheart.

Sitting at his desk, he pulled the manila folder from the drawer and fingered through the writings. He removed the first entry, the one that had started this whole journey, and read it over again. The words had never seemed more like his own. After all, they were his, weren't they? Written with his own hand. He still hadn't a clue who Samuel Whiting was. For all he knew, *he* was Samuel Whiting.

Samuel Travis was Samuel Whiting.

They were one, in spirit if in nothing else. Separated by over a century but bonded in will.

Grabbing a pen from the penholder Eva had made him last year for Father's Day, Sam scribbled his own message on the bottom of the sheet and signed his name to it. That solidified it. He and Samuel Whiting were now one in purpose as well.

Fifty

TOMORROW WAS THE BIG DAY. THE MISSION WOULD BE fulfilled, and then maybe Symon could get some answers. Answers to questions that had begun to gnaw at him, to eat away at his mind like termites—questions about who he was, where he'd come from, and why he knew so much but felt nothing. He had this overwhelming, almost sickening, desire to be someone, anyone. A name, an identity, a history. He yearned for it like a starving man craves sustenance of any kind. He *needed* it. And he'd do anything for it.

Symon studied his own eyes in the rearview mirror. They were familiar yet strangely alien. Dark shadows colored the skin beneath them. He'd slept in the Intrepid last night, or at least attempted to sleep. The front seat didn't recline far enough, and his head kept rolling to one side, giving him cramps in his neck, but the back-seat was much too small. He was used to sleeping flat on his back, with legs outstretched and hands folded on his chest—like a stiff in a coffin.

His eyes were green, with flecks of brown and gray. He thought it odd that you saw your own face multiple times a day and never failed to recognize it, but when you looked at your eyes, really looked at them, they seemed so much like the eyes of another. There was something about his eyes, something that almost frightened him. To look deeply into them was to peer into the soul of someone—or something—evil, dark, malevolent.

He thought about the gunshots that had done him in. He remembered them clearly now. He was standing in that trailer, and the bruiser had shot him. Three times in the chest. Why three? Why did Symon feel a need to shoot his targets three times? It failed to make sense to him. He had a trio of circular scars on his chest, each about the size of a nickel. Entry wounds. One just above his left nipple, two near his right collarbone. Clearly they hadn't been fatal, but they would have certainly put him in the hospital.

The hospital? Another memory shot through his mind…

Bright lights, voices, flat and businesslike, white walls and ceiling, gloved hands, the smell of latex and rubbing alcohol. And pain, searing pain, throughout his chest cavity. It felt as if he'd been run through with a hot poker. He tried to scream, but his throat produced no sound. Something was jammed down it. He tried to suck in a deep breath, but it was like breathing through a straw. Strong hands held his arms and legs as he thrashed and flailed about. Then there was nothing.

The memory faded just as quickly as it had come.

Symon rubbed at his eyes and glanced in the mirror again. He looked so tired. His hand moved to the scars on his chest. They were still soft and pliable yet no longer tender, and by this he figured they were months old, no more than a year.

Anyway, none of that mattered now. What mattered was completing the mission. The voice on the phone had finally directed him to a new location, a home where he could take the target after securing her. And the one he was looking at now was a good choice. It was a large, white, two-story, neoclassical Greek Revival, with four columns running from porch to pediment. A lane branched off Fairfield Road and traveled a good two hundred yards to a small crest before offering even a glimpse of the place. From there, it was another two hundred yards to the front steps. The occupants were two widows, sisters, both in their seventies.

Symon spent a few more seconds letting the Intrepid idle at the crest of the rise where he'd gotten that first glimpse of the house. Finally he shifted the car into drive and slowly covered the last two hundred yards. In front of the home he cut the engine and got out.

It was still raining lightly. Symon hated the rain and made quick work of the thirty feet to the porch.

Wicker furniture—a sofa, coffee table, and four chairs with flowered cushions—adorned the porch, but other than that it was bare and simple. He found the front door open and, without knocking, went in uninvited. A cavernous interior met him, distinguished by ten-foot ceilings, hardwood parquet flooring, Federalist furniture, and a winding staircase. The widows obviously hoped to live out the remainder of their days in comfort.

From the back of the house came the sounds of a classical piece, Beethoven's "Moonlight Sonata."

Symon followed the music. There, beyond the staircase, hall, kitchen, and great room, he found a sprawling sunroom with three glass walls overlooking a field that ran for acres to a distant tree line. Midway between the house and trees one leafless willow stood by a pond, its bare branches dangling like lifeless tentacles. In the sunroom the sisters sat in separate chairs, each lost in a book.

They hadn't yet noticed the stranger watching them.

Symon took one step closer, and a floorboard creaked under his weight. The plumper sister looked up, startled, and dropped her book in her lap.

"Oh, you scared me," she said.

The other sister spun around to face Symon. "Why...can we help you?"

He approached them with relaxed, even strides. He pointed beyond the glass to the willow. "Did you know willows are considered guardian trees? They're said to ward off evil and protect the good." He had no idea how he knew that.

The plump widow stood. "I had no idea. Are you the landscape gentleman we talked to on the phone?"

Symon smiled. "I hardly think so."

The sisters looked at each other, and he saw worry lines deepen on their faces. It must have been something in his voice. The thinner of the two started to stand as well.

"Please," Symon said. "Ladies. Please sit back down and relax."

The plump one straightened her shoulders. "I will not sit down. What's the meaning of this? What are you here for?"

Her sister sat slowly. "Margaret…please."

"Shush, Louise, let me handle this."

"Ladies, please," Symon said again, trying to sound cordial and regain control of the scene. "I'm afraid there's been a misunderstanding."

Margaret returned to her chair but kept her shoulders squared and her back rigid. She obviously did not like his intrusion and was not impressed by his knowledge of local flora.

Symon took a deep breath and bowed slightly. "My name is Hector Montoya, and I come bearing good news."

Louise's hands went to her chest. "Oh. Margaret, did you hear that?"

Margaret narrowed her eyes. "You don't look like a Hector Montoya."

"Yes," Symon said. "My mother didn't think so either. She wanted to name me Edward, but my father insisted. It was his grandfather's name."

"What's the good news?" Louise said. Her eyes were expectant and wide, and a smile stretched across her thin face.

Symon took two steps closer. "First, I must ask you ladies a question. Do I look at all familiar to you?"

His question caught them off guard, and they both studied him in stunned silence. Louise looked at Margaret then at Symon. "I don't believe I know any Hector Montoya."

"Regardless of the name, do I look familiar?"

She looked confused. "But you said your name was Hector, after your grandfather."

"Ladies—"

"Is your name Hector or not?" Margaret's tone more than hinted at her doubt.

"Forget the name," Symon said. His frustration was showing,

and he knew it. This couldn't last much longer. "Look at my face. Is it familiar to you?"

"I said you didn't look like a Hector Montoya," Margaret said.

Louise pointed a finger at him. "A Hector maybe, but not a Montoya. You must take after your mother's family."

Symon had had enough. Pulling the pistol from his jacket pocket, he pointed it at Margaret. The sisters said nothing; neither did they exchange a glance. They were startled into momentary paralysis.

After the initial shock passed, the sisters shared a glance and Louise said, "Is there no good news, then?"

"I'm afraid not." Symon sighed—a dramatic gesture, he knew, but it seemed appropriate. "I think there's only one thing to do."

He pointed the gun at Margaret and squeezed the trigger. The pistol spit, and before Margaret had time to flinch or holler she was punched back into the chair so hard that it toppled over and left her with legs pointed upward. Louise let out a weak squeal as Symon swung the pistol and put a round in her too. She jerked sideways and slumped in her chair.

The melancholy piano of "Moonlight Sonata" seemed to fill the room again. Symon walked from Margaret to Louise and made sure he finished the job with two more rounds each. It had to be three apiece. He stood in the middle of the room, gazed out at the willow, then down at the bodies—and felt nothing.

And it bothered him.

Fifty-One

Sam pulled his work truck off Steinwehr Avenue into a parking space at the Americana Motel. He entered the office and paid cash for a one-night stay in a room on the north end. When the middle-aged woman behind the counter asked for his name, he told her it was Anthony Mundis. He'd gone to elementary school with a Brian Mundis, but the name had no particular significance; it was just the first thing that popped into his head.

Room 230 was nicely furnished, with a mahogany desk, dresser, and TV stand. The bed was a queen-size job with a flowery comforter, flanked by brass lamps on nightstands. The room smelled like cinnamon and sugar.

Sam made sure the door was locked, then tossed the duffel bag onto the bed. He moved to the large casement windows. From here on the second floor he had a clear view east across Steinwehr, across Taneytown Road, toward the Gettysburg National Cemetery, its barren late-November trees, and the rostrum, a rectangular, brick platform on the cemetery's southeast end.

The view was perfect.

He went back to the bed and took the scope from his bag. Then he cranked open the window, removed the screen, and pulled the curtain closed so only a sliver of sunlight slipped through. Dropping to one knee, Sam held the scope to his eye. The rostrum was a good four hundred yards away, a distance he hadn't tried since he was a kid but used to hit regularly. His farthest shot with a scope was nearly five hundred yards. He'd hit a plastic milk jug, center left.

At this time in the morning, this time of year, the cemetery was mostly empty. One older couple stood by the Gettysburg Address memorial, directly behind the rostrum. They were holding hands, and the man was running his finger along the text engraved in granite. Sam had once visited the cemetery with Molly and Eva. He remembered Molly reading the speech aloud with such awe and reverence. Now he thought nothing of it. His mind was focused on the mission at hand.

After dumping his things in the room, he headed back to his truck and pointed it north toward Shippensburg. He needed to ditch this vehicle and get a replacement. He figured Shippensburg University, in a neighboring county, was as good a place as any. If he took a car after dark, its student-owner most likely wouldn't notice until well into the next day, and then the initial bulletin would only circulate countywide.

Shippensburg was a good forty minutes from Gettysburg, on tangled roads that wound through miles of apple orchards, Michaux State Forest, and over Piney Mountain. But Sam wasn't paying attention to the scenery. He was planning his next move.

On the edge of the forest he veered onto a seldom-used service road and steered the truck into a clearing. There he would leave it, white rag wedged in the driver's side door frame. Any drivers-by would assume the truck had either run out of gas or broken down. And it could be days before a forest ranger took notice.

He wasn't far from the campus here. He'd wait until sundown, then make his way over to the student parking lot.

The afternoon passed slowly for Sam, and he spent most of it avoiding thoughts of Eva and Molly. The patter of rain on the windshield lulled him into fitful sleep where he dreamt of Eva's voice outside the study door—*Daddy, please, I love you.* He awakened suddenly, sweaty yet chilled, breathing rapidly. Climbing from the vehicle, he stood in the cool rain until the stressful feelings passed, then got back in, turned on the engine, and cranked the heat until the arrhythmic tap-tapping of droplets caused him to doze again. Fortunately he had no encounters with Tommy and no fugues where he became a medium through which Samuel Whiting expressed himself. He was only haunted by his daughter's panicked voice.

A little after five o'clock the sky was darkened enough that Sam felt it safe to leave his truck and walk the two miles to Shippensburg University. Sticking to side streets and back alleys, he wove through the college town unnoticed.

Nearly soaked and shivering uncontrollably, he reached the campus and began checking vehicles in a dormitory parking lot. It didn't take him long to find a late-model, maroon Ford Escort with a spare key hidden in a magnetized box under the rear corner of the chasis.

He started the car and put the heat on max.

Fifty-Two

The night air was cool, borderline chilly, but Molly Travis didn't care. Poor Eva had spent the whole evening watching out the front window, waiting for Sam to come home, but he never showed. At eight, her regular bedtime, Eva all but threw a fit, something very unlike her, because her daddy still hadn't returned. She was convinced something had happened to him, something awful, or that he had done something very naughty.

Molly had climbed into bed with her daughter and sang her a lullaby. Eva was so tired from the worrying and pacing and questioning—oh, the endless questioning—that once she stopped fighting, she slipped into sleep with a shudder.

A quarter to ten. At last Molly could have a few moments of silence.

The rain had stopped, so she carried the cordless phone out to a seat on the patio and watched bats fly erratic circles in the night sky. She hoped her husband would call. For now, though, she was alone with her thoughts, a place she wasn't entirely comfortable being, especially with the direction her thoughts were taking her.

Sam's unpredictable behavior had grown quite disturbing. She knew some of it was caused by the brain injury, of course it was. Dr. Sullivan had told her to expect mood swings, depression, even sporadic psychotic behaviors such as hallucinations and paranoia. Now Sam was displaying all of them. It was a perfect storm of side effects, the meeting of every negative outcome. But there was something else about him, something unrelated to the brain injury, that wasn't right.

Something foreboding, dark, almost…

She hated to even think it, but the word kept surfacing, a buoy refusing to stay down.

Evil.

Just as Eva had done when sleep overcame her so suddenly, Molly shuddered. Her sweatshirt could not keep that chill from reaching her skin. Where was Sam? She'd tried calling his cell phone earlier, but he'd left it on the kitchen counter. She'd called his mother and a few friends, but no one had seen or heard from him. He'd simply disappeared. She knew they'd been arguing more than usual and that she'd been hard on him the last couple of days, but it wasn't like Sam to just quit on their relationship, on his family. On Eva.

From the large spruce at the corner of their property, an owl began its nightly questioning. It was a great horned. Molly and Eva had watched it before, through the binoculars. Big thing too. Two feet tall, at least, with deeply mottled feathering and large, round eyes. Eva thought the eyes were creepy; Molly couldn't disagree.

Again the thought of the evil entered her mind, like a virus finding its way into her system, and she tried to push it out. There was something in Sam's past that still haunted him, she was certain of that, something he had never wanted to talk about...and never completely overcome. She knew it had to do with his brother, Tommy, and a rifle. She'd been told Tommy was killed in a hunting accident, although lately she wasn't so sure.

And then there was the broken window incident. Sam wasn't telling the whole truth about that; he was hiding something, keeping secrets. Since that event, his whole personality had changed. He seemed so preoccupied, absorbed in...something. She didn't know what.

But it went back to Tommy. It all went back to Tommy.

Molly picked up the cordless and dialed Sam's mother for the second time that evening.

"Hi, Gloria." Molly never called her Mom. "It's Molly again."

"He finally came home, didn't he?"

"No. Not yet. But I have something else I need to ask you about."

"I'm sure he'll be home soon."

"Sooner or later. Um, what happened between Sam and Tommy?"

For a few seconds Molly thought Gloria would not answer.

Then: "Why do you ask?"

"It's not something Sam has ever talked about. I don't even think I can name three times he's mentioned Tommy's name. And lately I think something about it's been bothering him. Something that happened between him and Tommy. It might have something to do with why he's gone missing. What happened there?"

Gloria forced a laugh. "Oh, they were like any brothers, at each other. You know."

"I don't think I do. I didn't have any brothers. How were they 'at each other'?"

"Oh, just brother stuff. They didn't always see eye to eye. Tommy was...active, and Sammy didn't always go well with that. He was a more serious child, you know."

Molly swallowed before asking the next question. "Can I ask about Tommy's death? How it happened?"

"I really don't like talking about it, Molly. It's in the past, and that's where it needs to stay. I'm sure Sammy's gotten over it by now."

"That's the thing," Molly said. "I'm not sure he has. I think he still struggles with it, has issues that—"

"If he has issues, he sure hasn't ever said anything to me about them."

"Well, maybe he doesn't—"

"Molly, dear, I don't think this is something anyone wants to remember. It was so long ago. It's better left alone."

"I just—"

Inside the house a floorboard creaked. Molly spun in her chair and found Eva, in her pajamas, watching her through the kitchen's screen door.

"I have to go, Gloria. I'll let you know when Sam gets home." She clicked off the phone and stood. "Eva, baby, what are you doing out of bed?"

Eva stood motionless, arms at her side, stare fixed on her mother.

A tingle tickled the back of Molly's neck. She opened the door and looked into her daughter's glazed pupils. "Eva, are you awake?"

Eva nodded, then rubbed at her eyes.

Molly splayed the fingers on her hand. "How many fingers am I holding up?"

Her daughter's face was emotionless, as flat as undisturbed water. "The time is up," she said. Plainly she was sleepwalking. Her dull gaze moved past Molly's shoulder toward nothing in particular. "Daddy's time is up. He used it and went the wrong way...Jacob said...Jacob prayed for the time, when the time was up—"

"OK, baby, let's go back to bed." Molly took Eva in her arms and let the door slam behind them. Her daughter felt heavier than she remembered. She was growing up too fast.

Eva continued to mumble. "The man needs to be careful and watch for, and watch out for, he needs to watch...Jacob said, he prayed...Daddy, I need to tell him." The more she talked, the more agitated she became. Her voice was rising, her body stiffening. "Daddy needs to, he needs to know...Jacob can't tell him, I have to—"

Molly hurried up the steps to Eva's room.

"I need to tell him...love him...Jesus—"

She put Eva on the bed, and Eva tried to push her away.

"He needs to know...the man watching, talking...Daddy needs to know...Jesus—"

"Eva, please, baby." Molly tried to calm her, tried to hold her arms, but the more she did so, the more combative Eva got and the more she rambled.

"Jacob...Daddy...Jesus...Daddy needs to know, he needs

to know...love him—" Then, as if someone had hit a switch, she stopped struggling and looked up with clear eyes. "Mommy?"

Molly smoothed her hair. "Yes, darling, you were talking in your sleep again."

"Is Daddy home yet?"

Molly shook her head. "He will be soon, though. You go back to sleep, OK?"

A tear spilled from the corner of Eva's eye, tracked down her temple, and disappeared in her hair. "Jacob said Daddy's going to do something bad. I need to tell him I love him."

"Baby, Daddy's not going to do anything bad, and I promise he knows you love him."

Eva's eyes closed slowly and opened again. Sleep was overcoming her. "He needs to know."

"He does know, baby."

"Pray with me, Mommy. Pray for Daddy, please."

Molly prayed. As she did so, Eva fell back to sleep, but Molly feared it would be anything but peaceful. She hurried back downstairs, grabbed the phone, and pushed the buttons. She needed someone to talk to. She'd go plain nuts if she didn't.

As soon as Beth Fisher answered, the tears started to flow from Molly's eyes. At first she could say nothing; the words stuck in her throat as if glued there.

"Hello?" Beth said again.

Molly choked out a word. "Beth..."

"Molly, is that you? What's wrong?"

She drew in a deep breath and composed herself. "Sorry...sorry to call so late."

"No, no, it's no problem. I was up. What's wrong?"

"I just need to talk." Her words were strained and broken, squeezed out through tight vocal cords.

"Are you OK?"

"Yes."

"Are Eva and Sam OK?"

"I don't know. Can we talk?"

"Honey, I'm coming right over."

* * *

Molly and Beth sat out back, under the night sky, under the chasing bats, and Molly unloaded everything until the conversation came full circle back to her own past she'd been hiding from for thirteen years.

"Lately Sam's been acting so much like my father that I–I find myself resenting him for no reason."

Beth was quiet a moment. "Your father was abusive?"

Molly nodded. She'd known it for a long time, forever it seemed, but never voiced it to anyone besides Sam. "Not physically or sexually, he never did that, but there was verbal and emotional abuse. Plenty of emotional. And he had quite the temper."

Again, Beth was quiet. She tucked her leg up under herself and faced Molly. Her face was etched with concern and empathy.

Molly continued. "He'd get angry with us over the dumbest things, then not talk to us for days. One time my sister forgot to clean the hair out of the shower drain, and he threatened to throw her out of the house. She was thirteen. Once I came home late after school. I'd told him I would be late, helping set up for an art show, but he must have forgotten. When I got home he went wild, threw my clothes into the front yard, and made me sleep out on the porch that night."

"And Sam's been acting like that?"

Molly smiled. "No, not that bad. But the sarcasm, the irritability, the sharp comments—it's all the same. Just like my father. When we argue, it's like I'm arguing with my father and I have to win, like this is my chance to finally stick it to him and get the upper hand for once."

Beth reached over and put her hand on Molly's. "You still carry the weight of it, don't you? You've never let it go."

It was Molly's turn to be quiet. She had left this load strapped to her back for far too long, at times so heavy she thought she'd crumble under the weight of it.

"Molly, Sam's been under a lot of pressure lately. He's been through a lot. You all have. Give him some time. Whatever it is that's gnawing at him, he'll work it out. And when he needs your help or needs you to talk to about it, he'll make that move. Until then, give him some space."

"If he comes home."

Beth gave Molly's hand a squeeze. "Do you love him?"

The question seemed an odd one—of course she loved him—until Molly let it settle in, and then she was asking herself the same question. Did she love Sam? Really love him? Unconditionally? Unembarrassed by how long it took her to answer, Molly searched her heart and found a love that went back fourteen, fifteen years, a love so strong and resilient that the fires of hell could not crush it.

"Yes," she said. "With all my heart."

Beth nodded and smiled. "Then keep loving him. Tell him and show him. Pray for him. He's in a dark place and needs you now more than ever. Wherever he is, your love can find him there."

Fifty-Three

November 19, 7:20 a.m.

Senator Stephen Lincoln sat in the back of the Suburban and glanced at his watch. He'd been up since five going over his speech, jotting notes, doing last-minute revisions, and praying. Lots of praying. He knew full well this speech could be the biggest of his political career, and Stephen Lincoln was a firm believer in the hand of God guiding the affairs of men. He hadn't always been, but he was now.

He retrieved a photo of his family from his jacket pocket, the one taken a year ago as they vacationed in Maine. They'd stayed in a cottage on the coast, just north of Freeport, one of his favorite vacations ever. They even met the Bushes in Kennebunkport. Went fishing with 41.

He replaced the photo and phoned Emily, told her he was on his way. She'd be traveling separately to meet him there from their home in Lancaster County.

"Love you, honey," she said. "And Steve?"

"Yeah?"

"Be careful, OK?"

There was something about the hesitation in her voice and the way it cracked on the word *careful.*

"What's wrong?" Lincoln asked.

There was silence on the other end for a couple of seconds. "I don't know. Just a feeling I have. Just...be careful, OK?"

Emily wasn't dumb. She was well aware that there were death threats, not to mention nut-jobs out there crazy enough to make good on their threats.

"I'll be fine, sweetheart. Really. People give speeches all the time."

"But 'people' aren't you."

"I'll see you there, all right?"

"Yes. Do your best."

They said their good-byes, and he put the phone back in its jack.

It was raining outside, just a light patter on the limo's windows, enough to smudge the view of the world beyond the bulletproof glass and reinforced doors.

Taylor Blake leaned to her side and caught Lincoln's eye. "Sir, are you sure you want to do this now? I mean . . . "

"You mean we can always reschedule?"

"Yes. It's done all the time."

"Reschedule for when? And what happens when threats start popping up then? Reschedule again? Taylor, I appreciate your concern, but I won't back down because of a few crazies giving idle threats."

"It's not just the threats. It's the murders, the rain—"

"The rain? You really think I'd let a little rain stop me?"

She looked out the window. "No."

"And as for the murders, the locals have been planning this event for some time now. From what I'm told, they're ready."

"They are." She smiled. "But I still hope the rain stops."

Fifty-Four

7:25 a.m.

Sam still wasn't home, and Molly was more than a little worried. She'd called his mother again, a little after 5:00 a.m., waking her from a deep sleep. Gloria answered, mumbling something about needing to get out of the room while there was still time. She'd neither seen nor heard from Sam, though. Molly decided she would give him until lunchtime to show up. If he didn't surface by then, she'd call the police.

In Eva's room Molly sat on the edge of the bed and stroked her daughter's forehead. She had let her sleep as long as she could. "Hey, sweet girl, time to wake up. Gotta get ready for school."

Eva's eyes fluttered open. She stretched her arms overhead and wiped at her eyes with the backs of her hands.

Molly rubbed Eva's belly, then stood. "I have breakfast all ready for you, and your clothes are here on the bed. Get dressed and come downstairs, OK?"

"Did Daddy come home?"

Sitting back down, Molly combed her fingers through Eva's hair. "Honey, I'm afraid he didn't." She saw the look of fright pass through Eva's eyes. "I'm sure he's OK, though. Don't you worry about him one bit. He'll come home today. I'm sure of it."

"Then where is he? Where did he go?"

"I don't know, baby."

"Did you call Grandma? Maybe he spent the night there."

"Yes, I called her, and she hasn't heard from him either."

Moisture pooled in Eva's eyes. "He's not coming home, is he?"

Molly cupped her daughter's face in her hand. "Shh. Now don't talk like that. Of course he's coming home. In fact, I'm thinking he'll be back by the time you get home from school."

"I don't want to go to school."

"You have to go to school, darling. And you need to get up because Miss Beth's going to be here soon to pick you up. I let you sleep in a little later today."

Eva sat up and pushed back her covers. "But how will I tell him?"

"Tell him what?"

"How will I tell Daddy I love him and that Jesus loves him? Jacob said I have to tell him, that's the only thing that can help Daddy."

Molly touched the tip of Eva's nose. "Listen to me, baby girl. I know you're upset about this whole thing, but I want you to try to be brave and...let's not have any more talk about Jacob, all right?"

"But he—"

"Eva, I'm serious. No more, all right?"

Eva's eyes dropped. "OK."

Molly knew her daughter was struggling with the changes she'd seen in her father, but she didn't want to upset her by talking about it more than was necessary. Hopefully Sam would be home by noon, back to his old self. Cabin fever could do strange things to people. For the last four months he'd been stuck in the house, dependent on Molly for almost everything, and that was tough for a man used to doing things on his own. Maybe he just needed some time alone, time to spread his wings again and sort things out in his mind. She prayed that's all it was. Dear God, let that be all.

Beth arrived right on time, waving from her Volvo.

"She's here." Molly helped Eva with her jacket and book bag, then handed her the American Girl lunchbox they'd given her for Christmas. "Here you go, sweetie. I packed you turkey and cheese. Make sure you eat it all."

Eva gave her a kiss on the cheek and turned toward the door.

"Hey," Molly said, touching her arm. "You OK?"

Tears formed in Eva's eyes again. "Daddy's gonna do something bad. Ja—I know it. I need to tell him how much I love him. *Please*, Mommy, I need to tell him."

Molly took Eva in her arms. "Oh, baby girl. I wish you could. I do. But I promise you, Daddy knows how much you love him. And he loves you back the same. You know that, don't you?"

Eva nodded. "But I need to tell him."

Wiping a tear from Eva's cheek, Molly said. "You can tell him when you get home, OK? I'll tell him he better be ready for the biggest hug he's ever got. Sound good?"

Eva nodded again.

"Now, here." She handed over a tissue. "Blow your nose and settle yourself. And don't worry about Daddy. You just have a good day at school."

Eva fell into Molly's arms. "I love you, Mommy."

"I love you too, baby. More than anything. Do good at school, you hear?"

"OK. I will."

And then her little girl was gone, out the door and down the sidewalk. Molly waved at Beth as Eva climbed into the car. When the car had faded from view, Molly let the tears come.

Fifty-Five

8:05 a.m.

Symon had disposed of the widows, and their grand house awaited his return with the target. Now, to complete his mission. He sat in his Intrepid along Pumping Station Road, watching the raindrops dot the windshield. He was pleased this rural lane saw little traffic. The sky was overcast, and the morning light was slow to arrive, but this would make the forest-green Volvo's headlights easier to spot. If his timing was right, he should pull out in exactly five minutes. He'd angle his car cockeyed, blocking the path of the Volvo wagon, and then do his thing.

He went over it in his mind again. It should be an easy task.

"Easy as puttin' peanut butter on bread." That's what his mother used to say. Funny he should remember that. She also used to say, "Two heads are better than one, even if one's a cabbage-head," and though that had nothing to do with this mission, it was eminently important because it meant at one time he was *someone*. His mother's son.

Laying his head on the headrest, Symon shut his eyes and tried to clear his mind. But he couldn't. The faces were there, the faces of those he'd killed…

The Moellers—minding their own business that morning, with her cooking breakfast and him getting ready for another boring day. Thad Lewis—that hippie all alone in his trailer, just him and his books. Officer Ned Coleman—the dutiful civil servant, upholding the law, too young and cocky for his own good. The widowed sisters—living in a mansion with more than they needed, yet having nothing but each other.

Still, he felt void of sympathy, void of guilt or regret. And still it bothered him. He should feel something, shouldn't he? He'd murdered six people and was about to chalk up two more, but he felt no remorse, no disgust, no pity, no joy. If he felt joy over the killings, it would be sick, yes, and the world would be appalled, but at least he'd feel *something*.

The clock on the dash told him it was time. Symon pulled onto the road, using the Intrepid to block one lane and half of the other. He killed the engine, got out, and popped the hood. The rain felt cool on his head and face.

Exactly one minute later a pair of headlights appeared, coming over the rise. As the Volvo approached, he started waving his arms. It stopped beside his car, and the driver's side window lowered.

A woman was driving. And two girls were in the backseat.

One was the target.

"Looks like you're in some trouble," the woman said.

She looked just as the voice said she would—dark, curly hair, neatly applied makeup, small nose and eyes. He glanced back at the Intrepid, then at the woman. "Yeah, deer ran out in front of me, and I think I hit it. It happened so fast. You know how they are."

"I do. I had one hit me a couple years ago. Almost totaled the car. Is your car working?"

"No. I swerved off the road, hit something, maybe the deer, yanked it back, and it stalled. You wouldn't happen to have a cell phone I could use real quick, would you? Just want to call my mechanic and get a tow."

The woman glanced at her watch, then at the Intrepid. "Um, sure. Quickly, though. I have to get the girls to school." She retrieved the phone from her purse and handed it to Symon.

"Thank you so much. I'll be quick." He punched in some numbers, nothing in particular. "I've held out on getting one of these things. Hate technology, you know? But times like this I could shoot myself for not… Hello?"

There was no one on the other end, of course, but Symon put

on a real Oscar-worthy performance, detailing what'd happened and what his vehicle looked like. While he talked, another car appeared over the rise, a Honda SUV. It slowed, but Symon gave the driver a thumbs-up and waved him on. Young guy. Looked full of himself.

The woman seemed to be getting impatient. She glanced in the rearview mirror and said something to the girls. Symon folded the phone, handed it to her. "Thank you. And hey, this is really asking a lot, but would you mind giving me a ride into town?"

Her smile was as fake as he'd ever seen. He had an impulse to slap her across the face and erase the stupid, patronizing grin.

"I don't think so," she said. "I'm sorry."

"Then could you at least help me push this thing to the side of the road? It's kinda blocking traffic here."

She glanced at her watch again. "I really need to get going. We're already going to be late for school. I'm sure someone else will be along soon enough to help you, someone with more muscles than I can offer."

"Oh, but—" Symon pulled the Beretta from his coat. His left hand reached through the open window and grabbed her by the collar while his right shoved the pistol against her head. "I really wanted you to help."

The woman let out a weak little scream, and the girls in the back yelped. The woman twisted her face, grabbed the steering wheel with both hands, and the car lurched forward. Symon had a good grip on her jacket, but the momentum threw him off balance, and he nearly went down. The Volvo veered left and ran into the rear of the Intrepid. The woman screamed again as her car kept going forward, pushing his vehicle off the road. The moan of twisting metal grated against his ears.

Symon cocked back his hand and smashed the butt of the pistol into the woman's forehead. She slumped in the seat, and the Volvo rolled to a stop. Her head lolled to one side, oozing blood from a gash the size of a paper clip.

The girls whimpered. One of them screamed, "Leave my mommy alone!"

Symon said nothing.

He felt the woman's neck for a pulse and found it. He should have shot her right then and been done with her, but the look of the two girls in the back seat deterred him. He had a daughter of his own about their age.

Wait.

Symon took a step back, his peripheral vision going black. He had a daughter of his own? Yes, he remembered her. The girl in the park, pulling him toward the woods. She was his daughter.

He shook his head, tapped the Beretta against his skull. He didn't have time for memories now. Another car could appear any moment. In the driver's seat the woman moaned and rolled her head back and forth.

He tore open the door and put the pistol to her temple. "Move over."

She moaned again, a pitiful sound really, and lifted her hand to the gash.

Symon looked up and down the road. Still no other cars. But that wouldn't last long. They had to move. He nudged the barrel against the woman's head. "Now. Move it, or I'll give someone an awful mess to clean up."

Slowly—too slowly—she inched herself into the passenger seat. She tried to say something, but her words came out slurred and jumbled. Blood tricked down her cheek, and a line of saliva ran from the corner of her mouth to her chin. Her eyes were glazed, as empty as the windows of an abandoned house.

When she had cleared enough of the seat, Symon pushed himself in and shoved her the rest of the way over. He put the car in reverse, backed away from the Intrepid, shifted to drive, and put the pedal down. A short distance later he turned right onto a windy, tar-and-chip lane even less traveled than Pumping Station. Beside him the woman let out a low mewl, then turned to the girls in the backseat, but said nothing.

Symon glanced at them in the rearview mirror. They sat silently, holding hands. "How about a day off from school, girls?"

He thought of his own daughter then. More was coming back to him. She had his fair complexion and dark-brown hair, cut to the shoulders with bangs. Brown eyes too, like morsels of milk chocolate. And freckles. That's it; that's all he could pull from memory at the moment. Just a still shot of her face, smiling...no, laughing. She was laughing at something.

Around a bend they came to a shallow creek. A gravel lane ran parallel to it, then disappeared around a clump of locust trees. Symon turned onto it and stopped a half mile later near a fast-moving section of the water. He cut the engine, walked around to the passenger side, ordered the woman out. When she resisted, still bleary-eyed and dazed, he found that the barrel of a Beretta placed strategically along the side of the skull could be very persuasive. The girls in the back remained locked in by their seat belts, holding hands. They said nothing.

With the woman standing beside the car, Symon opened the back door and pointed the gun at her daughter. The girl did not move. The woman whimpered and made an awkward move toward Symon.

"Don't," he said, holding up a hand. "If you want your daughter to see her next birthday, don't." Then he turned to the girl. "You. Get out here and stand with your mother." And to the target, "And you stay put, or these two get it."

The first girl unhooked her seat belt and scooted out of the car. She was taller than Symon expected a second-grader to be. His own daughter was short for her age. Upon exiting, she ran to her mother, and they both hugged. The woman was crying now, tears leaving faint streaks of mascara down her cheeks.

"Why are you doing this?" she cried. "What do you want with us?"

"Have you ever seen me before?" Symon asked.

The woman gobbled like a turkey, stuttered, then swallowed hard. "I've never seen you before."

"Are you certain of that? I don't look at all familiar to you? Think way back."

She didn't even hesitate. "No. I promise. I've never seen you before. Please, let the girls go."

Ignoring her request, Symon said, "Then I guess I don't want anything with you."

He pointed the gun at her with every intention of squeezing off three rounds and dumping her body in the creek. But he couldn't do it, not with her daughter so close. Not with the target watching. He would feel no remorse over shooting the woman, he knew that; but he would forever regret doing it in front of the girls. He wouldn't want his own daughter, whoever she may be, wherever she may be, to witness such an act.

Instead he took three large steps—three, to maintain some order—and in one quick motion whipped the Beretta against the side of her head before she had time to flinch. It made a sickening thud, snapped her head to the left, and she crumpled to the ground on paper legs. Her daughter screamed and dropped next to her. The side of the woman's head lay open, bleeding freely.

Symon lowered the gun. "I could have killed her," he told the sobbing girl.

She neither looked at him nor acknowledged his presence in any way. His declaration of mercy inspired no gratitude.

Taking the woman by the wrist, he dragged her limp body down to the creek bank. The effort brought out a sweat on his brow. As she lay motionless on the moist dirt, he saw her chest rising and falling with quick, shallow breaths. She'd have a crusher of a headache when she came to, and most certainly a concussion, but she'd live. The tall second-grader would not lose her mother.

The girl, who had followed close behind, stumbled and slid down the embankment, then rushed to her mother and knelt beside her. The creek babbled and gurgled playfully, a strange backdrop to the mother-daughter scene on its bank.

"Stay with her," Symon told the girl. "You don't want Mommy to die, do you?"

She looked at him, open-mouthed. He could see the wheels turning, calculating. She would stay put.

Symon returned to the Volvo and checked the backseat. The target was still there, wearing her seat belt. Her eyes were wide, her mouth tight, but there was only a trace of fear on her face. She was trying to be brave.

"Hi, Eva," he said. "You and I are going to take a little ride. I have business to conduct with your daddy."

The look on her face said she already knew.

Fifty-Six

8:30 a.m.

Symon led the target into the Greco Revival mansion. The two widowed sisters were now locked from view in a heap at the bottom of the basement steps. He'd tidied the sunroom before leaving to get his target. Rearranged the furniture, cleaned the blood from the floor. Fortunately it was minimal; the poor old gals were so old they hadn't had much pumping through their veins.

"Now, Eva, let's go to the sunroom, and you and I can have a little talk."

Eva Travis, the target, was more darling in person than any picture could portray. Symon smiled, a genuine smile because his memories were slowly sifting back, and this child's calm demeanor reminded him of his own daughter, who took after her mother.

"Seriously, sweetie. We need to talk about your daddy and about Jacob."

That put a look of bewilderment on Eva's face.

"Oh, yes. I know all about Jacob." He had no idea how he knew, but there were lots of things he knew without any idea how he'd acquired the knowledge.

He led the way to the sunroom and motioned to one of the chairs. "Sit. Would you like a drink?"

Eva said nothing, neither nodding nor shaking her head.

"Very well, I'll take that as a yes." He went to the refrigerator and poured tall glasses of iced tea. He took a sip. "Oh, Southern sweet tea. I haven't had this in ages. You'll like this." He handed her a glass, then sat in an overstuffed chair across from her. "Now, let's talk about your daddy, shall we? Do you know where he is right now?"

She set the tea on a table and looked at him.

"Come now, Eva, we need to have a discussion here. That means both of us talking, sharing information, feelings, passions, all of it. Do you know where your daddy is?"

She shook her head slowly.

"Oh, that's too bad." Symon crossed his legs and folded his hands in his lap. "But you do know he's going to do something naughty, don't you?"

Again, no response.

"Well, don't you? Isn't that what Jacob told you?"

"How do you know about Jacob?"

"Ah, you do talk. I know many things, Eva. How I know isn't important."

She looked around the room, her eyes finding and searching every corner.

"He's not here," Symon said. "He can't come to this place. It's just you and me now."

"Where's my dad?"

"I know, I know. He needs to know you love him, blah, blah, blah. It's too late for that, sweetie. Your daddy is long gone, and he's not coming back. He's on a mission right now, doing something very important. And you, you are my insurance to make sure he does it. Now, what do you say we give your daddy a phone call and let him know what's at stake, shall we?"

Eva mumbled something.

"Excuse me, sweetie? I didn't hear what you said."

"I said it's not just me who loves him."

"Oh, yes, yes, many people love your dear old daddy. He's such a great guy, isn't he?"

"I need to tell him that Jesus loves him."

Heat crawled up Symon's neck and settled in his cheeks. "Eva, coming from most, that name would not bother me, but coming from you, I'm afraid I find it quite offensive. I'll ask you politely once to not use it again."

Eva appeared to think about that. Her eyes shifted around the room and finally landed back on Symon. He was impressed with her courage. With all sincerity, she said, "Jesus loves you too."

Symon vaulted from his chair and covered the space between them before she could flinch. His hand found her throat and squeezed. "Don't you ever even think about saying that name again in my presence. Do you hear me, you little brat?"

Eva's eyes bulged and her face reddened.

He looked deep into her eyes and there found real fear. "Do you hear me?"

She nodded.

He released his grip and dropped to one knee. His head began to throb. "I'm sorry, Eva. I probably shouldn't have done that. I... Let's just call your daddy. You know, someday you'll be proud of what he's about to do. He's about to change the course of history."

Symon took the phone from the table and dialed the number the voice had given him. The number for Sam's motel room.

Fifty-Seven

9:35 a.m.

"WE'LL BE THERE IN TEN MINUTES, SIR," TAYLOR SAID. SHE WAS seated in front of Lincoln in the Suburban, with her cell phone to her ear. "Your wife has just arrived and is waiting in her vehicle at the rostrum."

"How do things look?"

"Sir?"

"Security, what are they saying?"

Despite the confident appearance he put on for his staff, Lincoln couldn't help but be concerned about safety at the Gettysburg event. His concern wasn't for himself but for his wife. If anything happened to her because a few radicals hated him, he'd never forgive himself. His team rarely told him the details of the threats. He knew most were the routine batch that always came in, and only a few were taken seriously. Apparently this time there were more than a few.

This was a risk he would take, a risk they all took.

"The crowd is growing by the minute," Taylor answered, dropping her phone into the inside breast pocket of her jacket. "There's a group of protestors on the other side of Taneytown Road, but they appear peaceful. Taneytown and Steinwehr have been closed off. Security is covering the perimeter. Locals are patrolling the immediate area and rerouting traffic. So far so good. When we get there, we'll pull up right behind your wife's vehicle. The two of you will get out and take the platform together. There are chairs there for you and several local notables."

"Do you have their names?" Most politicians didn't care whom they shared their platform with so long as it reflected well on them, but Lincoln's concern was for the individual. That's why he'd gotten into politics in the first place, and knowing whom he was sitting with was important to him.

"I have the list here." Taylor dug a piece of paper from her pocket and unfolded it. "The mayor of Gettysburg, Milt Kyle; the president of Gettysburg College, Harry Lee; the president of the Lutheran seminary, George Wickham; a few honor students from Gettysburg High and Gettysburg College; and the pastor of a local Baptist church, Ed Mickley. They've all been cleared."

She looked to him for his approval to go on. He nodded, satisfied.

"Lee will speak first," she said, "followed by Wickham and Mickley. Then the mayor will introduce you. You'll take the podium, and you'll notice the first several rows of the audience are children. The kids of Lincoln Elementary School have been invited." She looked out the window. "Thank goodness it stopped raining."

Lincoln sighed. "Do the children have to be there? With the threats issued?"

"Security considered that but thought it best to go on with things as planned. Sir, you can be confident the area is secure. No one is coming or going without passing through multiple checkpoints."

He tightened his jaw and said a quick prayer.

Taylor's phone rang. She picked it out of her pocket. "Yeah." She turned and looked out the window, then to Lincoln. "We're here. You ready?"

Lincoln nodded. A flock of butterflies had taken flight in his stomach, looking for the fastest way out.

Fifty-Eight

9:50 a.m.

DESPITE THE TIME OF DAY, THE MOTEL ROOM WAS DIM AND dreary. The curtains were pulled, the lamps switched off, and a thick cloud cover blotted any direct sunlight. Sam Travis sat on the bed, brooding. The television at his back was tuned to local coverage of the senator's appearance. Some female anchor was going on about the importance of the speech and the significance of it being given in Gettysburg on this very date. Apparently this Senator Lincoln was a hit with a lot of people and had a good chance of winning the White House in a year.

Sam walked across the room and picked up his rifle. It felt lighter than usual but comfortable in his hands, as though molded to the shape of his palm.

He turned toward the TV, where cameras filmed a black SUV parking near the rostrum. The anchorwoman said it was the senator's ride. Men in black suits milled around, and one opened the back door. Sam had never seen Stephen Lincoln except in his campaign photos. He stepped from the SUV, middle-aged, tall, and lean. Full head of dusty brown hair. He waved and smiled as the vehicle door closed and security officers surrounded him.

A rush of hatred for the man caught Sam off guard, and he had to sit. The feeling made no sense to him. He knew little about this senator, this presidential hopeful. He did know he was conservative, outspoken, and half the country saw him as a godsend—things Sam would normally have no problem with—and yet still he hated him. But it was more than hatred, wasn't it? It was vitriol, contempt.

Stephen Lincoln was a malignancy, an abomination. He was the enemy, and he had to die.

Sam brought the rifle stock to his shoulder and looked down the barrel at the TV. The time would come soon. Within minutes. He walked over to the window. The scope was on the table. He attached it to the rifle and calibrated it to the proper distance.

He then parted the curtain just an inch and looked across Steinwehr, across Taneytown Road, at the rostrum. The rain had stopped, and a crowd had gathered around the platform, some sitting, most standing. He watched as Lincoln climbed the stairs and took a seat next to an old fat guy with a terrible comb-over. The fat guy smiled and shook Lincoln's hand, said something then laughed. His double chin jiggled grotesquely.

The room phone rang, and although it startled him, Sam didn't move.

It rang again. Still he didn't move.

On the third ring he let the curtain fall into place and crossed the room. The phone was on the table next to the bed.

Four rings. Who knew he was here? The answer was simple. No one. It had to be the front desk. If he didn't answer, they'd send someone to the room, and that could throw everything off.

On the fifth ring he lifted the receiver to his ear but said nothing.

A man's high-pitched voice came through. "Hello, Samuel."

The use of his first name and the sound of the man's voice kept Sam quiet. This was not a courtesy call from the front desk.

"I know what you're about to do," the man said, "and I applaud you for it." There was a brief pause. "But I'm not sure you're fully committed to the mission, so I bought a little insurance. Would you like to know what it is?"

"Who are you?"

"That's a good question. One I've been asking myself lately. Who I am is of no regard, though. Not to you. The pressing issue is, who you are and what you are about to do. Now, aren't you at all interested in my insurance plan? My sweet little insurance plan?"

Sam did not answer.

"Very well."

There was muffled static on the other end, the sound of footsteps, then, "Daddy?"

It was Eva. She sounded scared.

"Daddy? Are you there?"

Sam said nothing. The voice of his daughter on the other end was like the sound of some distant train whistle that hinted at life and freedom but was too removed for any real meaning.

"Daddy, please say something if you're there."

But he didn't. He couldn't. He dare not say anything, for her own good. It would be easier for her if he simply stepped out of the picture. He would fulfill his mission and then all would be right for Molly and Eva. He remained motionless, the phone to his ear, his heart in a vice.

"I love you, Daddy." She was crying now. "Please, I love you no matter what. And—"

Eva shrieked, then went quiet.

Sam clutched the phone with a shaky hand. The thought of Eva in the hands of that lunatic made his skin itch with rage.

"You see, Samuel?" The man was back on. "My insurance plan. Oh, I know you don't care at the moment, and that's how it should be, but just in case you feel compelled to care, remember this: if you don't follow through, dear little Eva here will die. She'll beg and she'll pray and she'll cry, but she *will* die. You do what you need to do, what you know you want to do, and I'll reconsider things for Eva."

The phone clicked off, and silence took over the line.

Sam sat on the edge of the bed, receiver still in his hand. He was a man torn between two impossible choices. If he took the shot, he'd surely be caught and imprisoned, losing both Molly and Eva. But if he didn't take the shot, he would most certainly lose Eva. He slammed the phone down, wiped the sweat from his brow. A knot tightened his throat.

At the moment it seemed there was only one way out, one way to both satisfy the darkness and save the life of his daughter.

He would take the shot.

Fifty-Nine

10:05 a.m.

RATHER THAN WALLOW IN FEAR MOLLY SPENT THE MORNING vacuuming the house, washing and drying two loads of laundry, and finishing the dishes from breakfast. She had just begun dusting when the phone rang. She caught it on the fourth ring, before the answering machine picked up.

"Hello?"

"Mrs. Travis?"

"Yes."

"This is Joan Petroski from Lincoln Elementary. Is Eva sick today, or will she be tardy?"

An eel of dread squirmed in Molly's stomach. "No, she... should be there."

There was a moment of silence on the other end. "She wasn't in homeroom at the beginning of the day."

"Beth Fisher, Lucy's mother, took her. We carpool."

Joan paused again. "Um, I don't know what to say. Lucy wasn't in homeroom either. You don't... do you think Eva could be hiding again?"

"And Lucy too?" It was possible. "Let me call Beth's cell and see if she dropped them off. I'll get back to you, OK?"

"All right. I'll wait for your call."

"Bye." Molly reset the phone and punched in the number for Beth's cell. It went right to voice mail. Great. She was either out of range or had the thing turned off. "Beth, it's Molly. Call my cell as soon as you get this."

She hung up the landline and put her cell in her pocket so it would be close when Beth called. Her mind locked up like rusted gears. Eva was missing again. If she was hiding…Molly checked herself. If Eva was hiding again, then there was something more going on than an imaginary friend telling her what to do. Something more serious. And now she'd pulled Lucy into it. Molly didn't even want to think about what it could be. She'd need to get Eva in to see a family counselor. They should all see a counselor.

For now she'd go to the school and talk to the principal.

Upstairs, Molly changed her clothes, put on sneakers, and was about to rush down the stairs when something stopped her. A feeling, an inclination, maybe intuition. Something told her to check in Sam's study. With the door already open, she entered and looked around. Nothing looked out of place or even oddly positioned.

From his desk, the manila folder he kept his writings in caught her eye. He hadn't willingly shown her those yet. Was there a reason for that? If she felt any hesitation in violating this boundary, it was washed away by her fear for her husband's well-being. Sitting in the desk chair, she opened the folder and skimmed the first page. It was a diary of some kind, a soldier's journal from the Civil War. Sam said he'd been working on a period piece. This was the bit she'd read the other morning when the window broke.

The soldier's name was Samuel Whiting. Molly had no idea if he was a historical or fictional character. The writing was gripping, though. Whiting was apparently going to assassinate the president. Abraham Lincoln. It was actually quite good. But what grabbed her attention even more than the writing or Whiting's account were the words scribbled at the bottom of the page. In Sam's handwriting, more sloppily written than the journal entries:

Kill Lincoln.

Her husband had signed his name below.

And that's when she noticed the second thing, the headline of the newspaper next to the folder: "Presidential Front-Runner to Give Gettysburg Address." That's right. Senator Stephen Lincoln was giving his speech in Gettysburg today.

She remembered Eva's warning from last night, while she walked in her sleep. *Daddy's time is up. He used it and went the wrong way.*

Molly could not have felt more chilled if someone stuck an IV in her vein and pumped in a liter of ice water. She began to shiver, and her palms broke into a cold sweat.

As she leafed through the other writings, she noticed the third thing, and it shoved her heart into her throat. On each page, misplaced uppercase letters were scattered throughout the text. She started with the first entry, quickly stringing the letters together. Then the second, the third, fourth, and fifth.

Oh, God. Please, no.

This wasn't happening. Again, Eva's words rushed back to her: *Jacob said Daddy's going to do something bad.*

Eva. Jacob. Sam. It couldn't be.

"God, please no."

She said those words over and over as she crossed the room and threw open the closet door. Sam's rifle was missing. She rummaged through every drawer of his dresser, remembering that Sam had told her he kept the magazine there, only it wasn't in any of them. Sweat beaded on her forehead and cheeks. Her pulse tapped out a quick rhythm in her neck.

She had to get to the school, had to get to Eva, but first she had to call the police. Her husband was going to do something very bad.

Sixty

Sam cranked the window so that the barrel of the rifle could sneak through the opening yet remain unnoticed. He lowered himself to one knee and propped the rifle butt against his shoulder. Wedging his left elbow against his chest to stabilize the stock, he peered through the scope and found the rostrum and Lincoln. The senator was still seated, a fake smile plastered on his face. A woman beside him, presumably his wife, had her hand on his. She glanced at him and smiled. The mayor was speaking, waving his hands about, and getting red in the face. The crowd cheered and clapped.

Sam put the crosshairs on Lincoln's head and steadied his hands, breathed in through the nose, out through the mouth, focusing himself. He wouldn't take the shot yet. No, he'd wait until Lincoln was standing and giving his speech. It'd be more dramatic that way, more memorable.

With the scope Sam scanned the crowd. Mostly he saw the backs of heads. A bunch of school kids were standing in front. Some paid attention, some shoved each other or whispered or watched the birds in a nearby tree. Running the crosshairs across the group, he noticed nothing out of the ordinary.

The air from outside was still and muggy, smelling of fresh rain and worms, and it reminded him of the air on the...

...hill, a little more than a hundred yards from home, Sam dropped to his stomach, heart beating like the hooves of stampeding horses, and pointed his rifle at the kitchen window. He had only one round in the chamber. He cursed himself now for not thinking to

bring the ammo box. He tried not to think about what he was about to do. If he thought about it, he'd chicken out.

Through the window he could see Tommy going off on Mom. His brother was swinging something wildly, knocking plates from the hutch and toppling chairs. It wasn't the hammer he had in his hand earlier. No, he'd traded it in for something Sam couldn't make out, something bigger than a hammer. Maybe the old billy club Dad kept hanging in the hallway.

Mom was scrambling and cowering, screaming hysterically. Tommy swung the club and missed; the momentum carried him into the wall, where he punched a hole. Sam tried to line up the sights, but there was too much movement in the window, nothing to put them on. And his hands were shaking so violently he could barely hold the barrel still.

He watched Tommy lunge at Mom and swing the club again, this time catching her in the back. She reared back and dropped out of view.

Tears blurred Sam's eyes. He had to do something. He had to stop Tommy. He thought about dropping the rifle and making a run for the house, bursting in and taking on Tommy hand to hand, but it would be futile. Tommy was bigger and stronger, faster too. In this crazed state he was more animal than human and would tear Sam limb from limb. The rifle was Sam's only hope, Mom's only hope. If he didn't take a shot soon, it would be too late.

Shutting his left eye, he drew in a deep, steady breath and blew it out. Tears and sweat made the stock slippery against his cheek, and he struggled to keep the rifle still. He pulled the stock away, wiped his cheek and eyes on his shirt, then tried again. This was crazy. If he missed, it'd all be over. Tommy would know what Sam had attempted, and he'd kill both his brother and mother.

In the kitchen Mom appeared again. She was staggering around the old farm table, Tommy on her heels. He no longer had the club. He caught Mom from behind and punched the back of her head hard, hard enough that it made Sam, a hundred yards away, flinch and shudder. She snapped forward, but he kept her from falling and punched her again. Sam's stomach writhed until he was sure he would vomit. He sucked in another deep breath and sighted the barrel against the window again.

Tommy had Mom's head on the table, his hands on her neck. His face was twisted and screwed up into a devilish grimace. The muscles in his arms were taut cords. Sweat soaked his shirt and matted his hair to his forehead. He was killing her.

Sam had a perfect line of fire. He pressed the butt of the rifle harder against his shoulder. This was it. He had to take the shot now, his only chance.

Suddenly the gravity of what he was about to do hit him, and it felt like someone had reared back and punched him in the chest. This was his brother he was about to shoot…with the intent to kill. His brother. Tommy.

No! That wasn't his brother. It looked like Tommy, but it wasn't him. It was something else, something evil, and Sam had to take the shot before Tommy killed Mom.

Sam curled his finger around the trigger, but even as the fat pad began to squeeze against metal, Tommy lifted his head and seemed to look directly through the scope at him.

Sixty-One

Concealed behind the heavy motel drapes, Sam Travis continued to observe the events on the rostrum through the lens of the scope. It was like watching an old silent film, and he found it disorienting. At this distance even the slightest drift or quiver of his hand caused Lincoln to disappear from view. The mayor must have said something funny because Lincoln laughed, looked at his wife, and took her hand in his.

Suddenly a guy in a gray suit was beside Lincoln, speaking into his ear. Sam hadn't seen where this man came from. He did see Lincoln shake his head and wave the man off. The man put his hand to his ear, then leaned close again. Lincoln shook his head, this time more emphatically.

The suit, obviously flustered, looked over his right shoulder, scanned the crowd, and held his hand to his ear again. He passed behind the senator and said something to the wife. She glanced at her husband, who nodded and squeezed her hand. Worry lines formed on her forehead. She rose and walked off the rostrum. Lincoln watched her leave. They were on to him; Sam knew they were. Somehow they'd gotten word.

Molly. It had to be. He'd left the writings on the desk—his writings, Samuel Whiting's writings—and she must have found them, put two and two together.

Thoughts of Molly invited thoughts of Eva. Sam tried to push them back into the darkness, but they filtered through like pinpricks of light.

Daddy, please, I love you.

If he was going to save her, he had to take the shot now. His heart thumped in his chest, and he blew out a breath to steady himself.

Lincoln rose, looked left in the direction of his departing wife, and approached the podium. On the ground more men in suits swarmed the rostrum like worker ants, some at its base, some on the platform itself. Their movements were methodical, precise, yet hurried.

Sam had to take the shot.

Daddy, I love you.

He coughed, and the scope jumped to the crowd full of families and children and older couples holding hands. They were all focused on Lincoln, oblivious to the threat just four hundred yards away. Sam panned the scope back toward the rostrum, slowly, so as not to further disorient himself. There, in the crowd near the school children, a man was turned and looking his direction—no, looking directly at him.

From this distance the man's face was shadowed with a look of...of what?

Sadness.

It couldn't be. He had to be looking at someone or something else. But he wasn't, was he? How was this possible? There was no way this guy could've spotted him. Sam wanted to pull the scope away from the man. He had to take the shot but found he couldn't, his attention drawn instead to this stranger. The man wore jeans and a flannel shirt, untucked. He looked to be about Sam's age, thirty-something, with wavy brown hair and sorrowful eyes. But there was something else about him, something odd. His skin, it had an unusual quality to it. It...

Sam's hands went numb, and his mouth felt like it'd been stuffed with cotton. He tried to swallow but couldn't.

The man, his skin shimmered like glitter.

What had Eva said about Jacob? That he looked like he'd been dipped in glue and rolled in glitter?

Jacob.

It couldn't be, but he was standing right there in the midst of the crowd, still staring Sam down through the scope. No, it couldn't be. It was another one of Sam's hallucinations. Tommy was gone, and now Jacob had replaced him. The stress of the moment was causing his mind to go haywire, to conjure up some image of hope.

But as much as Sam tried to focus on the mission, on the task at hand, Eva's voice wormed its way into his mind again.

I love you, Daddy.

Despite his awful treatment of her, she still loved him. And now she was in the hands of a nut-job—and what was he doing about it?

Those tiny points of light slowly grew as Eva's voice in his head drew nearer.

Daddy, do you know I love you?

Yes. How could he deny such unconditional love?

Perspiration rolled down the back of Sam's neck, between his shoulder blades. His hands began to quake again. He moved the scope to the rostrum and found Lincoln still speaking. The suits around him scanned the crowd and talked into their lapel mics.

He had to take the shot. Had to take it now.

Nevertheless he hesitated, filled with thoughts of Eva's arms around his waist and Molly sweeping up broken glass. Thoughts of family, of love. Of hope.

He placed the pad of his finger on the trigger, put the crosshairs on Lincoln's head, dead center. With the scope, it was an easy shot. There was no way he'd miss.

I love you, Daddy. Please, I love you no matter what.

No matter what.

The voice of Eva's abductor filled Sam's ears as well, that high-pitched tone. Creepy and dark.

But the shot was here, and he felt a great urge, a *need*, to take it, to end all this. Besides, if he wanted Eva safe he had to take the shot, didn't he?

Or was there another way?

A thought came to mind, just a glimmer of hope, but growing

brighter. Eva was calling him, drawing him. Her voice was a rope pulling him up from the murky waters, up toward the light.

There *was* another way. And he would take it.

He shut his eyes, opened just the right one, sighted through the scope, inhaled, exhaled, and squeezed the trigger.

Sixty-Two

STEPHEN LINCOLN GRIPPED THE PODIUM WITH BOTH HANDS. He'd insisted on presenting the speech even after Tony Wu told him of the call they'd received. A woman claimed her husband was going to make an assassination attempt. They had no validation of the threat, just a wife's panicked phone call. To be safe, Lincoln told Tony to get Emily off the platform. Tony wanted to shut the whole thing down, call it quits, and get Lincoln and Emily out of town as quickly as possible, but Lincoln refused. Twice. And Tony wasn't happy about it.

Now, as exposed as a lighthouse on a rocky point, Lincoln felt a fear like never before. But he couldn't show it. He couldn't let the crowd notice even a waver in his voice, a shadow of anything less than confidence in his demeanor. This was his time, his message, his passion. He had to deliver it with full and true conviction.

But the fear was still there. At any moment he expected the crack of a rifle shot and the sharp punch of a bullet.

He paused, said a quick silent prayer. His eyes surveyed the crowd. He doubted the shooter would be among the spectators. Security was too tight for anyone to sneak a weapon past the checkpoints. He considered the schoolchildren in front of him and had second thoughts about continuing with the speech. What of their safety? He threw a glance at the agent on the ground to his right. He didn't even know the man's name. He was tall and well built, had to be over two hundred pounds. His hand was at his ear, his eyes focused on a strip of shops and hotels to his left.

Lincoln glanced at his notes. He'd memorized his speech and delivered it to himself countless times, but suddenly he felt he knew none of it. This was ridiculous. The threat may be nothing at all, just the paranoia of a bitter wife. It was not validated, that's what Tony said. But obviously they were taking it seriously.

"My fellow citizens," Lincoln began. "Men and women, young and old, we stand here together on hallowed soil, on the fields of ancient battle where Americans shed their blood for the right to liberty and justice for all. For freedom.

"I too long for freedom, for personal choice, and in fact have fought for that right during my political career, only to have my world and my beliefs shaken last year by—"

To Lincoln's left the brick pillar supporting the rostrum's roof exploded in a spray of red dust and mortar, even as the crack of a distant rifle pierced the air. He flinched and ducked. Pandemonium broke out. Two agents were on him before he could turn around, pulling him to the platform's deck. Men scrambled. People screamed and yelled. Cursed. Children cried. Panic was in the air like a pelting rainfall.

How many shots had there been? Lincoln had heard only one, but in the commotion following there may have been another; he couldn't be sure. The men on top of him were hollering something, but he couldn't make out what it was. Though he tried to get up, they had him pinned.

Emily. All Stephen Lincoln could think of was Emily.

Had she made it to the car?

Sixty-Three

Sam never saw the chaos unleashed by his shot. He'd missed intentionally for just that purpose: to cause a distraction. A major distraction. As soon as his finger pulled the trigger and the bullet left the barrel, he tucked the rifle into his duffle bag and bolted from the room.

He headed for the motel's back exit. Behind him people poured out of their rooms into the hallways, wondering what was going on—was that a gunshot? Where was the shooter? In the distance sirens gave mournful wails. He had to hurry before the roads out of town were barricaded.

Down the steps he ran, taking them two, three at a time, almost falling more than once. He burst into the parking lot. The Escort was there waiting for him. He had no time to think about what had just unfolded, about Eva's voice in his head, in his heart, about the man with the glittery skin—Jacob—about the shot, the assassination that never was, about his daughter in the hands of a madman. He just ran.

He unlocked the Escort's door, tossed the duffle bag onto the passenger seat, and climbed in behind the wheel. The car started without hesitation, and he had to remind himself to stay calm, follow the plan, avoid drawing attention to himself.

It was beginning to rain again, sporadically, fingernail-sized drops here and there on the windshield. And he had no idea where he was going. He needed to get to Eva. If the psycho who had her was watching the speech on television, which seemed safe to assume, then he had seen the shooting and whatever holy mess had followed. No doubt the senator had been tackled to the ground for his own protection, as the whole area erupted in bedlam. Reporters wouldn't know for hours whether the senator was hit or not.

Sam's nightmare, though, was not knowing his daughter's whereabouts.

He needed to get out of town, get clear of the activity around the cemetery that was already rippling outward like shockwaves after a bombing.

Taking side streets, trying to stay close to the posted speed limit so as not to draw attention, he managed to find Fairfield Road and head south out of town beyond any erected roadblocks. Beyond the town line, he pulled the car to the side of the road and gripped his head with both hands. The adrenaline rush was waning and opening the door for his emotions to emerge. He had to keep it together; this was no time for a breakdown.

A township police car, one of the decked-out Chargers, headed toward him, siren and lights on full display. Sam scrubbed his face and held his breath, but the cop behind the wheel didn't even glance over as he sped by.

A sense of panic overtook Sam. Eva, his baby girl, his little buddy, was in the hands of a psycho, and there was nothing he could do about it. He couldn't go to the police, not now. They'd see right through him. Besides, if Molly was the one who called in the warning, the authorities were already looking for him. He'd have to find Eva on his own. But how? How? The question pounded in his skull like a jackhammer chipping away at granite.

Sam gripped the steering wheel and paused to pray. Nothing eloquent or elaborate, just a simple plea for help. But it was something. It was a start.

About a quarter mile ahead, a figure was standing alongside the road. The water on the windshield blurred Sam's view, and he swept the wipers once over the glass, revealing an oddly familiar man whose skin seemed to shimmer in the rain.

And he was pointing to Sam's left.

Sixty-Four

SYMON RUBBED THE TIPS OF HIS FINGERS AS HE PACED THE sunroom. While waiting for Sam Travis to take action, he'd squeezed the arms of the overstuffed chair so hard that he numbed the ends of each finger.

Then Sam had taken the shot.

A spray of red.

The senator dropping to the deck.

Sam had done it, actually hit his mark. On the television the pandemonium that unfolded was almost comical. In fact, it *was* comical. With Lincoln down, Symon had let out a sharp yelp, like a coyote, and startled Eva. She understood what had taken place and sat in stunned silence, watching with Symon as the news reporter, in a shaky voice, tried to comment on unfolding events.

Someone had taken a shot at Senator Stephen Lincoln. Of course, Symon knew full well who that someone was. So did poor little Eva. Her daddy was now the most wanted man in America. A very bad man indeed.

With eyes still fixed on the plasma screen, Symon patted her tiny shoulder. "It's OK, darling Eva. Daddy did the right thing. You'll come to understand that in the future."

He backed away from her and sat in a wicker chair. It creaked under his weight. Outside, the rain left silvery tracks down the glass panes. On the TV they were replaying the moment before the shot—Lincoln speaking, looking down at the podium, at his notes, glancing to his right, then flinching and going down, instantly covered by security agents willing to take the next bullet in his stead. At normal speed it looked like a clean shot, but when replayed at half-speed, Symon saw something that sent waves of heat through his blood. There, to Lincoln's left, an instant before he flinched and went down, something struck the brick support column and erupted in a spray of red dust.

Sam Travis had missed. Intentionally or not, he'd missed.

Anger flared in Symon like a stoked fire. The flames licked at his nerves. He sprang from the chair and rushed the television, kicking it over and shattering the plasma screen. Eva flinched and hunched down into the chair.

Symon paced the room like a criminal on death row whose time had come. His nerves burned, itched, twitched. His mind raced in all directions at once. This wasn't part of the plan, and he had no idea what to do next. He looked at Eva in her chair, so small, so vulnerable, and again thought of his own daughter. He'd warned Travis that if he didn't complete the mission Eva would die, but now he found himself unable to carry out that threat. She was too much like his own child, his Bethany.

Bethany.

That was her name, wasn't it? Now he had not only a face but also a name. He said it aloud, "Bethany." It felt comfortable, natural, coming out of his mouth. Like he'd said it a million times before, imprinting each syllable in the muscles of his tongue and lips. "Bethany." He was somebody. He was a father, a dad.

Bethany's daddy.

From the chair Eva said, "Who's Bethany?"

"We need to move, Eva. Daddy did a very bad thing, and we need to leave this place." He reached his hand toward her and had an image of doing the same thing with his Bethany. "We need to move now."

Sixty-Five

In spite of his once-active faith, Sam Travis had never believed in miracles, at least never believed they would happen to him, but what he saw, *whom* he saw, standing in the rain on the gravel shoulder along Fairfield Road made him a convert.

Jacob. It couldn't be, but it was. It had to be. He was the same man from the crowd, the man who'd found Sam in the window from so many yards away.

He was looking directly at Sam, pointing at something to his right. From this distance Sam couldn't tell what it was, but it had to be something off the road.

On a far hill, the flashing lights of another police car appeared. Sam knew he needed to get moving. He checked his side-view mirror and pulled onto the pavement. Just ahead, the road was empty. Jacob was gone. Sam hit the steering wheel hard. Had he been duped by another hallucination? Despair overtook him, tearing at him like the teeth and claws of ravenous wolves. The police car was upon him now, heading toward town where some nut had taken a shot at the senator. He had a sudden impulse to jump out of the Escort and surrender, to give himself wholly to these wolves. But the cruiser howled past in a blur of lights.

Up ahead, where the Jacob apparition had been pointing, a gravel lane cut off the main road, its deeply worn ruts divided by a grassy median. Maybe there was something to this after all. Sam decided to see where it led. What harm could that do? He had no other grand scheme to fall back on. No other way of finding Eva.

Gravel crunched beneath the tires, and dry grass scraped the car's undercarriage. His wipers were beating steadily now to battle the increasing rain.

The lane stretched out through grassy fields, its destination obscured by a rise. On the crest Jacob stood next to a tree. He was pointing over the slope. This time, as Sam grew closer, Jacob did not disappear. He was no more than fifty feet away now. Nevertheless, Sam was still convinced he was a hallucination, an image his brain had conjured from the descriptions given him by Eva. Thirty feet now, and Jacob's skin glimmered ever brighter, despite the downpour. It seemed to catch and refract whatever light was in the air, as though encrusted with miniature diamonds. Ten feet, and Sam could see the color of Jacob's irises, a brilliant azure, the stuff of the clearest, bluest skies on the sunniest of days. They were radiant, seeming to create their own light.

Now Jacob was right outside the car.

Sam thought of stopping and rolling down the window but didn't. It didn't feel right. Instead he met Jacob's eyes and felt warmth pour over him, a hot shower after being caught in the cold rain for too long. Those eyes spoke of hope, love, assurance. They had a quality that pierced Sam through his flesh, muscle, tendons, organs, all the way to his soul, infusing him with something he couldn't quite put a finger on. But it was good. This was no mirage, no hallucination. Sam didn't know what Jacob was—an angel? He'd probably never know, not really, but at the moment it didn't matter. Jacob was telling him that he was on the right path, heading in the right direction, to Eva, and that there was still light in the darkness, still something to grab hold of and hang on to. There was still hope.

Pushing the accelerator to the floorboard, Sam crested the hill. He glanced in the rearview mirror as he passed Jacob and saw that he had vanished again. But up ahead, another two hundred yards along the gravel path, a capacious white house appeared through the trees, the kind of mansion seen on plantations in the South—the kind where psychos hid with their abductees.

Sixty-Six

Symon grabbed his jacket and dragged Eva along, his hand large enough to overlap his first knuckles and thumb around her wrist. He had no plan, but he did have the advantage. He had a hostage. And if he played the game correctly, he might yet persuade Travis to complete the mission. Although now the mission was less important to him than surviving this whole thing so he could find his Bethany. And Eva would be his ticket for survival.

Out the front door they fled into the chilly November air, damp and thick with humidity. Overhead, the rain pattered on the porch roof in a syncopated rhythm, like a chorus of finger-tappers drumming on school desks.

Symon stopped and his breath caught in his throat. A car was approaching, and quickly, no more than a hundred yards away. It was him. Travis. Coming for his daughter.

Eva let out a sharp gasp and yanked free, but Symon caught her by the jacket before she made it off the porch.

"That's my dad," she cried, fighting his grip.

He yanked her hard, and she fell. "Come, Eva; we must be on our way." When she refused to get her legs under her, he stooped low, hoisted her with one arm wrapped around her waist, and carried her against his hip. She lashed and flailed like a salmon snatched from its upriver journey.

The car stopped, the door opened, and Travis popped out, holding his rifle at shoulder level.

In one quick and anything but smooth motion, Symon ripped the Beretta from his jacket pocket and pressed the barrel against Eva's head. Time seemed to freeze, as if the inner workings of the earth's machinery had frozen tight and ground to a sudden halt. Raindrops fell in slow motion, each one impacting the earth with such force that the sound reminded Symon of tribal war drums. Travis had his elbow propped on the open car door, rifle pointed in their direction, crosshairs on Symon's forehead (he could *feel* those crosshairs on him, tattooed on his flesh), while Symon had Eva in his grasp, the cold metal of the Beretta against her skull. He'd never shoot her. No, it would be like offing his own daughter, and he would never, ever, do that.

But Travis didn't know that.

Symon began working his way slowly back across the porch to the front door. If he got inside, he would have the advantage.

"Let her go," Travis yelled. His voice sounded shaky.

Symon only gripped Eva tighter and backpedaled faster.

"Daddy!" Eva yelled.

Symon shook her and told her to shut up.

"Let her go," came the order again.

Symon did not answer. He felt he had the upper hand here, and if Travis hadn't taken the shot yet, he wasn't going to.

"I love you, Daddy."

Symon squeezed his captive harder, so hard she squealed. "Shut up, Eva. I mean it." At last his heel bumped the doorjamb. The door was still open, and he ducked inside, around the corner from Travis's line of vision.

Sixty-Seven

SAM CURSED HIMSELF FOR NOT TAKING THE SHOT. HE'D PUT the crosshairs on the nut's forehead and had the angle, but the guy was moving around too much and holding Eva high and pressing that pistol to her head.

That pistol. The sight of it caused Sam's breathing to become erratic, hitched. His nerves were stretched wires, ready to snap. The shot was too risky. He'd only get one chance, and it had to be dead-on, had to be perfect to shut down the brain before it could send a signal to the trigger finger.

And now they'd disappeared into the house.

Panic clamped a vice around Sam's lungs, making it even harder to breathe. The rain was coming down faster now. His hair was stuck to his head, and he had to wipe at his eyes to clear the water from them.

Leaving the car door open and engine running, Sam headed from the stolen vehicle for the house. On the porch he paused and listened, hoping to hear Eva's voice inside.

Met by silence, he stepped through the doorway, past a small woven rug bearing a family crest of some sort. The two-story foyer echoed the sound of water dripping off Sam's elbows and striking the hardwood floor. The only other sound in the cavernous house was the soft ticking of a clock in another room. No breathing, no footsteps, no Eva.

He held the rifle chest high, ready to aim and fire in a fraction of a second. Cautiously, with his wet shoes squeaking on the varnished floorboards, Sam followed the hallway toward the back of the house. To his right a curved staircase led to the second floor. He doubted the psycho would take Eva there. That would be a trap, no escape route. To his left glass-paned French doors led to a formal dining room, and a glance revealed that it was empty. He passed a large kitchen and reached a great room on the right.

Still no Eva.

Sam stood on the carpet so that the sounds of his dripping clothes were muted. The ticking clock, he realized, was in this room, an ornately carved grandfather clock tucked into a corner. The television in the other corner was on the floor, its cracked screen facing up.

Fanning off from the great room was a wide sunroom. The transition from original house to this addition was seamless. Beyond the glass walls recently harvested fields stretched toward a pond and—

Movement on his right caught Sam's eye. There, more than halfway across the field already, the abductor had Eva in tow, practically dragging her along.

Sam ran out onto a brick patio and lifted the Winchester Model 70 to his shoulder. They were close to three hundred yards away by now, a difficult shot under the circumstances, with his heart tripping in his chest and the rain beating on his face. It would test every ounce of his skill.

You're a natural, Sammy.

Sam sighted the man in the scope, put the crosshairs on his head.

As if anticipating the impact of a bullet, the man flinched, stopped, and spun around. He faced Sam now, holding Eva's wrist with his left hand and the pistol to her head with the right. For a moment he stared at Sam across the field, his face slack, mouth slightly agape. Then he turned, still holding the gun to Eva's head, and walked with a hitched, clumsy gait toward the tree line another four hundred yards away, a good seven hundred yards from the house. In these conditions, an impossible shot for Sam.

Sixty-Eight

Molly felt as though she'd climbed out of her skin and into someone else's a thousand miles away. This wasn't happening, wasn't reality. But she'd already tried waking herself from the nightmare and met only disappointment.

It was all too real.

She stood in the parking lot of the motel, the Americana, where Sam had registered under a phony name, taken a shot at a senator and presidential hopeful, and fled in a stolen car. Sam...her husband, the man she'd married and loved and trusted and shared her life with. The man she'd nursed and cared for when he couldn't even dress himself or wipe himself on the toilet. And if that weren't enough to knock the air out of anyone's lungs, her Eva had been abducted.

Thankfully, Beth and Lucy had been found by a state trooper, Beth teetering on the edge of a coma, Lucy in hysterics. But it only underlined the danger Eva now faced. Molly's world was crumbling, and she had no footing, no handhold, no purchase. She was losing it.

She stood beside a police cruiser, umbrella in hand. Activity buzzed around her. US Capitol police, local cops, state troopers, anyone in a uniform or with credentials of some sort. Her mind kept going to Eva—Lucy said she'd been abducted, taken in Beth's Volvo. Then to Sam—her husband gone off the deep end. She had no more tears to cry. She was numb, in shock, maybe even in denial.

She thought of her baby girl in the hands of some creep, some demon...

Her husband, once so strong, so sure, her rock, now...

Molly chewed on a nail and looked around. Law enforcement

officials talked to each other, into phones and radios, and shouted orders. It was all a blur to her, the motion, the activity, like one massive organism rather than a thousand different moving parts. A chopper whizzed overhead, circled the area. Flying low, it flogged the ground with its powerful downwash, spraying water every which way and beating the air with its *wump-wump-wump.* Then a tall man in a suit was walking toward her, a phone to one ear and his hand against the other. He was leaning forward, squinting. He lowered the phone and bent low to meet Molly's eyes under her umbrella.

"Mrs. Travis?"

She nodded, unable to speak.

"They found 'em."

Sixty-Nine

Sam knew this was his best chance. The man was taking Eva farther away, headed for the tree line. He had to take the shot before too much distance was put between them, but he was shaking from the cold and rain and adrenaline. The crosshairs bounced around on the back of the man's skull. Sam couldn't risk jerking the rifle and putting Eva in its sights. He had to be sure.

She turned and looked at him, her eyes wide and sad, her hair soaked. Her skin was pale, almost translucent. Her mouth dipped at the corners in a pitiful frown. He remembered her words, the words of Jacob.

Jacob said Daddy's going to do something bad.

He'd done something bad all right. He'd failed his family, failed his dear Eva, rejected her love, and proven he was everything she feared he was. He'd failed Molly as well, cast her aside like yesterday's leftovers, and treated her worse than an enemy. He should turn the gun on himself right now and end it all, save everyone from further heartache. His life was ruined anyway.

Behind him a voice called his name, then another. He didn't turn. He had to keep the psycho with his daughter in the crosshairs.

"Sam Travis," the first voice said. It was a man's, deep and authoritative. "This is Officer Richardson of the Gettysburg Police. Put down your weapon."

Sam knew he had to act quickly. They'd found him, the man they believed had taken a shot at the senator with intent to kill, and they wouldn't wait around for him to explain himself and his circumstances.

"Sam." It was Richardson again. In the distance, the thrum of helicopter blades grew louder. "Put the weapon down and let us take care of this."

Within seconds the chopper was there to his left, hovering no more than thirty feet off the ground.

Eva's abductor stopped his forward progress and swiveled around.

Sam choked on his own saliva and nearly dropped his rifle.

No!

The psycho was Tommy. He was older now, his face more mature and angular, but there was no mistaking him.

Why hadn't Sam noticed this earlier? Because, of course, this was impossible. It wasn't Tommy; it couldn't be. Tommy was long dead. He rubbed the water from his face and let out a guttural moan. He found the duo in the scope again. It still appeared to be Tommy, and he was still holding that pistol to Eva's head.

Through the scope Sam detected the fear in his daughter's eyes. But behind the fear he saw love, deep love. He'd heard it on the phone earlier, yet to see it for himself was indescribable. In spite of all he'd done to her and all he'd become, in spite of how low he'd sunk and how despicable he'd acted, there was still love there.

She said something and he read her lips: "Daddy."

Richardson was still talking, his voice just audible above all the racket. "We'll handle this, Sam. Let us handle it."

The Tommy figure pulled Eva in front of him, pressed the barrel of the pistol harder against her head, and shook her. He yelled something that Sam couldn't hear over the pounding chopper blades and downpour. To his left the helicopter landed and cut its engine. The blades continued to beat at the air but slowed.

Sam put the sight on…

…Tommy's forehead. It was there in his scope. It was a nearly impossible shot, unlike any he'd ever taken. At this distance, through a pane of glass, it would require a miracle to pull it off. And besides that, my goodness besides that, this was his brother he was taking aim at, his blood, his kin, his big buddy. They'd played, laughed,

listened to music together, hunted, camped, worked, gotten spanked and grounded together. He thought of the time they'd shot Old Man Gruber's dog by accident. He'd shot at the same groundhog the dog was hunting. The dog lived, but when they got home Dad was waiting with his belt and delivered a pair of whoopin's like never before or after.

This was his brother he was going to pull the trigger on. Only it wasn't Tommy. It was something much worse. Tommy was already gone.

Sam steadied his hand, his darn shaking hand, drew in a long breath and held it. Tommy was still choking Mom while looking directly at Sam, taunting him, daring him to take the shot.

And Sam did.

He squeezed the trigger real steady, and that Winchester 70 popped and kicked back against his shoulder. Tommy's head snapped so violently that for a second Sam thought he'd blown it clean off, but then it came back up, and Tommy stood there motionless, the left side of his cranium missing and his skull teetering on his neck like a bobble-head doll. He wore a stupid grin on his face. A heartbeat later, Tommy buckled at the waist and fell forward, landing on Mom and rolling off to the side.

Freezing cold, Sam dropped his rifle and ran for the house. His legs were so weak and wobbly he almost went down more than a couple times. His arms hung numbly at his sides. When he reached the house, he heard Mom whimpering and coughing and sputtering inside. From the doorway he could see Dad lying in the hallway, his head a bloody mess. Sam rounded the corner into the dining room and found Mom on her knees over Tommy. Her face was tomato-red, smeared with tears and snot and Tommy's blood. She was rocking back and forth, her hands on her oldest son's back.

"Mom," Sam said. His voice seemed small, almost a whisper.

She looked at him through glassy eyes, twisted her face, and screamed, "You killed him! You killed my son."

"Sam, don't." The voice was muffled but familiar. Molly.

Sam didn't look at her, didn't pull his eyes from Tommy and Eva, but her voice burned in his ears. Tommy smiled at him—that same stupid grin—then tightened his grip on Eva's arm and shook her again.

"Please, Sam. Please." Molly sounded like she was crying.

"Sam, we can take care of it." Richardson. "Put down the weapon."

But he couldn't. Not now. He was the only one who could take the shot, or at least that's what he'd convinced himself of. He was the only one who *had* to take the shot. As if Tommy knew Sam's intentions (of course he knew, they were brothers), he crouched low and hid behind Eva. There was no shot now, not without a huge risk of hitting Eva.

Behind Sam Molly groaned, a pitiful sound squeezing through tight vocal cords.

He had to do something, but he had only one option. He thought of that shot he'd taken all those years ago, the impossibility of it, and weighed his chances of pulling it off again. He might be a good shot—*You're the one, Sammy*—but not that good. It'd be like hitting a soda can at four hundred yards in the pouring rain...and the can was on his daughter's head. His baby girl. There was no margin for error. Even the slightest movement, the smallest of muscle twitches, could be tragic.

That was it. He couldn't do it. He started to lower the rifle.

Molly's voice stopped him. "Sam, wait."

With the rifle still against his shoulder, he pulled his eye away from the scope. He looked down the barrel at the psycho with his daughter in the middle of the open field. The rain fell in sheets now, harder than it had all day.

"You can do this. You can save her. Eva." Molly's voice quivered like she was freezing. "God loves you, Sam. He loves you so much. You have to trust Him."

Trust was something Sam hadn't thought much of in the past months. He hadn't trusted anyone, let alone God. But Eva's love had changed that today, a lifeline lifting him out of that pit of despair and reassuring him there was one thing in this world that was OK to trust—unconditional love. How, though, could God still love him?

Do you know Jesus loves you?

How could that be? Sam had done nothing to earn such love. In fact, he'd done everything to reject it.

And yet he did know it. He'd known it since he was a kid.

Sam pressed his cheek against the rifle stock, blinked away the rain, found his brother and daughter in the scope. Tommy was on his knees behind Eva, one arm around her shoulders, the other holding the pistol to her head. Only a sliver of his face showed, one eye and an ear. He was trapped and desperate, a cornered wolf with its teeth at the neck of a rabbit. Any hint of a threat, and he might pull that trigger. It'd be suicide, but someone like Tommy might see that as the only way out.

Sam would only get one shot. If he squeezed off a round and missed…

He blinked again. Then he saw it, his shot. It was his only hope. But it was an impossible mark and way too risky.

"Trust him, Sam." Molly's voice was hoarse, but to Sam it was a shelter in the midst of the deluge. "He loves you."

Sam matched his breathing to his rapid heartbeat. *God, I trust You. I trust You. Jesus, help me.*

"I love you too, Eva," he whispered, and during the pause between two beats he pulled the trigger.

Seventy

THE BULLET PIERCED SYMON'S PALM LIKE AN AWL THROUGH leather, throwing the Beretta behind him. He spun to his left and fell back on his haunches, shaking his hand in an effort to ward off the imminent pain. First he noticed the blood, then the agony of white-hot jolts that shot up his arm to his elbow. Grabbing his mangled appendage, he curled onto his side and moaned.

■■■

Molly saw the rifle kick back against Sam's shoulder before she heard the blast. By the time she realized what had happened, Eva's abductor was spinning around and crumbling to the ground, holding his hand. Eva had broken loose and was on her way toward Molly and Sam.

Molly let out a shrill scream and took off for her daughter.

■■■

Symon lay still, processing what had just happened, letting the drizzle cool his face. His hand had been shot, nothing more. The pain was severe, yes, and reminded him of…of something, of the flashes from the pistol the big guy had in the trailer. That was the last time Symon had been shot. But it also reminded him of something else…

A voice said his name. The woman, kneeling over him, looked into his eyes. Her lips mouthed it this time. His name.

"Albert."

His name was Albert. He was Bethany's father. He was *somebody*. Albert, Bethany's daddy.

Albert.

Cradling his aching, bleeding hand, he propped himself up on his right elbow and found the Beretta in the wet grass not five feet from him. To his right the girl was running. She was in a full sprint and looked so much like his Bethany that it brought tears to his eyes. She was running from him, his Bethany. He couldn't lose her again. Albert scrambled to his feet, slipped on the slick grass, went to one knee, and got his feet under him once more.

Eva—Bethany—turned and looked back at him. There was sadness in her eyes. Deep sadness. She didn't want to leave him.

He wobbled and swayed, then took one step toward his Bethany. He had to go after her. He would risk everything to be with her again.

Something punched him in the chest, and he stumbled backward. Bethany and her mother both flinched and ducked their heads. Beyond them Albert saw a line of men in dark uniforms. He stumbled backward, felt another blow, this one higher up on his chest and to the left. It corkscrewed him around so that he lost his balance, went to his knees. His vision blurred, and he suddenly felt very heavy and tired.

He'd lost her, lost his Bethany.

■ ■ ■

Sam lay on his back on the patio, rain spattering his face. He opened his eyes, squinted. The tears were coming now, faster than the falling rain—tears of relief, of joy, of sadness, of emotion unimaginable. He saw a police officer bending over him, and...

...with one hand on Sam's shoulder, the officer squeezed.

"You OK, son? You all right?"

Sam tried to talk but couldn't. What had he just done? What horrible crime had he committed? Had he really shot his own brother? He looked at his mother bent over the dead body of Tommy, and her tear-stained, reddened face filled him with such remorse that it nearly buckled his knees. He steadied himself against the door frame.

And nodded absently.

The cop patted his shoulder. "You did what you had to do, son."

Sam sat up and felt the cop's hand slide off his shoulder. Then Eva was there, falling into his arms, tumbling them both backward.

"I love you, Daddy," Eva said. She was crying but smiling at him. Water ran down her face and dripped off the tip of her nose.

Sam hugged her close and said, "I love you too, Eva. My baby girl."

Then Molly was there, on her knees next to them. She cupped his face in her hands and smiled at him.

"I love you, you crazy man." She punched his chest and said it again.

The darkness within him was gone now, driven out by the light that shone through his wife's smile and his daughter's eyes.

The light of love.

Seventy-One

Trial Excerpts

The following excerpts were taken from the transcript of the federal court case trying Mr. Samuel Michael Travis for the attempted assassination of Senator Stephen William Lincoln.

The examiner is prosecuting attorney Mr. Richard Albright. The witness is government-appointed psychiatrist Dr. Millard O'Connor.

Albright: In your estimation and professional opinion, Dr. O'Connor, at the time of the alleged assassination attempt did Mr. Travis possess the mental capacity to determine whether his actions were morally wrong or not and whether they violated the law?

O'Connor: In my estimation and opinion, I believe not, sir.

Albright: You believe not?

O'Connor: That is correct, sir.

Albright: Are you not certain?

O'Connor: Absolute certainty is hard to come by in this field. But I believe with some guarded certainty that Mr. Travis suffered from a form of brief reactive psychosis or temporary schizophrenia.

Albright: Could you elaborate on those diagnoses, Dr. O'Connor?

O'Connor: Certainly. Both involve temporary bouts of psychosis during which the individual suffers from delusions, paranoia, hallucinations, mood changes, and a variety of other irrational behaviors.

Albright: What causes the onset of such mental disturbance?

O'Connor: Usually stress, a specific psychosocial causative

stressor. The patient, under an enormous amount of stress, copes by retreating into a state of psychosis.

Albright: And how long does this state of psychosis usually last?

O'Connor: It can vary from a few days to weeks, but almost always less than a month. In rare cases it can become a chronic condition.

Albright: Can become a chronic condition?

O'Connor: If there are preexisting personality disorders.

Albright: And to your knowledge, did Mr. Travis have any preexisting personality disorders?

O'Connor: To my knowledge, no, sir, he did not.

Albright: What was the specific psychosocial stressor that may have triggered this temporary psychosis?

O'Connor: Mr. Travis endured a fall on the job and suffered a closed head injury. The injury left him unable to return to his line of work. He's a self-employed carpenter.

Albright: How long ago did this fall occur?

O'Connor: Thirteen months ago.

Albright: Dr. O'Connor, what led you to believe Mr. Travis suffered from this temporary psychosis?

O'Connor: His own testimony, sir. Mr. Travis believes he was visited, influenced, if you will, by a captain from the Civil War.

Albright: Visited?

O'Connor: Yes, through journal entries. He believes this Captain Samuel Whiting was contacting him through these writings and influencing him, guiding him, to assassinate Senator Lincoln.

Albright: And how did this soldier contact him through these writings?

O'Connor: Mr. Travis believes that while he was sleeping or daydreaming, he wrote the journal entries.

ALBRIGHT: He wrote them, as in Mr. Travis wrote them?

O'CONNOR: Correct.

ALBRIGHT: And he believes this Samuel Whiting was using him as a medium of some kind, possessing him?

O'CONNOR: Mr. Travis didn't use those terms, but, yes, that is the sense of it.

ALBRIGHT: And is it true that he believes this to be the same Samuel Whiting, in fact Jefferson Samuel Whiting, who himself was found guilty of plotting to assassinate President Lincoln in 1863?

O'CONNOR: A little-known fact, but yes, sir, the same Jefferson Samuel Whiting.

ALBRIGHT: The prosecution has submitted as Exhibit A the journal entries, handwritten by Mr. Samuel Travis. What else did Mr. Travis say, Dr. O'Connor?

O'CONNOR: He believes he was visited by his deceased brother, Thomas.

ALBRIGHT: And did Mr. Travis elaborate on the circumstances surrounding Thomas Travis's death?

O'CONNOR: He did.

ALBRIGHT: Can you share what he said with the court?

O'CONNOR: Mr. Travis said his seventeen-year-old brother had gone insane and attacked their parents. After beating their father to near-death, Thomas then began assaulting their mother. Mr. Travis, fifteen at the time, fled with his rifle and from outside the home shot his brother in the head while he was beating their mother.

ALBRIGHT: The prosecution would like to enter as Exhibit B the police records dated April 12 to April 21, 1987.

ALBRIGHT: Dr. O'Connor, to the best of your knowledge, did Mr. Travis have a bout of temporary psychosis when he shot and killed his brother?

O'CONNOR: That's really impossible to know—

ALBRIGHT: To the best of your knowledge.

O'CONNOR: To the best of my knowledge, no, he did not.
ALBRIGHT: So Mr. Travis has a history of completely sane violence with a rifle.
O'CONNOR: I don't know that I'd—
ALBRIGHT: Thank you, Dr. O'Connor. No further questions.

■■■

The examiner is defense attorney Mr. Allen Sutter. The witness is Officer Glenn Richardson, Gettysburg Police Department, PA.

SUTTER: Officer Richardson, you were the first one on the scene at the house at 120 Fairfield Road, correct?
RICHARDSON: That's right.
SUTTER: Can you elaborate on how you found Mr. Travis?
RICHARDSON: When we received word that there'd been a credible tip about an assassination attempt, we blew the phones up, put out an APB on the vehicle description Mrs. Travis had given, an '02 white F150 with lettering on the doors: Samuel M. Travis, general carpentry. We all figured he'd be driving something different, though, something stolen. So I called the surrounding counties and checked for any reports on stolen vehicles. There was one, an '08 maroon Ford Escort, that caught my attention because it was stolen from the campus of Shippensburg University, not three miles from where some hunters came across Travis's truck ditched on state lands. I was now looking for an '08 maroon Escort...a million of them on the roads. I drove down Fairfield Road, en route to set up a perimeter barricade, and noticed down the lane to the old Beaufort place a maroon Escort. I ran the plates, and bingo, it was our car. Dumb luck, really.
SUTTER: And what did you find at the residence?
RICHARDSON: I found Travis in the backyard with his rifle

pointed at Drake.

SUTTER: For the record, Officer Richardson is speaking of Albert Drake. Officer Richardson, was Mr. Travis's daughter, Eva, with Mr. Drake?

RICHARDSON: Yes, sir. He held her in front of him with one arm and held a handgun to her head with the other.

SUTTER: And how far away were Mr. Drake and the girl?

RICHARDSON: A good four, five hundred yards, I'd say. Pretty good ways off. Just beyond them was a tree line.

SUTTER: What did you do when you got there?

RICHARDSON: First, I got on the horn and told the feds I'd found them, Mr. Travis and his daughter. Then I told Travis to drop the rifle.

SUTTER: Did he comply?

RICHARDSON: No, he did not.

SUTTER: Officer Richardson, did it appear to you that the girl, Eva Travis, was in imminent danger from Mr. Drake?

RICHARDSON: He had a gun to her head.

SUTTER: But did it appear to you to be an urgent situation?

RICHARDSON: He had a gun to her head. That's pretty urgent.

SUTTER: Go on, Officer Richardson; what happened next?

RICHARDSON: The feds and staties were there within minutes, like they'd climbed out of the ground. Sharpshooters were set up to get a bead on Drake, but with the way he was positioned behind the girl, a safe shot was impossible. They didn't want to use the chopper either because of the girl. If Drake got spooked, there was no telling what he might do.

SUTTER: And what was Mr. Travis doing during this time?

RICHARDSON: Nothing. I mean, the same thing. He was on one knee aiming his rifle at Drake and the girl. We didn't want to spook him either. It was touch and go.

SUTTER: Officer Richardson, was this a protocol kind of situation?

RICHARDSON: Absolutely not. Whenever a child is involved, extra caution is taken. Plus, we all thought we knew the motive behind Travis's actions, with his daughter being held hostage by Drake. We wanted to take him alive.

SUTTER: Would you say Mr. Travis was acting much like any father would to protect his daughter, that he was only doing what he thought necessary to prevent harm or even death from coming to her?

RICHARDSON: I would say that, yes.

SUTTER: When did Mr. Travis take his shot?

RICHARDSON: It was soon after the feds arrived. Quite a shot too. Right through the hand holding the weapon.

SUTTER: How difficult a shot was that?

RICHARDSON: Under those conditions, for a military-trained sniper it would have been a tough shot, not impossible, but tough. Hitting a four-inch by four-inch target at five hundred yards, in the pouring rain, with a hunting rifle? For a civilian, I'd say an impossible shot.

SUTTER: So in your estimation and professional opinion, Mr. Travis is a pretty good shot.

RICHARDSON: Good or lucky.

SUTTER: Lucky? But he didn't seem like he was willing to gamble his daughter's life on luck, did he?

RICHARDSON: No, he didn't.

SUTTER: So it was a good shot, a remarkable shot even, not luck. Would you agree?

RICHARDSON: Yes.

SUTTER: For a marksman like Mr. Travis, would hitting a human target at, say, four hundred yards be difficult?

RICHARDSON: No. Most sharpshooters would say that was a chip shot.

SUTTER: So if a sharpshooter missed at that distance, there

would be probable cause to believe he missed intentionally.

RICHARDSON: I would certainly think so, unless he had a malfunction with his weapon or something caused him to lose his focus.

SUTTER: But it's probable.

RICHARDSON: Yes, definitely probable.

SUTTER: Thank you, Officer Richardson.

Seventy-Two

Letters From Prison

Baby girl,

I feel like I didn't really get a chance to explain things to you, partly because of circumstances, partly because I've been afraid to, not that I doubted your ability to understand, but rather my ability to offer an accurate explanation. Listen to me, making excuses already. I was scared, plain and simple. Scared of myself, scared of what I went through, scared of where I was, scared of the truth.

It started that night the window broke. I can't explain it, but something happened to me then. A darkness surrounded me and closed in. Day after day it grew darker and more oppressive. Scared me to death. Man, it scared me. The darkness, it overcame me, controlled my thoughts, my feelings, my attitudes, everything. It was like I was somebody wholly different. And you noticed it, didn't you?

I treated you terribly, and for that I don't know if I will ever forgive myself. Looking back on it now, it was like a nightmare. I remember bits and pieces, like those ice floats you see in the Arctic Ocean, moving here, moving there, but there's so much more under the surface. I don't know if you can understand it now, but I pray someday you will—that was not me, not your daddy. It was something dark. I was lost in it.

But you found me. No matter how dark it got, there was always a ray of light, and it was your love.

Thank you, Eva. My baby girl. I may not be able to hold

you in my arms right this moment, but I'm holding you in my heart. You're my hero; you know that? You gave me the gift of love, your love, God's love. That'll satisfy me for a thousand Christmases.

Can't wait to see you again.

Your dad

▪▪▪

Baby girl,

I've been thinking about something, wanting to tell you, but I don't half believe it myself. I haven't told anyone, not even your mother. It's time, though. It's time to tell at least you, and then if you want to tell Mommy, you can. I suppose I'll get around to telling her myself sooner or later.

I saw him. You know who I'm talking about. The first time was there in the crowd when the senator was talking. He looked right at me. It was then I knew you were telling the truth all those times you said you saw him and talked to him. I'm sorry I didn't believe you. So sorry.

Then I saw him again when I was coming after you. He showed me where you were. He looked just like you described him too. Like someone dipped him in glue and rolled him in glitter.

I don't know who or what he was, but I do know that if he hadn't shown me the way, I wouldn't have found you when I did. Have you seen him since that time? I've looked for him, can't stop myself from looking. In the crowds here, in the yard, in the mess hall, but I don't see him. I'm starting to doubt I'll ever see him again.

See you soon.

All my love,

Dad

■■■

Molly,

I know we didn't get a lot of time to talk following the mess I made of things, and there's so much I want to say to you. So much happened. It's hard for me to think about it all at one time. I find myself remembering snippets here and there, trying to fit them together like lost pieces to a puzzle. One by one I put them in place. After a while, the full picture will start to emerge, I'm sure, but for now it's just fragments I'm going off of.

When we're together again and I have the full story in my head, I'll tell you everything. You deserve to know. One thing I remember crystal clear, though, is your voice breaking through the static that day behind the old house. You told me to trust. When I find a quiet place here (which is nearly impossible) and close my eyes and listen extra hard, I can hear your voice just as real as if you are next to me.

"Trust Him, Sam," you said. "God loves you."

And I did. Sure as I'm writing this letter, I did. I thought of you and Eva, and how much you both needed me and I needed you. I thought of Eva, and how there was no way I was letting that guy leave with her. And I thought there was no way I could make that shot on my own. I had to trust Him. And you told me to.

I need you, Molly. I know that more now than ever. You're everything to me. Thank you for sticking by me. Thank you for loving me no matter how unlovable I can be.

There's one more thing. When I get home again, I'm going to tell you everything about my childhood and Tommy. You deserve to know that. You need to know it.

Love you,

Sam

❊❊❊

Molly,

Hi, babe. Life here is slow and monotonous. I have so much time to think and pray. Lately my mind has been on the others who were caught up in this horrible web. The Moellers, the widows, that cop, and poor Thad. I miss him, you know. He was there for me when I needed a friend. Can you put some flowers on his grave for me?

There's one thing I haven't told anyone, not even the lawyer. Don't ask me why I didn't tell, probably was just too scared. Everyone was trying to paint me as something I wasn't. The prosecuting attorney wanted to make me sane, my attorney wanted to make me a devoted, protective father doing what he had to do to rescue his daughter. I don't know if I was sane or not. I really don't. I suppose it doesn't matter now.

You remember me saying I was seeing my brother, Tommy, right? In our house, that day at the battlefield, at the old house. Well, I saw him there at the end too. I thought he had Eva, that he'd somehow come back from the dead and finally got his revenge on me by taking my daughter. I was so scared. If you'd cornered me then, I would have sworn on my own grave that it was him. Even now I'm not totally convinced he wasn't there. I know it sounds strange, and no, I'm not going insane now, but every cell in my body knew it was him in that field with Eva. He was there. The man I shot, the hand, it was Tommy's.

Anyway, I guess that doesn't matter now either. I just had to get that off my chest. Isn't that the most idiotic thing?

And there's something else. My mother came to visit me here a few days ago. Can you believe it? She actually came the whole way up here to see me. I asked her a lot of questions, and we had a good talk. She finally opened up to me. Then she hit me with a real shocker. She told me there was something I needed to know about Samuel Whiting. Apparently he's family. A great-great-great uncle on my mom's side or something like that. She said there were other family members who'd gone off the deep end too. Isn't that the weirdest thing?

So that got me thinking. Whiting, Tommy, me. This darkness has been in our family, moving from generation to generation. Molly, it's like it had been following me, waiting for the right time. I try not to think about it anymore.

Can't wait to see you again.

Love,

Sam

Seventy-Three

Other Notes

Appearing in the *Milwaukee Journal Sentinel*:

> GETTYSBURG—Albert W. Drake, 42, passed on Friday, November 19. He was the husband of Nicole Drake, of Jonesville, WI, whom he married on July 17, 1990. Albert was a graduate of Glidden High School. He was the son of Thomas and Florence Drake. In addition to Nicole, Albert leaves behind a daughter, Bethany. A private service will be held for the family only, at an undisclosed location.

❖ ❖ ❖

Excerpt from the transcript of the radio show *Mitch Lewis Live*, which aired February 10. The host is Mitch Lewis, and the guest is "Lucretia Billows."

Lewis: OK, all you fans of conspiracies and cover-ups, boy, have I got a tale to tell you. This one's right out of the books, a real barn burner. Remember back in November when that Travis fella took a shot at Senator Lincoln? If you've been watching the news, you know he claims he missed on purpose and that he was trying to save his daughter who'd been kidnapped by one Albert Drake, the man allegedly responsible for six murders in and around the Gettysburg area in the week preceding November 19.

Drake, as you've heard, was shot and killed by the police. Well, there's more to the story than meets the eye. Mr. Drake, it seems, is a man of mystery, a man who died twice. A year and a half ago he went missing. Witnesses said he'd been shot and killed and his body dumped in Lake Michigan, off South Shore Park, in Milwaukee. A search commenced, but his body was never found. Regardless, he was pronounced dead. Then, a few months ago, he shows up again on some murder spree that ended with the kidnapping of a little girl and his own death—the second time.

With me today on the phone is Lucretia Billows. That's an alias. She's asked that her real name not be used for her own protection. Lucretia knew Mr. Drake before he died the first time and has some light to shed on his mysterious identity and proclivity for death.

Lucretia, welcome to *Mitch Lewis Live*. We're happy to have you on the show.

Billows: Thanks, Mitch. Um, I'm glad to be here.

Lewis: Lucretia, why don't you start off by telling us your relationship with Drake?

Billows: Sure, um, Albert—he liked being called Albert—and I were both part of a group called the Marxist Brotherhood. As the name implies, we were Marxists. There were a couple hundred of us altogether. We were a small group as far as those kind of groups go, but we had some big ideas.

Lewis: What kind of ideas?

Billows: Government takeover, mainly. We were…we were planning to take over the government by infiltrating it with Marxists. I can't get into how we were going to do it, but that was our plan. Um, when Albert joined our group, he was kind of an outsider from the start. The other guys were really gung ho about the mission, you know, and Albert, he–he just wasn't. He was brainy, really smart, knew all kinds of things, useless stuff even, and the other guys, they teased him a lot but kept him around because he was useful.

LEWIS: So what were the circumstances surrounding his death the first time?

BILLOWS: We were supposed to meet, to get together in one of the guy's homes, a trailer. Is it OK if I don't mention names? I have to be careful.

LEWIS: Absolutely.

BILLOWS: OK, um, we were getting together at this guy's trailer, and Albert was one of the first ones there. He got in an argument with another guy, said he was leaving the group and spilling his guts. The other guy...shots were fired, bam, bam, bam—it was so loud in there—and Albert was hit three times in the chest. I can still see it. He stumbled back a couple feet and fell against the door. He looked at his chest, and then at me, like he was surprised or something. Then he went down.

LEWIS: In the house, the trailer? He was shot inside?

BILLOWS: Yeah, shot dead. Or that's what I thought at first. I panicked, but the other guy, he was real cool about it, made some phone calls, and before I knew it they were taking Albert's body away in an ambulance.

LEWIS: And did they dump his body in Lake Michigan?

BILLOWS: No, some guy was paid off to tell the cops that he'd seen Albert shot, and another was paid off to say he saw a body that looked like Albert's being dumped in the lake off South Shore Park.

LEWIS: So what happened to Albert's body?

BILLOWS: Well, apparently he wasn't dead when they took him away. And the ambulance, it wasn't even real, at least not real in the sense that they took him to a hospital. They took him to our headquarters. At the time it was located in downtown Milwaukee.

LEWIS: Wait a minute. So let me get this right. The ambulance was a real ambulance, lights and everything, but the drivers had been paid off too? Or were they part of your group?

BILLOWS: I'm not sure. They were either paid off or threatened. We had friends in some very high places.

LEWIS: Such as?

BILLOWS: Name it. The police, local government, big government, judges. Everywhere. They weren't officially part of our group, but they helped us, like, sympathized with us.

LEWIS: Unbelievable. So, in a sense, you'd already infiltrated the government, the ball was rolling.

BILLOWS: Oh, yeah. We had our fingers in every aspect of social life. But the guys, they wanted more, they wanted the whole thing.

LEWIS: OK, so the ambulance takes Drake's body away. Then what?

BILLOWS: A group of doctors we worked with nursed him back to health and reprogrammed him. That's what they called it.

LEWIS: Reprogrammed? Can you be more specific?

BILLOWS: I don't know how specific I can, I can be. I wasn't there for all the training sessions, but basically, I mean what they did was brainwash him. Erase his brain and start over. It was big-time stuff, a lot of torture, isolated confinement, sleep deprivation, stuff like that.

LEWIS: And were they successful?

BILLOWS: Not totally. That's when I started getting uncomfortable. Some of the guys, they were so desperate to make this work, they, um, got involved in occult kind of stuff. Weird stuff. Creeped me out. They wanted to assassinate Lincoln, said he was a major obstacle, that if he won the presidency, which it looked like he would, he would ruin everything they'd done so far. But Albert just didn't have the skills to pull it off. Mentally he did, but physically he just wasn't ready. So they went looking for someone else, someone obscure, and found Travis. That's when they were at their deepest with the occult stuff. Finally I had enough and left the group. I've been in hiding ever since. Beyond that, I don't know what they did or how they pulled it off.

LEWIS: Wow. Wow. What a story. So if we put the pieces together, we can assume Drake was sent to Gettysburg to kidnap Travis's daughter as leverage to get Travis to take a shot at Lincoln while he gave his speech on national television. Travis had the physical skill they needed—he was a crack shot with a rifle—and he was unassuming.

BILLOWS: And he was...he was vulnerable. They prey on the weak.

LEWIS: Wow. All I can say is wow. Lucretia, thank you for joining us. I hope someday you can share your story in its fullest without fear of retaliation. You take care and be safe, OK?

BILLOWS: Thanks, Mitch. I'll stay on the move.

Excerpt from an Associated Press article that appeared in the *Washington Post*:

> In a move that raised many eyebrows around the country, President Lincoln visited his would-be assassin in the high-security Allenwood Federal Correctional Complex in Allenwood, PA. Prison officials said the meeting between President Lincoln and Samuel Travis, the man who attempted to assassinate then-Senator Lincoln, lasted a little more than an hour. Later the same day Mr. Lincoln exercised his right as president and granted Travis a full pardon, cutting short Travis's eighteen-year sentence.

Seventy-Four

THE SKY HAD NEVER SEEMED BRIGHTER TO MOLLY, THE AIR never cleaner. The smell of cut grass was in the air, and somewhere in the distance a lawnmower hummed. Overhead, a couple starlings bantered with a hawk. By Molly's side Eva gripped her hand tightly and smiled up at her. She'd gone through a growth spurt in the last year and lost some of her baby fat. She was looking more and more like a little lady.

"You ready for this, sweetie?"

"Ready, Mom. I can't wait to see him."

Molly looked at her watch: 9:03 a.m. He should be emerging from the building anytime now. The Allenwood correctional facility was an imposing structure, and every time Molly visited Sam here, she felt intimidated by its size and coldness. But today it didn't seem so big or chilly.

She combed her free hand through her hair, pushed a few loose strands behind her ear. "How do I look?" she asked Eva.

"You look pretty, like you always do. How do I look?"

"Beautiful. Like an angel."

Then, just like that, the glass door swung open, and he was standing there in street clothes, jeans and a blue T-shirt, duffel bag in one hand. A free man.

Eva let go of her hand and said, "Daddy's back." Then she took off toward Sam.

Tears blurred Molly's eyes and put a lump in her throat.

■■■

No sooner had Sam passed through the door and into the shade of the building's overhang than Eva was on her way to him, arms open wide. She was smiling big and bright, and tears were rolling down her cheeks. Sam released his duffel bag and dropped to his knees. He took her in his arms and almost fell over backward. Over the past year and a half he'd seen her only a handful of times and hadn't been able to touch her at all. She smelled great, like soap and shampoo, and fit perfectly in his arms.

"I love you so much, Daddy. I'm so glad you can come home with us."

"Me too, baby girl. Me too."

Then Molly was there, and Sam released Eva and stood. When his wife smiled at him, it was as if beams of light radiated from her pores. She looked stunning. Without hesitation she threw herself at him, and he was there to catch her. They held each other for a long time without saying a word. They'd been through so much, so much darkness, but things were different now—and always would be.

"I love you," Molly whispered into his ear.

Sam squeezed her. "I love you too. Let's go home."

With one arm around his wife, he reached over and put his other around his daughter, who had hoisted his duffel bag over her shoulder. Together the three of them stepped out from the shade into the light.

Note to the Reader

As of the writing of this, I have three daughters and a fourth on the way. By the time it meets your eyes I will have four daughters. I know well the love between a daddy and his girls. I know the love a daddy has for his children. Many of you do too. And every day it reminds me of the love my heavenly Father has for me.

Reader, friend, God loves you. I know it's become somewhat of a bumper sticker cliché in recent history—Smile, God loves you—but it's a cliché that rings true. He does love you. In fact, He loves you more than you could ever love Him back. We've never experienced that kind of love before. Human love, even at its best and purest, is still flawed. It has to be because we are flawed, and imperfect people can't offer perfect love. But God can, and He does.

I know many of you don't want to be preached to—that's not why you pick up a novel—but some things just need to be said. God's love for you is unconditional; it has no bounds, no limits, no prerequisites, and knows no bias. Nothing you do, nothing you have done, can quench His love. It's a fire burning brightly, and no amount of water can extinguish it. This is the love you've been searching for your whole life.

So what's the one thing He asks for in return? Simply that we accept His love.

His love for us—for you—drove Him to set into motion the most astounding act of sacrifice this world has ever seen. He sent His Son, Jesus, to this world to take the punishment for our crimes, our selfishness, our hatred, our sin. His love produced the greatest gift mankind has ever known—the gift of eternal life. And all we have to do is accept it.

OK, that's my preaching. Now a personal message. Thank you. I've said it before and I'll say it a million times, until my mouth goes dry and blisters and I can't speak any more—I have the greatest readers in the industry. Many of you have been with me from the beginning, from my first announcement right before *The Hunted* released that I was diagnosed with colon cancer. You've supported me, encouraged me, and prayed for me. And though it's impossible for me to know you all by name, please know that I appreciate every one of you and pray for you. And I pray your numbers will increase and more people will be exposed to these stories of hope and redemption, faith and forgiveness. Stories of love.

—Mike Dellosso

Coming in 2012 from Mike Dellosso—*Frantic*

One

The night Marny Toogood was born it rained axe heads and hammer handles.

His grandfather made a prediction, said it was an omen of some sort, that it meant Marny's life would be stormy, full of rain clouds and lightning strikes. Wanting to prove her father wrong, Janie Toogood named her son Marnin, which means "one who brings joy," instead of the Mitchell she and her husband had agreed on.

But in spite of Janie's good intentions, and regardless of what his birth certificate said, Marny's grandfather was right.

At the exact time he was delivered into this world and his grandfather was portending a dark future, Marny's father was en route to the hospital from his job at Winden's Furniture Factory where he was stuck working the graveyard shift. He'd gotten the phone call that Janie was in labor, dropped his hammer, and ran out of the plant. He wanted to be there when his son was born. Fifteen minutes from the hospital his pickup hit standing water, hydroplaned, and tumbled down a steep embankment, landing in a stand of eastern white pines. The coroner said he experienced a quick death; he did not suffer.

One week after Marny's birth his grandfather died of a heart attack. He too didn't suffer.

Twenty-six years and more than a couple lifetimes of hurt later, Marny found himself working at Condon's Gas 'n Go and living above the garage in a small studio apartment George Condon rented to him for two hundred bucks a month. It was nothing special, but it was a place to lay his head at night and dream about that dark cloud that relentlessly stalked him.

But one thing his mother told him every day until the moment she died was that behind every rain cloud is the sun, just waiting to shine its light and dry the earth's tears.

Marny held on to that promise, those last words of his mother, and thought about them every night before he succumbed to sleep and entered a world that was as unfriendly and frightening as any fairy tale forest—the place of his dreams, the only place more dark and doomful than his life.

The day reality collided with the world of Marny's nightmares and those storm clouds grew darker than he'd ever seen them, it was hotter than blazes, strange for a June day in Maine. The sun sat high in the sky, and waves of heat rolled over the asphalt lot at Condon's Gas 'n Go. The weather kept everyone indoors, which meant business was slow for a Saturday. Marny sat in the garage bay, waiting for Mr. Condon to take his turn in checkers, and wiped the sweat from his brow.

"Man, it's hot."

Mr. Condon didn't look up from the checkerboard. "Ayuh. Wicked hot. News man said it could hit ninety today."

"So it'll probably get up to ninety-five."

Mr. Condon rubbed at his white stubble. "Ayuh."

He was sixty-two and looked every bit of it. His leather-tough skin was creased with deep wrinkles. Lots of frown lines. Marny had worked for him going on two years but felt like he'd known the old mechanic for decades. George Condon had one daughter in the area. She lived upstate, near Caribou. His other daughter married a navy man and lived in Japan. He rarely spoke of either, but once Marny caught him staring at a faded photo of the three of them when the girls were but children. He kept the photo in a drawer of his desk.

Mr. Condon made his move, looked at Marny, and squinted. Behind him, Ed Ricker's Dodge truck rested on the lift. The transmission had blown, and Mr. Condon should have been working on it instead of playing checkers. But old Condon operated at a speed all his own and kept his own schedule. His customers knew that, and not one ever complained. George Condon was the best, and cheapest, mechanic in the Downeast Region. He'd been getting cars and trucks through one more Maine winter for going on forty-five years.

Marny studied the checkerboard, feeling the weight of Mr. Condon's dark eyes on him the whole time, and was just about to make his move when the bell chimed, signaling someone had pulled up to the pump island. Condon's was the only full-service station left in the Downeast, maybe in the whole state of Maine.

Despite the heat, Mr. Condon didn't have one droplet of sweat on his face. "Cah's waitin', son."

Marny glanced outside at the tendrils of heat wriggling above the lot, then at the checkerboard. "No cheating."

His opponent winked. "No promises."

Pushing back his chair, Marny stood and wiped more sweat from his brow, then headed outside.

The car at the pump was a 1990 model Ford Taurus, faded blue with a few rust spots around the wheel wells. Marny had never seen it before. The driver was a large man, thick and broad, who filled out most of the driver's side of the cabin. He had close-cropped hair and a smooth, round face. Marny had never seen the driver before either.

He approached the car and did his best to be friendly. "Mornin'. Hot one, isn't it?"

The driver neither smiled nor looked at him. "Fill it up. Regular."

Marny headed to the rear of the car and noticed a girl in the backseat. A woman, really, looked to be in her early twenties. She sat with her hands in her lap, head slightly bowed. As he passed the rear window she glanced at him, and there was something in her eyes that spoke of sadness and doom. Marny knew that look because he'd seen it in his own eyes every night in the mirror. He smiled, but she quickly averted her gaze, obviously uncomfortable with the small attention he'd shown her.

As he pumped the gas, Marny watched the girl in the backseat, studied the back of her head. She was attractive in a plain way, a natural prettiness that didn't need any help from cosmetics. Her hair was rich brown and hung loosely around her shoulders. But it was her eyes that held him captive. They were as blue as the summer sky but so sad and empty. Marny wondered what the story was between the man and girl. He was certainly old enough to be her father. He looked stern and calloused, maybe even cruel. Marny felt for her, for her unhappiness, her life.

He caught the man watching him in the side view mirror and looked at the pump's gauge. It was going on thirty dollars. A second later the nozzle clicked off, and he returned it to the pump. He walked back to the driver's window. "That'll be thirty-two."

While the man fished around in his back pocket for his wallet, Marny glanced at the girl again, but she kept her eyes down, on her hands.

"You folks just visiting?" Marny said, trying to get the man to open up a little.

The man handed Marny two twenties but said nothing.

Marny counted off eight dollars in change and gave it to the driver. "Lots of people come to Maine for vacation. They call it Vacationland. It's right on our license plate."

Still nothing. The man took the money and started the car. Before pulling out he nodded at Marny, and there was something in the way he moved his head, the way his eyes sat in their sockets, the way his forehead wrinkled ever so slightly that got Marny shivering despite the heat.

The car rolled away from the pump, asphalt sticking to the tires, and exited the lot. Marny watched until it was nearly out of sight, then turned to head back to the garage and Mr. Condon and the game of checkers. But a crumpled piece of paper on the ground where the Taurus had been parked caught his attention. He picked it up and unfurled it. Written in all capital letters was a message:

HES GOING TO KILL ME